"Far be disappoint a lady—in anything."

He strode toward her, reached out, took her hand and lifted it to his lips. He pressed a gentle kiss upon her knuckles, then raised his eyes to regard her. "You, my lady, are the most surprising young woman I have ever met."

Her cheeks flushing, she tugged her hand away. "Hardly a compliment, sir knight. I'm not impressed."

He lifted the corners of his mouth in the sort of lazy smile he gave a woman after they had made love. "I assure you, a man likes to be surprised by a woman, and a truly surprising woman is a very rare creature."

For the briefest of moments her eyes widened with shock, and he wanted to shout with triumph.

But then her eyes flashed with scornful fire. "Creatures?" she demanded. "Is that what women are to you— creatures?"

* * *

In the King's Service
Harlequin Historical #675—October 2003

Praise for *USA TODAY* bestselling author MARGARET MOORE'S titles

The Overlord's Bride
"Ms. Moore is a master of the medieval time period."
—*Romantic Times*

The Duke's Desire
"This novel is in true Moore style—
sweet, poignant and funny."
—*Halifax Chronicle-Herald*

A Warrior's Kiss
"Margaret Moore remains consistently innovative,
matching an ending of romantic perfection
to the rest of this highly entertaining read."
—*Romantic Times*

MARGARET MOORE

IN THE KING'S SERVICE

HARLEQUIN®

TORONTO • NEW YORK • LONDON
AMSTERDAM • PARIS • SYDNEY • HAMBURG
STOCKHOLM • ATHENS • TOKYO • MILAN • MADRID
PRAGUE • WARSAW • BUDAPEST • AUCKLAND

ISBN 0-373-29275-9

IN THE KING'S SERVICE

This edition published by arrangement with Harlequin Books S.A.

® and TM are trademarks of the publisher. Trademarks indicated with ® are registered in the United States Patent and Trademark Office, the Canadian Trade Marks Office and in other countries.

Visit us at www.eHarlequin.com

Printed in U.S.A.

Available from Harlequin Historicals and
MARGARET MOORE

*Warrior Series
†The Viking Series
‡Most Unsuitable...

Other works include:

Harlequin Books

Mistletoe Marriages
"Christmas in the Valley"

The Brides of Christmas
"The Vagabond Knight"

Please address questions and book requests to:
Harlequin Reader Service
U.S.: 3010 Walden Ave., P.O. Box 1325, Buffalo, NY 14269
Canadian: P.O. Box 609, Fort Erie, Ont. L2A 5X3

With many thanks to the astute and delightful
Melissa Endlich.

Chapter One

Sir Blaidd Morgan, knight of the realm, trusted friend of Henry III, champion of tournaments and reputedly able to whisper a woman into his bed, drew his horse to a halt and wiped his nose with the back of his gloved hand. Water dripped from the soaked hood of his woolen cloak, and his boots were spattered with mud. The scent of damp leaves arose from the wood on his left; on his right, some cows stood in a meadow beneath the shelter of an oak, looking as miserable as he felt. At least now, through the teeming downpour, he could make out a village and a castle just beyond.

"That has to be Throckton Castle, thank God," he said to his equally drenched squire. "I was beginning to fear that we'd taken the wrong fork a few miles back and would have to bed down in the forest for the night."

His squire pulled the hood of his cloak farther over his head. "I thought you Welsh were used to the rain."

"Used to it, aye, Trev, I am, and because of your father's ideas about training, too. But that doesn't mean I like it."

Blaidd and Trevelyan Fitzroy's fathers were old friends, and Trev's father, Sir Urien, had trained Blaidd in the arts of war, which included drilling in all kinds of weather.

Sixteen-year-old Trev nodded at the fortress looming in the distance. "I thought Lord Throckton wasn't an important man, but that's quite a castle."

"It's more impressive than I thought it would be, too," Blaidd confessed.

On closer inspection—or as close as one could get from this vantage point through the rain—it seemed a massive creation, with inner and outer walls, an impressive gatehouse and a large keep in the center. Blaidd hadn't seen many castles to rival it, and he wondered if King Henry would be equally as surprised to learn the extent of Lord Throckton's fortifications, or if he already knew. That might explain the king's suspicions.

"Not every important man goes to court," Blaidd noted as he nudged his black gelding, Aderyn Du, to a walk. "Our fathers don't. It's likely to have some comfortable accommodation, though, thank God."

"Do you think Lady Laelia will be as beautiful as they say?" Trev asked.

Blaidd gave his companion a brotherly grin. "Probably not, but there's no harm in looking."

"We've come all this way because you only want to *look?*" Trev asked, incredulous.

Blaidd wasn't about to share the real reason Henry had sent him, so he grinned wider. "What else should a chivalrous knight do but look? I've heard enough tales of Lady Laelia's beauty that I decided it was worth a journey to see if they were true. My mother is truly starting to despair that I'll never find a wife and settle down."

"So if Lady Laelia's as beautiful as they say, you'll marry her?"

Blaidd's deep bass laughter sounded above the rain and the squelching of the mud beneath their horses' hooves. "Beauty's not the only thing a man should think about when it comes to marriage."

"I suppose not," Trev replied dubiously.

"Definitely not."

"So you've thought about it before, then?"

Aderyn Du skirted a large puddle in the middle of the rutted road. "Aye, of course," Blaidd said. "But I've never found the right woman."

"Is that why you've been with so many?"

Blaidd slid the youth a wry look. "I haven't *been with* that many. I'll not deny I like women's company, but I'm not quite the amazing lover gossip paints me."

"But Gervais says—"

"Your brother has no more knowledge of what I do with my nights than you do."

A more subdued Trev remained silent as they rode across a stone bridge leading into the village. Blaidd was rather glad of that. He didn't enjoy discussing his relationships with women with anyone, let alone a sixteen-year-old.

Because of the rain and the spring runoff, the river was high, the water frothing and splashing as it hit the bridge's foundations. This bridge was a finer piece of engineering than Blaidd had expected to find in a place this far to the north and west of London, too.

Mercifully, the rain began to abate and he could better note the state of the village. It was comprised of several cottages of wattle and daub and thatch. Shops and stalls, many with living quarters above, lined the green.

He'd seen villages in worse repair, but he'd seen plenty better, too. The village church wasn't much, either, leading him to suspect that little of Lord Throckton's income from his tenants' tithes was given away in charity. More likely it was spent on stones and mortar and master masons for his castle.

The green was deserted, but Blaidd felt he was being watched nonetheless. No doubt the unseen villagers were speculating about who they were and why they had come.

From Blaidd's mount and his accoutrements, his bearing from years of training as well as the broadsword slapping his thigh, they would surely guess he was a soldier, at the very least. The presence of a squire and the device on his shield would reveal that he was a knight. Anything else would be pure speculation.

The rain stopped completely as they neared a larger building that looked to be an inn. Blaidd was thinking he wasn't sure he'd fancy spending a night there any more than on the open road, when a blowzy, dark-haired, unkempt woman appeared in one of the un-shuttered windows on the second level. She leaned so far out of the window that her ample breasts, barely covered by her loose shift, seemed likely to be completely exposed at any moment.

She brazenly grinned at Blaidd, then whistled. In the next moment, several other women, equally slatternly, appeared at the other windows.

"Ain't he a fine, bold one now?" the black-haired one said in a loud voice. "I bet he's bold in bed, too."

The women cackled like chickens, and another declared, "Lovely weapon you've got, m'lord, I'm sure. I'd love to see it up close."

"I like the pretty young one," another called out.

Blaidd glanced over his shoulder. His face red as holly berries, Trev stared straight ahead. Blaidd stifled a smile that was both amused and sympathetic as they drew abreast of the building.

"I'm sorry, my dears," Blaidd said, as if he were addressing the queen of England, "but my squire and I must decline your charming and generous offers."

"Ooh, listen to him, will ya?" the black-haired harlot cried. "Ain't that the loveliest voice you ever heard! Welsh, too. I've heard good things about them." She made a gesture that demonstrated what exactly she had heard. "Come here, my buck, and whisper something naughty in my ear. It's the least you can do if you ain't gonna stay."

Blaidd put his hand on his heart and bowed. "Alas,

I fear I cannot. I have business at the castle and must not tarry any longer.''

He again nudged Aderyn Du into a walk, but before they had gone, a young woman—probably not much older than Trev—came to stand in the doorway. Her blond hair was a tousled mess, her relatively clean gown clung to her shapely body and her eyes were a startling shade of green. But while she had the face of an angel, the way she leaned against the frame of the door and the leering smile she gave Blaidd told him that she was an old hand at this game. As he rode forward, he sighed for the loss of innocence, even if he understood that poverty offered many women few choices in life but this one.

He realized he didn't hear Trev's horse behind him, and twisted to look over his shoulder. Trev's horse hadn't moved, and the squire was staring at the young woman like a man bewitched.

Blaidd swore under his breath, then barked, ''Fitz-roy!''

Jolted by the explosive summons, Trev kicked his horse's sides and was soon riding beside him toward the castle's gatehouse.

''She's a whore, like the others,'' Blaidd said.

''I know that. I'm not a baby,'' Trev muttered, not looking at him. ''And I've got ears. I heard what they said.''

''Then you know you must forget about that girl.''

Trev flushed. ''I've got money.''

''Whether you can afford it or not is beside the point. That's not a fit place for you to go. Aside from fleas and bedbugs, a lot of women in such places will gladly rob you blind, and it is a sad fact that most of them are probably diseased. A wise man stays out of stews.''

''You sound just like my father.''

''Thank you for the compliment,'' Blaidd replied, keeping his voice light, ''and I *am* responsible for you while you're in my service. If your father found out I'd let you go to a brothel, he'd probably have a fit— but he'd still be able to break my head before he succumbed. I'm not about to risk that.''

''Have *you* ever been to a brothel?''

Blaidd was glad that he could answer honestly. ''Never wanted to, never had to.''

Fortunately, they reached the gatehouse of Throckton Castle, effectively ending the conversation. He had a job to do here—one that had nothing to do with courting Lady Laelia—and he didn't want to have to play tutor to Trevelyan in matters such as these, as well.

Blaidd studied the raised portcullis, a huge wooden grille with pointed ends. Sentries patrolled the wall walk above. At the other end of the gatehouse was a closed second gate that led to the outer ward. It was made of solid oak, inches thick and studded with brass.

Lowering his hood, Blaidd rode beneath the portcullis and into the gatehouse, passing under the murder hole. If enemies got trapped between the wooden grille of the portcullis and the solid inner gate, defenders could pour boiling oil or throw rocks through that hole. He shivered, and it had nothing to do with the fact that he was wet with rain. He had seen a child accidentally burned by hot sheep's tallow once, and the thought of a great vat raining such a doom from above was the stuff of nightmares.

Arriving at the inner gate, he pulled his horse to a halt and dismounted. Trev followed suit, and Blaidd handed him Aderyn Du's reins.

Before Blaidd could call out a greeting, though, a panel in the right half of the door slid swiftly back. No doubt the sentries on the wall walk had notified the guards below that they had visitors.

A thin face wreathed in a rough, dark brown woolen hood appeared. The guard's brilliant blue eyes regarded Blaidd as if he wanted to accuse him of cheating. "Who are you and what do you want?" a slightly husky voice demanded.

"It's a woman!" Trev cried in what was meant to be a whisper, although it was loud enough to be heard twenty feet away.

After the first moment of astonishment had passed, Blaidd did what he always did when he met a woman. He smiled. "I wasn't aware Lord Throckton had Amazons in his garrison."

With an expression that looked suspiciously like scorn, the blue eyes surveyed him slowly, from the top of his soaked head, over his woolen cloak and leather jerkin, past his sword belt and breeches to the soles of his black boots. Then her expression changed to one of approval—because she'd caught sight of Aderyn Du.

Blaidd stiffened. Aderyn Du was an undeniably fine animal, but he wasn't used to having his horse meet with more favor than he did.

Turning her attention back to Blaidd, the woman said, "I asked you who you were and what you want here."

"He's Sir Blaidd Morgan," Trev declared incredulously, as if the whole world must know that.

Blaidd, however, knew that the whole world did not know of him, and it was very possible that his fame, such as it was, hadn't traveled this far north of London and east of Wales.

"As my squire has said, I am Sir Blaidd Morgan," he replied, once more his calm, genial self. "I've come to pay a friendly visit to Lord Throckton, provided you'll let us through the gate."

The woman sniffed. "You've come to court the Lady Laelia, like so many men before you. Well, good luck."

"I do hope I have good luck, if Lady Laelia proves to be worth courting."

"Well, well, no false modesty in you, sir knight, is there?" the woman replied. "It should be interesting to see how a Welshman fares. You *are* a Welshman, aren't you?"

By now, Trev was fairly hopping with indignation. "Are you going to let her talk to you like that? Do we have to stand here like a couple of peddlers asking to come in?"

Blaidd continued to smile, and while he ostensibly replied to Trev, he didn't take his steadfast gaze from what he could see of the woman's face. "As a matter of fact, since she is keeper of the gate, I *am* going to let her talk to me like that, and keep us waiting, if she likes."

The woman laughed, a low and rather cynical chortle. "I'll give you credit for your manners, Sir Welshman," she said. "Enter, then, and be welcome."

She slammed the grille closed, and they heard the sound of the heavy bolt being drawn back.

"And about time, too!" Trev muttered. "God's blood, Blaidd, that's the rudest—"

"Never mind, Trev. We're here without a specific invitation, so we can hardly be offended if the welcome is less than warm."

"I hope Lord Throckton is more polite."

"I'm sure he will be. It's a nobleman's duty to extend hospitality to a fellow nobleman."

His squire didn't respond; nonetheless, Blaidd could fairly feel the annoyance shooting out of him.

In truth, he was a little annoyed by the woman's brazen manner, too, but he had had more experience with disrespect. His father was not nobly born, and it had taken winning several tournaments, as well as the friendship of the king, before Blaidd was truly accepted at court.

So while this was far from his usual reception both at castles and with women, he wasn't as quick to take offense as Trev. As for the woman, he was very curious to see the whole of her face. If it was half so fascinating as those vibrant blue eyes, his time here might be more interesting than he had anticipated.

Although he mustn't lose sight of his true, and important, purpose.

The gates slowly swung open, and he and Trev proceeded through, entering a wide, grassy outer ward. Beyond was the inner curtain wall of the castle, with towers at the corners.

Several armed guards—all men—stood at attention beside the gatehouse. The blue-eyed woman shrouded in a long brown cloak waited closest to the gate, as if she had personally drawn back the bolt. Her face was thin, her skin pale, and her blue eyes seemed rather too large for her face. But her features themselves weren't too bad, and when he considered her lips, the first thought that came to mind was kissing.

"I hope you'll forgive my questions, sir," she said as she bowed low. "We so seldom have any visits from the king's minions that naturally I was suspicious."

Minion? Blaidd was no longer moved to excuse her insolence, vibrant blue eyes or not, and as for kissing her, he'd sooner kiss Aderyn Du.

"He's not a minion!" Trev cried, echoing his thoughts. "He's a friend of King Henry's."

"Trev, please, allow me to deal with this *underling,*" Blaidd said as he slowly ambled toward the woman until they were less than a foot apart.

She stiffened as Blaidd perused her in a leisurely manner.

"What's your name, wench?" he asked with deceptive tranquillity before he gave her a smile that his opponents in armed combat had learned to dread.

Her chin jutted out with defiance. "Becca."

"Tell me, Becca, do you always speak this way to your superiors?"

"Usually I don't speak to anybody who considers himself my superior."

She was, without doubt, the most insolent wench he'd ever encountered. "If this is the welcome nobles can expect at Throckton Castle, it's no wonder to me that your lord is not held in high esteem at the king's court."

The woman's steadfast gaze finally faltered—but only for the briefest of moments. "If he isn't, that merely confirms what I think of the English court."

"What do you know of the English court?"

Her eyes widened with what he recognized as a completely fraudulent innocent bafflement. "I never said I knew anything about the English court, sir. I said it confirms what I *think* about it."

She bowed again, with an unexpected grace. "I'm sorry if I've offended you, Sir Blaidd."

He tilted his head as he studied her, not at all taken in by her change of manner. "Are you?"

"If what I've said causes trouble for Lord Throckton, I am."

Then she smiled, with so merry an expression, it was like finding a flower blooming in the dead of winter. "But if my honesty means you think I'm an insolent wretch who ought to be punished, I'm not sorry a bit."

Under the force of that smile, Blaidd's anger

melted away. "Perhaps I'll be merciful and not tell Lord Throckton about his impertinent gatekeeper."

"Perhaps he won't be surprised." Her smile dimmed, but she didn't sound worried.

Then she wrapped her cloak more tightly about her slender frame. "Aren't you in a hurry to meet the lovely Lady Laelia?" She gave him another smile. "I think *you* might actually stand a chance."

"Well, then, since I've apparently won your good opinion, I'll consider myself nearly betrothed."

The look in her sparkling eyes shifted again, becoming serious. "You may not have had much competition in anything before, Sir Blaidd Morgan of Wales, but you will now. I wish you luck, if you think Laelia and her dowry will make you happy."

He asked the next question without thought. "Will I be seeing you in the castle?"

"I hope not," she replied, in a way that left no doubt that she meant it.

The guards nearby stifled smiles and tried not to laugh.

Sir Blaidd Morgan enjoyed having people laugh *with* him, and women most of all. But he hated being laughed *at,* and it had been years upon years since anybody had dared.

He turned on his heel, marched back to Aderyn Du and threw himself into the saddle. "Let's go, Trev," he snapped.

His squire immediately obeyed. "Do you suppose she really is a gatekeeper?" he asked as they rode into the ward.

"Whoever she is," Blaidd answered grimly, "I don't think she's right in the head, and I hope I never see her again."

As Sir Blaidd Morgan rode away, Becca glanced at the castle guards, and the tall, gray-haired man in mail at the head of them. "Poor man. I don't think he expected my reception."

They burst out laughing.

"That's enough, lads," the commander of the garrison ordered, although Dobbin was having trouble keeping a straight face himself. "Back to your duties."

Exchanging muffled words and snickers, the men returned to their posts, while Dobbin joined Becca in the room in the gatehouse where the guards spent their time while not on patrol or sleeping. The plain stone walls were as stark as the battered trestle table upon which, over the years, men off duty had scratched their signs or initials. A couple of stools provided the only seating. A single shelf held materials for cleaning metal and leather, a task often performed here. The scent of the polish lingered, and helped add to the cozy feeling of the room, which was warmed by a fire.

Becca and Dobbin hung up their drenched cloaks on pegs near the door and returned to their stools by the small hearth.

Dobbin stretched out his legs and sighed. "I'm getting too old to stand in the rain," he muttered, his words betraying his childhood spent in the dales of Yorkshire.

"You could have stayed inside."

"Too risky."

"They were hardly on the attack."

Dobbin gave her a shrewd look. "But what might you have said if I wasn't there?"

She smiled, for he was quite right. She might have been even more impertinent toward yet another knight who'd arrived to see if the beauty of Throckton lived up to that name, and to court her if she did.

"Big fellow, he was, for a Welshman," Dobbin noted. "Sits his horse well. A man with shoulders and legs like that would probably be some fighter."

"I daresay he probably is a champion of tournaments," Becca agreed as she spread her damp skirts to enable them to dry more quickly. The ring of keys at her belt jingled with the movement.

"He's a handsome one, too, even with that hair. I've never seen a nobleman with hair to his shoulders like some kind of savage."

"Maybe all Welshmen wear it that way."

"I've never seen 'em do it," Dobbin replied, "and I've met a fair few at tournaments and such."

Becca clapped a hand on his shoulder. "I'll ask him, shall I?"

Dobbin nearly fell off his stool. "You'd better not. He looked angry enough to strangle you before. I thought he was going to, the way he got so close to you."

Becca tried not to remember how her heart had

pounded when the handsome knight with the incredible physique had strolled toward her, a look on his face as if…as if…

Well, she'd never had a man walk up to her with that look on his face. "Very well, I won't ask." She gave Dobbin a grin. "Judging by that smile of his, I wouldn't be surprised if Sir Blaidd expects to win Laelia with nothing more than a wink and a grin."

"I just hope his lordship ain't going to be angry when he hears what you said to a knight from King Henry's court."

"I expect he will be." Becca hunched her shoulders, lowered her chin and gruffly spoke in imitation of the overlord of Throckton Castle. "Ignore her, Sir Blaidd. She's flighty and foolish—a woman, that's all."

Dobbin shook his head. "You'd better take care, my lady, or one of these days you might push your father too far, and then where will you be?"

Chapter Two

While Trev finished taking their baggage to the chamber they would share, Blaidd waited for Lord Throckton in the great hall. He stood with his back to the massive hearth, and the heat felt so good, he barely managed not to squirm like a pig in mud.

His mood continued to improve as he surveyed the chamber, which, like the rest of the fortress, was larger and more indicative of personal wealth than he had expected. After entering the cobbled courtyard, he'd taken note of the huge building that had to be the hall, and the chapel beside it, judging by the windows. The rooms on the second level of the half-timbered stables were surely barracks for the garrison and living quarters for grooms and stable boys. Blaidd guessed the two-story building on this side of the yard, adjoining the hall, contained the apartments where the family and the other servants slept, as well as the lord's solar. The other buildings he could readily identify were the kitchen, attached to the hall and with a large chimney louvered so that rain couldn't put out the fire below, and the blacksmith's shop. The keep, a huge circular building to the left of the entrance, probably doubled as the armory, and would serve as a last redoubt should the walls be breached.

The keep was decades old, and the inner walls, too. Blaidd estimated that the hall, the chapel, the outer wall and the formidable gatehouse were new, built within the last five years. The second floors—the apartments and barracks—were likewise of recent construction.

As for the interior of the hall, the only place Blaidd had seen to rival it belonged to the king. Heavy and finely wrought tapestries covered the walls, depicting battles and hunts, their bright green, scarlet and gold threads catching the light. The benches and tables were relatively new, free of scars, scratches and gouges, and polished to a high sheen. Clean rushes covered the floor, and the light scents of rosemary and fleabane reached his nostrils.

Huge oak beams supported the ceiling, and banners of knights who owed allegiance to Lord Throckton moved in the shifting air like lazy maidens dancing. It was quite a collection—far more than Blaidd would have expected for a lord of Throckton's apparent standing—and most of them were unfamiliar. Should the king's suspicions about Throckton's possible disloyalty prove well founded, he would have to remember them.

One of the hounds slumbering near the fire twitched, drawing his attention. They had stood growling and quivering at him when he had first entered, until one of the male servants had commanded them to sit and be quiet.

That wench at the gate had practically snapped and growled at him, too. What would *she* look like asleep, her bright blue eyes closed and her breasts rising and falling in gentle rhythm? He recalled hints of the form beneath that damp cloak she held so tightly about her, and realized she was quite shapely.

His body warmed more, and not from the fire, as he imagined the spirited Becca in his bed. She wouldn't lie there unmoving, he was sure. If she decided to give herself to a man, she would—with zest. He would be free to tease and suggest and play, and she would probably respond in kind.

He began to harden, and forcibly reminded himself he had important business here that had nothing to do with women, even if he was supposed to be interested in Lady Laelia. And he should no more dally with a maidservant than Trev should go to that brothel, no matter how interesting or challenging the maidservant might be.

"Welcome to Throckton Castle, Sir Blaidd!" a deep voice called out.

Blaidd swiveled toward a curving stairway at the far end of the hall. A robust man with thick gray hair and broad shoulders strode toward him. He was well-dressed, wearing a long tunic of indigo blue belted with gilded leather. By his manner and confidence Blaidd assumed he was the lord of the castle.

When Lord Throckton reached the dais, he came to a halt and smiled pleasantly, revealing fine teeth.

Blaidd, however, had spent years among hypocritical courtiers so he quickly realized that the friendly smile did not reach the man's hazel eyes. They were as wary as the girl's at the gate.

The hairs on the back of Blaidd's neck tickled, as if he was trying to pick his way across swampy land, yet he betrayed nothing of his foreboding. After all, what man wouldn't be suspicious of a knight who arrived without warning? And it could be that his own disinclination for subterfuge was making him more suspicious than he should be. "Greetings, Lord Throckton," he said as he bowed.

"Nasty weather for traveling," the nobleman noted.

"Which is why I'm thankful for your hospitality."

"Think nothing of it, man! It's my pleasure." Lord Throckton's smile grew, but his eyes did not lose their shrewd wariness. "Still, I doubt it's merely chance that brings you so far from the main road."

"No, it isn't," Blaidd replied with his friendliest smile. "However, my reason for coming here is one that I would prefer to speak of in private, if we may."

"Of course! We can discuss what brings you here in my solar."

Lord Throckton led Blaidd toward the staircase he had just descended, glancing over his shoulder to ensure that he was following.

They reached a landing, and Lord Throckton opened the door leading off it. He gestured for Blaidd to enter the chamber first, and when he did, he found himself in a very comfortable room that provided more evidence that Lord Throckton was rich and liked his creature comforts. More colorful tapestries covered the walls, and the chairs, of pale new oak, sported silken cushions in bright, jewel-like colors. A trestle table was covered with parchments, vessels of ink, several quills and a silver candleholder. An open chest painted blue and green revealed parchment scrolls, likely the records of tithes and other estate business. A bronze brazier glowed with coals and a carpet covered much of the stone floor. Linen shutters over the tall, narrow windows shut out the chill spring breeze.

It was like being in a warm, comfortable, Oriental cocoon, and a far cry from many a nobleman's plain, chilly solar.

With a sigh of pleasure, Lord Throckton sank onto the scarlet silk cushion on the ornately carved chair decorated with vines, leaves and grapes behind the table. He gestured for Blaidd to sit in a slightly less intricately carved chair opposite.

"Are you related to Sir Hu Morgan, by any chance?" Lord Throckton asked when Blaidd had done so.

Blaidd didn't hide his surprise that the man knew who his father was. "I'm his son. Have you met him?"

Lord Throckton's eyes crinkled as he smiled again. "No. As I'm sure you're aware, I don't go to court. Westminster and London are too noisy and crowded for my taste. But I've heard of him nonetheless. He has many important friends.''

''My father rarely goes to court, either,'' Blaidd replied, electing to say nothing of his father's friends, some of whom were very powerful indeed. ''He shares your dislike of cities, and he prefers to stay at home.''

''With your mother, who was reputed to be the most beautiful lady of her time,'' Lord Throckton added with a chuckle. ''A wise and happy man.''

Blaidd inclined his head and didn't disagree.

''I recall many people were shocked that Lady Liliana married a man who had been born a shepherd.''

He didn't speak with obvious disrespect or malice, but Blaidd's jaw clenched regardless. He didn't reply until he'd mastered the flash of anger such statements about his parents' marriage always elicited. ''My father was a knight when she wed him.''

''And a very handsome fellow himself, like his son. So I suppose that you've come to woo my beautiful daughter?''

''Word of the lady's qualities have reached the court, and I am unwed. I hope you won't hold my father's birth against me, but will allow me the privilege of meeting her, at least.''

''Indeed, I shall. I have a great respect for men who have risen above their station,'' Lord Throckton replied with every vestige of sincerity. ''So does my daughter.''

''Then may I also have your permission to woo her if she's willing, my lord?''

Lord Throckton toyed with the thick gold ring on his left hand and ran a measuring glance over Blaidd's clothes. The atmosphere in the room shifted subtly. "You haven't asked about her dowry, Sir Blaidd."

"From all that I've heard about your daughter, Lady Laelia herself will be the true prize."

Lord Throckton looked pleased. "Naturally, I agree, but I don't think it'll trouble you to know her dowry won't be small. Nor will it be the largest you've ever heard of. But I've had many offers from many men for Laelia, from the time she was twelve years old, and not a one of them complained about her dowry."

Blaidd bestowed a smile on his host. "Despite my attire, I'm not a poor man who seeks only wealth when it comes to a bride, my lord. I'm dressed thus because it's prudent when on the road, to avoid tempting outlaws."

"I should warn you, Sir Blaidd, it's not Laelia's heart you have to win over. It's *my* head. Be you knight or commoner, comely or not, and friend of the king or no, it's me you have to impress, not her. *I* have refused every man who asked for her. Are you still willing to try to woo and win her?"

Blaidd nodded. "If you are willing to allow me the opportunity, my lord."

"I am, and you are welcome to stay for as long as you like." Lord Throckton put his hands on the arms of his chair and hoisted himself to his feet. "Now that we've reached an agreement, Sir Blaidd, the evening meal should be ready, and I am near to starving. Shall we?''

Blaidd rose and followed the man back down to the hall, which was now crowded with tables, benches, servants and soldiers. Trev was waiting near one of the tables, and after a nod to Blaidd, the lad continued his survey of the impressive hall and bevy of servants.

The hounds, now roused and hungry, prowled among the tables, noses aloft. Several of the men didn't look much different, and Blaidd couldn't blame them, for the aromas wafting out of the corridor that led to the kitchen smelled heavenly. His stomach growled in response, for his last meal had been half a loaf of bread that morning, accompanied by a drink from a stream.

''Here is my lovely Laelia already waiting,'' Lord Throckton said.

Blaidd's gaze followed the man's gesture toward the dais, and then his breath caught in his throat. He had met many a beautiful woman, especially since more than one went out of their way to be introduced to him. But he had never, ever seen a woman who was as truly, absolutely beautiful as this one was. Dressed in pale blue velvet raiment, Lady Laelia was like an angelic vision, with perfect features, a graceful swanlike neck and shining blond hair cascading in curling waves over her slender shoulders. The picture was made perfect by her attitude of modesty, her head lowered as she stared at the rush-covered floor.

''Is she not a beauty?''

"Indeed, my lord, words fail me."

Lord Throckton chuckled with pride and continued through the assembly like a horse through high grass.

Blaidd looked at the dais again—and got a second, even stronger jolt of shock that made him check his step.

What the devil was that wench doing seated at the high table? Wasn't she a servant? This meant she couldn't be, and if she wasn't, what the devil was she? What had she been doing at the gate?

Perhaps she was a friend of Lady Laelia's, and her interrogation of him had been her idea of a joke.

But then why would she be seated while Lord Throckton still stood?

The woman's blue-eyed gaze locked on to him, and even from this distance, he could tell that she was amused by his surprise. As she continued to regard him with that mocking merriment, energy and deter-mination fairly hummed in Blaidd's veins. Whoever she was, and whatever she thought she was doing, she was going to rue the day she'd made Sir Blaidd Morgan feel like a fool.

Lord Throckton reached the dais ahead of him and took the blond beauty's hand, leading her a little for-ward. "This is my daughter, Lady Laelia. Laelia, this is Sir Blaidd Morgan, from the king's court."

The lady didn't raise her head or her eyes—a blessed change from being looked at as if he were a trained bear sent solely for someone's amusement, Blaidd decided.

He bowed low and took her right hand, as limp and

cool as a fish in a basket, and brought it to his lips to kiss. "My lady, reports of your beauty don't begin to do you justice," he said as he straightened.

It was an easy, unoriginal compliment. Usually he enjoyed exerting himself for a lady's good regard, especially a beautiful one, but it must be the presence of that insolent wench that made his mind incapable of coming up with better flattery.

"You're most welcome to our hall," Lady Laelia replied, raising grass-green eyes to look at him, her tone high-pitched and breathless, like a little girl's. Or a woman trying to sound younger than she was.

He couldn't remember anybody ever saying how old Lady Laelia was.

The brown-haired young woman loudly—and rudely—cleared her throat. Was she some sort of mad relative? That would explain her place, and her bizarre behavior.

Lord Throckton's thick gray brows lowered and he frowned as he looked at her. "Sir Blaidd, this is Rebecca. My other daughter."

Daughter?

No one had ever mentioned that Lord Throckton had another daughter, perhaps because she wasn't as beautiful as her sister, and was decidedly insolent.

Her lack of beauty might explain her rudeness, though. Envy may have twisted her into a bitter shrew.

"What, no compliment for me, Sir Blaidd?" Lady Rebecca asked as she tilted her head and gave him a merry smile. "Granted, I'm no match for Laelia, but aren't all you courtiers trained in flattery? Surely you won't disappoint me.''

Rising to the challenge, Blaidd laid his hand over his heart and let his voice drop to the low, sultry tone he usually reserved for a clandestine rendezvous. ''Far be it from me to disappoint a lady, in anything.''

He strode toward her, reached out, took her hand and lifted it to his lips. He pressed a gentle kiss upon her knuckles, then raised his eyes to regard her. ''You, my lady, are the most surprising young woman I have ever met.''

Her cheeks flushing, she tugged her hand away. ''Hardly a compliment, sir knight. I'm not impressed.''

He lifted the corners of his mouth in the sort of lazy smile he gave a woman after they had made love. ''I assure you, a man likes to be surprised by a woman, and a truly surprising woman is a very rare creature.''

For the briefest of moments, her eyes widened in shock, and he wanted to shout with triumph.

Then her eyes flashed with that scornful fire that was becoming familiar. ''Creature?'' she demanded. ''Is that what women are to you—creatures?''

He tensed and became the knight who had won many tournaments. ''Women who would make a mockery of a stranger and a guest are creatures to me, yes.''

''Becca, I think we're heard quite enough from you at the moment,'' Lord Throckton declared. He strode past her and sat in his thronelike chair. "This man is our guest and should be treated accordingly."

She turned away from Blaidd to address her father. "I'm treating him as I treat all the men who come to see Laelia."

The way Lady Laelia's lips turned down seemed to confirm that.

"Damn it, Becca, that's the trouble! When will you learn to behave? Why can't you be more like your sister?"

"Because I am not my sister?"

"You know what I mean!" Throckton gestured at the seat to his right. "Sit down, Sir Blaidd, sit down. Don't mind Rebecca. Where's the damn priest? Let's have grace."

Wondering if this sort of exchange occurred frequently, and deciding that it probably did, if they would speak that way in front of a stranger, Blaidd did as he was told, taking the place accorded to honored guests. That also put him between Lord Throckton and Lady Laelia. Lady Rebecca was to her father's left and, miraculously, once the grace was said, she seemed content to be silent.

Or maybe it was the fact that the conversation, such as it was, consisted of her father's descriptions of the vast array of suitors who had sought Lady Laelia's hand. Whenever there was a lull in the recitation, Laelia stayed silent or answered Blaidd's questions as briefly as possible, no matter how he exerted himself to be charming.

If somebody were to tell him this place was bewitched and everything he did had the opposite effect than usual—repelling rather than attracting a woman—he could believe it. On the other hand, he had to stay at Throckton Castle for some time, so if courting the lady was an uphill climb, it would give him a good excuse to linger.

He looked around the hall for Trev and found him engaged in conversation with a serving maid who looked a little younger than the squire. She had a jug of wine balanced on her hip and swayed while winding a lock of ruddy-brown hair around her finger.

Ah, the universal sign of feminine interest. Perhaps a reminder of their duties as guests wouldn't be amiss. And perhaps it would have been better if he'd come here alone, Blaidd thought.

"Then I sent that young buck packing," Lord Throckton declared, interrupting his musings. The man's voice was slurred from the copious amount of wine that seemed necessary to keep his throat lubricated for the long enumeration. "That was the last of them till you."

That meant his recitation must be at an end, thank God, Blaidd realized as he turned to his host with a smile pasted on his face.

Lord Throckton put his broad hands on the table and heaved himself to his feet. Blaidd started to rise, too, but Lord Throckton waved him back down. "Just off to the garderobe. That French wine goes right through my English guts." He gave Blaidd a rather sodden wink. "But it tastes too good not to drink it."

With that, he made his way out of the hall, leaving

only an empty chair between Blaidd and Lady Rebecca.

He couldn't resist the temptation. "So, my lady," he said to her, "do you often play castle guard?"

She regarded him steadily, obviously not the least embarrassed by his question. "No, sir knight."

"But today you thought to amuse yourself at my expense?"

"Not only myself. The garrison enjoyed it, too. I'm sorry you didn't see the humor in it."

He didn't believe she was sorry at all. "Nobody likes to be made a fool of."

"No, and handsome young knights with all the world at their feet most of all. But humility is good for the soul, is it not, sir?"

"Yes, it is. It's a pity you don't possess that quality yourself."

She reared back slightly. "How can you say that? Of course I'm humble. How could I not be, when I must compare myself to my sister every day?"

"What else could it be but arrogance to think you have the right to make a knight play the fool?"

"If I am arrogant, what are you—a man who smiles at every woman he meets as if she must be fairly salivating with desire for him?"

"Becca!" Lady Laelia gasped.

Blaidd had forgotten she was there. "It's all right, my lady," he assured her. "I take no offense."

Nevertheless, Lady Laelia's expression hardened and her lips thinned. No soft and gentle maiden was she now; she was at war. He had seen women at such battles often enough to recognize the signs.

"If you're so disposed to talk, sister," she said through clenched teeth, "why don't you tell him about the time you fell out of the apple tree?"

Lady Rebecca flushed as her eyes flashed with anger. Blaidd suddenly had the sensation that he was caught between two enemy lines, without even a dagger to fight with.

"Would you like to hear that story, Sir Blaidd?" Lady Rebecca asked with a serenity distinctly at odds with the look in her eyes. "It's really terribly amusing."

Blaidd was quite sure it was anything but. "I think I have listened to enough stories for tonight. May we have some music instead?"

Lady Rebecca continued to regard him with her steadfast and bold gaze. "I've heard that Welshmen are excellent singers. Perhaps you would prove the point, sir knight?"

"He's a noble guest, not some troubadour," Lady Laelia protested.

Blaidd gave them both a friendly smile to show he took no offense. "It's true that most Welshman can sing, something we are justly proud of. If you wish to hear my humble attempt at a ballad, I'll be happy to oblige you."

Lord Throckton came staggering back and threw himself into his chair. He looked from one daughter to the other, and his eyes narrowed. "What's been going on?"

"Becca has—"

"Been my usual annoying self," she interrupted. "Sir Blaidd has just offered to sing us a Welsh ballad."

"Has he now?" Lord Throckton cried, ignoring the first part of her comments. "Wonderful! I've always wanted to hear a Welshman sing. But before that, what do you say to some dancing?" He shouted at the young serving woman Trev had been talking to. "Meg, fetch Rebecca's harp! Bran, Tom, take down the tables!"

It became too noisy for conversation as Meg disappeared up the stairs leading to the household apartments. The two male servants the lord had addressed quickly marshaled some others to help them take down the tables. The high table they would leave for last.

"Your daughter plays the harp?" Blaidd asked when the worst of the noise abated.

"Aye, and well, too." Lord Throckton leaned toward Laelia, forcing Blaidd back in his chair. "But not so well as my Laelia dances!"

That explained the urgency to have dancing. The man wanted his daughter's talents on display.

Meg reappeared, bearing a small stringed instrument. The reverent way she gave it to Lady Rebecca suggested that she was particular in its handling, as if it were very valuable. Yet the harp was plain, and although the wood had been polished to a bright sheen, it did not look to be worth much in itself. It must be the value its possessor placed on it that made the servant treat it with so much care.

While Lady Rebecca tuned the instrument, Blaidd rose and held out his hand to Laelia. She limply placed hers in his and allowed him to lead her to the cleared space.

Then Lady Rebecca began to play.

How she played! Her fingers flew along the strings, coaxing out marvelous sounds and quick rhythms perfect for a round dance. As she played, she bent over the instrument, swaying, lost in the music with the true joy of the naturally gifted.

If she were in Wales, she would be far more valued than Lady Laelia for her talent. As for Lady Laelia's dancing, it was excellent, but she moved with all the joy of a soldier on a long forced march.

The dance came to an end and, applauding enthusiastically, Blaidd left Lady Laelia and approached her sister. "That was wonderful, my lady. You play very well indeed. If you dance as well as you play, you would astonish even the court. I hope you will dance next with me."

Instead of being pleased, Lady Rebecca looked as if she'd like to strike him dead on the spot. She slowly got to her feet, clutching her harp so tightly her knuckles whitened. "If you will excuse me, Sir Blaidd, I'm going to retire."

Then she limped out of the hall.

Chapter Three

Slipping into the cool darkness of the chapel was like diving into the river at night, Becca reflected as she closed the heavy door behind her. Before her accident, during the warm summer months, she would sometimes sneak out of the castle for a night dip in the pond below the mill.

That sort of risky escapade had ended with the tumble out of the tree.

Putting those happier, carefree days from her mind, Becca moved forward slowly, one hand against the cold stone wall to guide her steps, the hem of her garments slapping against her booted ankles and making small sounds in the stillness.

The air smelled of damp and incense, and a single votive candle burned in a niche holding a statue of the Blessed Virgin. Weak shafts of moonlight penetrated the narrow windows, and one feeble beam illuminated the altar.

Becca knelt before it, the stones hard and cold and unyielding, and pressed her hands together.

"Dear Father in Heaven," she prayed, "let it be a fine day tomorrow, so that I may ride out. Let me leave the castle for a little while."

Her voice turned grim. "If I can't, grant me the grace to guard my tongue and not say hateful things I regret the moment they leave my lips. Help me not to be jealous of Laelia, Father. She can't help it if she is beautiful and I'm not. Help me to overcome my anger and bitterness because I can't hope to have a suitor like…"

She drew a deep breath and her knuckles whitened. "To have any man want me," she corrected. "I don't want to make people hate me but to have yet another knight ride up to our gate seeking Laelia and to know that it will never be thus for me is getting so hard to bear!" Her voice began to rise again with her rancor. "And when such a man smiles so, and has a voice that makes me feel like I'm wrapped in a velvet cloak and cradled in his arms… When the merest touch of his lips to my hand heats my blood near to boiling—"

Her breath caught and, ashamed, she bowed her head. "Oh, God, take away these lustful thoughts and feelings! Please, God, let me accept my fate and be *quiet.*"

In the silence following her fervent plea, she heard the chapel door creak open. Then the dull thud as it closed.

Startled, she tried to stand quickly despite her twisted and shortened leg, which had not healed properly and never would. A spasm of pain racked her at the sudden motion, but she pressed her lips together to make no sound as she cautiously continued to rise. Turning, she swiftly searched the small building.

A man stood silhouetted against the window to her left. There could be no mistaking who it was; no one else in Throckton Castle wore his hair to his shoulders.

Was this God's idea of a joke, to send her the very man who roused such lust and remorse and bitter jealousy in her while she was at prayer?

It crossed her mind to flee, but her pride simply wouldn't permit her to hobble from the chapel like a crippled coward. "What do you want, Sir Blaidd?" she demanded, her voice loud in the quiet.

"How did you know who it was?" he inquired as he walked toward her.

She squared her shoulders. "Your hair is very distinctive, in a savage sort of way. And everyone who has ever stayed here and attended chapel knows how that door creaks, and would take care to prevent it if they wanted to enter in secret."

He came to a halt a few feet away. "I have no need to be secretive. I was looking for my squire and saw you slip in here. I thought it might be a good time to apologize for any offense I've caused you."

He sounded absolutely, completely sincere. Yet he didn't have to apologize at all, and she couldn't think of any other knight who'd stoop to express regret to anyone, let alone her.

"You didn't know I was crippled," she said. She decided she could be a little magnanimous, too. "I'm sorry if I upset a guest in my father's house. In hindsight, it wasn't the behavior of a lady.''

"What say we begin anew, my lady?''

She made her away around the simple wooden altar that bore a carved wooden crucifix until it was between them, like a defensive wall. "Very well, Sir Blaidd, I agree. We'll forget my insolence at the gate and your request to dance, and begin again.''

"Excellent!''

He sounded as if he was truly pleased, which would mean he would have been disappointed if she'd refused. That was unexpected. And rather delightful.

Perhaps she was making too much of his apology and enthusiastic tone. Maybe he simply wanted to avoid conflict of any kind while he was a guest of her father's, which would be wise. "Now that we've come to an understanding, Sir Blaidd, you should leave. It isn't seemly for us to be here alone together.''

"I suppose not. But first, will you answer one question?''

She didn't see any harm in that, since she could always refuse when she heard what it was. She nodded in agreement.

"Do you play the gatekeeper often, or was that a special welcome?''

"No, not often." She wasn't going to admit that she'd watched the knight and his squire riding up to the gatehouse through a loophole after the sentry called out that someone was approaching. She wouldn't confess that she'd turned to Dobbin and wryly said, "Here comes another one. Let me see if he's as arrogant as the rest."

Dobbin had started to protest, but she'd given him a devilish grin and he'd thrown up his hands in surrender.

Sir Blaidd bowed. "Then I'm honored I had at least that much to single me out from the vast horde who've come to see your sister."

"Yes, sir knight, you're one of many."

"So you wanted to confront me and take my measure first, before your younger sister. I hope I passed muster, for no doubt your opinion means a great deal to Lady Laelia."

Becca crossed her arms. "I'm not the eldest. Laelia is."

"Forgive me," he said, obviously taken aback. "She seems less...mature."

Becca didn't know if she should take that as a compliment or not.

"That explains the necessity of getting her married, though, so that you'll be free to accept offers for your own hand."

She stared at him, dumbfounded. Nobody had ever suggested that she hadn't married because of Laelia's spinster state. "There have never been any offers for my hand."

"What, not a one?"

He sounded genuinely shocked.

She struggled to regain her usual self-possession and changed the subject. "You said you were looking for your squire."

"Yes. I want to make sure he's not getting into any mischief."

An honest answer. "Are you expecting him to?"

"I'm hoping he's got more sense, but he's young and high-spirited, and this is his first time away from the care of his parents or older brothers—his first taste of freedom, so to speak. Like many young men in such circumstances, he may be tempted to act without considering all the consequences."

"He's not likely to steal anything, is he?"

"Oh, no, he'd never do that."

"Then what…?" She fell silent as she considered the comely youth in the hall who'd been talking to the young and pretty Meg.

Becca bit back a curse and started toward the door. "You're right to be concerned, Sir Blaidd, for if there's the slightest implication he's been bothering any of the female servants, I'll ask my father to order you both to leave at once. I've seen the trouble a handsome young nobleman can cause—"

Sir Blaidd put his hand on her arm to halt her, his grip warm and strong and irresistible. "I don't think you need be overly upset. Trev's a good lad, and when I find him I'll give him a stern warning about—"

"What, you'll order him not to seduce the maidservants?" she demanded skeptically.

"That's exactly what I mean," he said firmly.

She could well believe that would be enough to nip any such behavior in the bud. Nevertheless, the servants here were her responsibility and she would ensure they weren't taken advantage of. "Be that as it may, that doesn't mean he'll obey your warning. He's young and so's Meg, and neither one of them may consider the consequences," Becca said as she yanked open the door.

She was about to step into the courtyard when she saw Meg exit the kitchen. Alone.

Hopeful that the maid had enough sense to ignore whatever honeyed flattery a handsome young squire offered, Becca drew back into the chapel and peered out the door. As she watched Meg continue toward the maidservants' quarters, Sir Blaidd came to stand behind her. Close behind her. His powerfully masculine body couldn't be more than a few inches away from hers.

"What is it?" he whispered, his hot breath stirring the wisps of hair on the back of her neck.

"There's Meg," Becca murmured, nodding toward the girl and trying to ignore the unfamiliar sensation of having a virile male so near her—and failing utterly.

Without so much as a backward glance, Meg hurried up the outer steps toward the maidservants' quarters and disappeared inside.

Sir Blaidd's sigh of relief echoed Becca's feeling and seemed to come all the way up from his toes. "That's the one he was talking to, I'm sure of it. He's probably gone to bed already. It was a long day's ride."

The words had no sooner left Sir Blaidd's lips than the same door opened and his squire stepped into the courtyard. He hesitated, obviously looking for something.

Or someone.

The lad surveyed the courtyard for a few more moments, then, his shoulders slumped with disappointment, turned on his heel and went back into the kitchen.

Sir Blaidd muttered something that sounded like a Welsh curse. "I'll certainly be speaking to Trev about how I expect him to behave while we're your father's guests."

"Good," Becca said, closing the door and facing him.

"I give you my word as a knight of the realm that I'll tell Trevelyan that if he doesn't conduct himself honorably, I'll send him home to his father in disgrace."

"That may not seem like much of a punishment to a boy that age," she noted.

"You don't know his father. Have you heard of Sir Urien Fitzroy?"

"Doesn't he train men in the arts of war?"

"Yes, he does. He trained me, and believe me, my lady, if he thinks his son has behaved unchivalrously, the punishment *will* be severe."

Becca suddenly regretted getting so annoyed. "I hope it doesn't come to that, and your warning will be enough. I'll speak to Meg, too." She hesitated, then decided to explain her reaction. She didn't want him to think she was completely hotheaded about everything. "We had a serving girl here a few years ago, Sir Blaidd, named Hester. She was as pretty as Meg, and just as coquettish—well, perhaps a little more brazen than Meg.

"A young knight arrived, supposedly to court Laelia. One day, he left without so much as a farewell. At first we thought it was because my father hadn't seemed inclined to consider his suit. A few weeks later, though, we discovered that Hester was carrying his child. He'd made all sorts of extravagant promises to the poor girl. He'd even said he'd marry her. We'd seen enough of the man to guess that he would have said whatever it took to get Hester into his bed. But Hester wouldn't give up hope that he'd return, so I asked my father to send a messenger to the knight to tell him about the baby. I tried to believe he'd at least send her a word, some money, *something,* but the lout's response was that he should be thanked for 'breaking her in' and teaching her how to please a man."

Becca shivered with revulsion. "That man's callousness destroyed Hester." She sighed, saddened as always when she recalled those terrible days. "If her baby had lived, things might have been different, but she lost it, and with it, every gentle part of her."

Becca looked away, unable to meet Sir Blaidd's concerned, steadfast gaze. "She's a whore now, in the village. I see her sometimes, and when I do, it breaks my heart." She raised her eyes, defiant and commanding once more. "I won't have that happen to Meg."

Sir Blaidd caressed her chin with his strong, callused palm. "I see it isn't only your sister and the gates of this castle that you guard, my lady," he said softly. "I trust your care is appreciated."

She moved back, away from him and his touch and his deep, sympathetic voice. "Of course it is."

"I give you my most solemn vow that I will ensure that Trevelyan doesn't do anything so disgraceful."

"Thank you," she murmured, her breathing fast and shallow as she told herself she should get away from the knight.

He reached out and put his hands lightly on her shoulders. She opened her mouth to tell him to let go, but the words wouldn't come. No one had ever touched her like this, as if she was fragile and precious.

She didn't make a sound as he pulled her close. She not only couldn't find the voice to protest, she couldn't find the will. She slid her arms around his waist, silently agreeing to what was coming.

So he kissed her. His lips brushed hers, a gentle, tentative whisper of soft flesh to soft flesh. Her embrace tightening, she leaned into him, permitting him to kiss her more deeply, as she was kissing him.

Oh, how wondrous, after all these years in Laelia's shadow, to think a man might desire *her!* He made her believe that she was a normal woman, and an attractive one at that. She felt whole and unbroken and wanted. His desire inflamed her own until she couldn't think.

His hand meandered down her back, cupping her buttocks and pressing her close to him, while the other held her steady. She needed that support, for her body softened and throbbed with yearning as she ran her hands over his shoulders and back, feeling the taut muscles through his tunic.

His body. His strength. His desire, matching her own.

A call rang out, signaling the changing of the watch. Reminding her of where she was, and who she was. Becca wasn't the beautiful Laelia; she was plain, crippled Rebecca, and this handsome, seductive man was here to court her sister.

So why was he kissing *her?* What did he hope to accomplish? Seduction? Power? *Control?* She would let no man use her for his own purpose, whatever that might be.

She shoved him back. "Is this your idea of honorable conduct, sir knight?" she demanded. "Do you think that because I'm crippled and homely I must be desperate and so easily, willingly, seduced?"

"God's wounds, no!" he said as he regained his balance. "I swear to you, my lady—"

"Swear all you want, but kissing me seems an odd way to woo Laelia. Or am I a means to practice your technique?"

Sir Blaidd stiffened, his back as rigid as a lance. "I had no intention of kissing you when I came here, and I'm not in the habit of seducing my host's daughters, however tempting they may be."

"Then what was that kiss about?"

"If you don't know, then it was a stupid mistake,

and one I won't make again,'' he retorted, his deep voice fiercely angry.

Good. Angry men she was used to and could handle. Men who tried to seduce her, however... ''I wouldn't try seducing Laelia, either,'' she warned. ''First, I'm onto your game. Second, Laelia may look and sound a bit dim, but I assure you, when it comes to men and their tricks, she's seen them all.''

Sir Blaidd sidled closer, seeming taller, more menacing, every inch the fierce warrior and champion of tournaments. ''If it's impossible for me to seduce either of you—supposing that was my despicable plan—then your warnings are quite unnecessary, aren't they? And I must say that kiss was rather amazing for a modest young maiden of limited experience, which leads me to wonder what exactly you were doing here at this time of night. You don't strike me as devout, so a sudden urge to pray seems unlikely.'' He ran a haughty, impertinent gaze over her body. ''Did I interrupt something? Were you waiting for somebody else?''

''How dare you suggest such a thing!''

''How dare *you* suggest that my motives are dishonorable?''

''You kissed me!''

''You kissed me back!''

''I had no choice.''

''Of course you did. You could have stopped me at any time. But you didn't, and what's more, you *enjoyed* it.''

"Oh, you are an expert on women's feelings, are you?"

"Expert or not, I know when a woman's desire matches or exceeds my own."

"*Exceeds?* Of all the arrogant, pompous, self-righteous—"

"Yes, you certainly are."

"You…you base, loathsome blackguard!" she cried, wrenching open the door, determined to get away from him. "Don't you ever come near me again!"

She limped off into the night.

"Trust me, I won't!" Blaidd muttered as the chapel door creaked to a close.

Every Welsh curse he knew tumbled out of his mouth in a low rumble of frustration and anger. How dare she call his honor into question? Granted, kissing her had been a little…well, a lot…

Well, he shouldn't have.

He let out his breath slowly. God save him, he'd been an idiot. An idiot totally overwhelmed with desire. An idiot so overwhelmed with desire that he'd forgotten that he was here because King Henry himself had sent him to verify if Lord Throckton was plotting treason or not.

He wouldn't be able to do that if Lord Throckton sent him packing the day after he'd arrived because he'd presumed to kiss the man's daughter. He should have been able to control himself, no matter what the circumstances or how tempting the lady. After all, he was no youth anxious to experience love, like Trevelyan.

"Fool," Blaidd mumbled under his breath as he left the chapel and headed toward the apartments.

He reached the chamber he and Trev were sharing and cautiously opened the door, which didn't squeak like the one in the chapel. He quietly crept into the comfortable room with its two beds. A brazier stood nearby, along with a chest for their baggage, and a small table bearing a ewer and basin for washing. There were no tapestries or carpet, or even a stool to sit on, but Blaidd had slept in worse places.

Someone was in one of the beds—Trev, to judge by the tousled hair. Blaidd hoped the lad had already fallen asleep, thereby sparing him the need to explain anything.

Trev was not asleep. He sat up abruptly and said, "Where have you been? I was starting to get worried."

"I was looking for you," Blaidd truthfully replied.

Trev hugged his knees and regarded him quizzically. "I've been right here for a long time."

Blaidd sat on the end of his bed. He might as well make a point, and incidentally turn the conversation away from his own whereabouts. "And before that, you were looking for that maidservant, Meg."

Trev blushed. "How do you know?" Then his eyes widened. "Were you *spying* on me?"

Blaidd was in no mood for more indignation, especially from a stripling youth. "I happened to see you looking for her in the courtyard, as anybody could have.''

"How did you know I was looking for her? Maybe I was searching for *you*."

"I saw her leave the kitchen, and you came hot on her heels. If you were looking for me, I don't think you would have been so disappointed when you didn't find me.''

Trev stared at his toes and shrugged his shoulders. "All right. I wasn't looking for you.''

"She's a servant, Trev,'' Blaidd said not unkindly. "You're a young nobleman who's a guest in her master's household. She wouldn't want to risk offending you.''

He saw dismay flash in Trev's eyes, and took pity on the boy. "Look, Trev, I'm not saying that's the only reason she talked to you. It could be she really likes you. But you're not equals. You have power and rank, and she has none. And we *are* guests here. It would be an abuse of your host's hospitality to dally with his maidservants.''

"What if a woman…you know…what if she's interested?''

Blaidd recalled what his father had said to him about such situations. "With such things come responsibilities, provided the man is honorable and not some lustful lout. What if the woman got with child?''

"Oh.''

"Yes, oh. Have you enough silver to give her a tidy sum to raise it? Would you be ready for a young man to show up at your gate one day claiming to be your son? Would you be willing to acknowledge a bastard?''

''I hadn't thought of all that.''

''No, I didn't think you had.''

''But with a whore, there wouldn't be—''

''You're not going to go with any whore while you're my squire. Do you understand me?''

Blaidd didn't often use that tone of command, but when he did, it always got results, and this time was no different. Trev swallowed hard and nodded.

A twinge of guilt assailed Blaidd. He'd hardly acted as an honorable knight himself tonight. And given the possible repercussions, it might be wise to prepare Trevelyan for a likely departure, as well as give him as much of an explanation as necessary. ''We might have to leave tomorrow.''

Trev's mouth fell open. ''Why? Because I was looking for Meg?''

''No. Because I quarreled with Lady Rebecca.''

A devilish gleam lit Trev's eyes. ''After all your warnings and admonitions to me about the proper behavior of a guest?''

Blaidd bent down and pulled off his boots. ''Yes.'' He glanced up. ''And no, you don't have to gloat. I know that was a stupid thing to do.''

Trev didn't gloat. ''She seems a very quarrelsome woman,'' he said comfortingly, ''and it didn't look to me as if her father or sister like that about her. Perhaps they'll take your side.'' He grinned. ''Especially Lady Laelia.''

Blaidd hadn't expected to find solace in the observations of a youth, but he did. "Well, we'll find out come the morning," he said as he rose to finish disrobing. "Go to sleep, Trev." He gave the lad a wry smile. "We *may* have a long journey tomorrow."

Trev made a face. "I hope not. I don't want to go home yet. I've had enough training."

"A knight can never have enough."

"You say that only because you don't have to do it anymore," the lad said as he snuggled beneath the covers.

When Trev's eyes closed, the rueful smile left Blaidd's face. If they did have to leave in the morning, how was he going to explain his failure to the king?

Chapter Four

In their bedchamber the next morning, it was obvious that Laelia was in a foul mood. Becca had long ago learned that the best way to dissipate a conflict with her sister was to keep quiet until Laelia deigned to speak. It went against the grain, but she stayed silent while Meg helped Laelia put on a beautiful gown of emerald-green velvet trimmed with golden bands of embroidery, and a gilded girdle about her slender hips. Laelia then sat on a stool before her dressing table, which was covered with little pots of perfumes and unguents, a silver-handled brush and a small cedar box holding ribbons to adorn her hair. Another wooden box, inlaid with ebony, held her jewelry.

Becca had no ribbons or baubles, and her jewelry, worn much less frequently, was in the bottom of her embossed chest on the other side of her bed. Laelia's bed was made up with fine linen sheets, a thick feather bed and large pillows, and curtains of scarlet damask kept out the chill night air. Becca's bed was just as sumptuous. She didn't feel the need to dress richly, but she wasn't about to turn up her nose at being warm and comfortable.

When they were children, she and Laelia had shared the bed that was now hers alone. They'd had many a whispered conversation together after the curtain had closed, punctuated with giggles. That had changed when Becca fell from the tree. Laelia couldn't share her bed for some weeks after that, and her father had purchased a new one for her.

Becca could easily guess why Laelia was upset this morning. She was furious that Becca had stormed out of the hall—well, stormed out as dramatically as a woman who limped could—coupled with her greeting of Sir Blaidd at the gate. Laelia had heard about that meeting before the evening meal, and her verbal jousting with Sir Blaidd in the hall would have raised her ire even more. Fortunately, Laelia had been asleep when Becca had returned from the chapel, or at least she'd pretended to be, sparing a quarrel last night, but letting her annoyance fester all the more, probably even as she slept.

Becca had been tempted to wake her sister and tell her that Sir Blaidd had kissed her, to warn Laelia that the man was up to no good. Becca had considered speaking to her father in the morning, too, and telling him to send Sir Blaidd away. Surely he shouldn't be courting Laelia.

But now, in the light of day, and considering how rarely her father ever paid heed to her concerns, she decided that the less said about what had happened last night, the better. There was no reason yet to believe that Sir Blaidd would be deemed any more worthy of Laelia's hand than any of the other myriad suitors who had come to Throckton Castle.

She hadn't exactly been a model of ladylike behavior herself. She should have left the chapel the moment Sir Blaidd arrived. Regardless of his manner and his voice and his apology, she should have fled.

Therefore, rather than risk unnecessary conflict, she decided to say nothing of her nocturnal encounter with Sir Blaidd Morgan, unless and until it seemed he was in contention for Laelia's hand.

"You were very rude to Sir Blaidd yesterday," Laelia suddenly declared as she regarded Becca's reflection in her mirror. "And as for that business at the gate—I suppose Dobbin put you up to it?"

"Of course he didn't. It was my idea," Becca replied firmly as she tied the side lacings of her overtunic. She wore a gown of plain brown wool beneath it, and a linen shift under that, and rarely required assistance to dress.

"That makes it even worse. And then to march out of the hall like a…like…I don't know what! If Sir Blaidd decides to leave today, it'll be all your fault!"

Becca didn't appreciate being scolded like an errant child. "You sound quite taken with the Welshman. I didn't think you could be so easily impressed."

"*Easily* impressed?" Laelia repeated indignantly as Meg finished brushing her hair and began to braid it as quickly as she could, clearly wanting to finish her duties and be gone. "I'm not *easily* impressed—

but he's handsome, he's charming *and* he's a courtier. Even you must admit that it's rare we get a man from court coming here, given Father's opinion of Queen Eleanor.''

It sounded as if Sir Blaidd had already found favor with Laelia. ''Ah, yes, for a moment I forgot how much you yearn to be presented at court.''

''While you would rather stay here in this…this *wilderness,* consorting with the peasants,'' Laelia replied.

''I enjoy consorting with the peasants,'' Becca said evenly as she began to make her bed.

Laelia pulled a face. ''Will you never have any regard for your rank and title?''

''I do, as well as for the responsibilities that go with it. But I have no wish to marry a man just so I can be presented at court.''

''That isn't the only thing I like about Sir Blaidd. I daresay the only thing that *you've* noticed about him is that he's a man, and you hate men.''

''I don't hate men.''

''You certainly do!'' Laelia exclaimed as Meg tied the first braid with an emerald-green ribbon. ''No man who's come here has ever found favor with you.''

''That's because they've all been vain, spoiled and arrogant.''

''Even you can't think Sir Blaidd is vain. His clothes are plain, his accoutrements, too, and he didn't seem very arrogant to me.''

He had been very simply dressed when Becca had first seen him at the gate, the sodden cloak clinging to his broad shoulders, his damp breeches to his muscular thighs. Later, he'd changed into a simple tunic with a narrow trimming of embroidery about the hem and a plain white shirt beneath. "Maybe he dresses that way because he's poor," she said, which would mean he would certainly not be considered a fit husband for Laelia.

"He's not. Father says so."

It was on the tip of Becca's tongue to point out that their father had been known to make a few mistakes. His vocal condemnation of the king's wife at feast times and other public gatherings was hardly wise. However, Becca didn't think it was time to bring him into this argument. "What about that hair of his? That hardly seems a fitting style for the king's court."

Laelia considered, as if the question were of national importance. "It looks well on him, so perhaps it is. If not, should we marry, I'll ask him to cut it."

"What if he won't?"

Laelia gave Becca a superior little smile that never failed to annoy her, for it hinted at a vast and secret feminine knowledge she would never possess. "I'm sure he'll do it if his wife asks him." That thought seemed to put her in a forgiving mood. "To be sure, he's a bit rough around the edges, but I can fix that."

Becca imagined Sir Blaidd with his "rough edges" smoothed out until he was like every other bland and smooth-talking nobleman she had ever met. She didn't think that would be an improvement.

Perhaps she should at least give some hint that he

might not be as wonderful as her sister seemed to think he was. "If I'm not in favor of him as a husband for you, Laelia, it's precisely because he is so charming and good-looking. He's probably had scores of lovers, and likely keeps a mistress—maybe more than one. He'll probably never be faithful."

Laelia regarded her reflection without a hint of distress. "I wouldn't be surprised if he has lovers now. But once he's married to me, he won't be tempted."

"I don't think marriage to anybody would make much of a difference. If he's a lascivious scoundrel, chances are he'll be one after marriage, too, no matter who his wife is, or how much he claims to love her."

Her coiffure now complete, Laelia gave a long-suffering sigh as she rose. "You would think an archangel would make a terrible husband."

Before Becca could point out that archangels didn't marry, Laelia gave her a pointed look, silently reminding her it was time to be on their way to the chapel for morning Mass.

"You go ahead," Becca said. "I need to talk with Meg for a moment."

"Very well, but don't be late."

Again, Laelia spoke as if Becca were a child. Her jaw clenched as Laelia sailed out the door and closed it firmly behind her.

"I ain't done nothing wrong, I hope, my lady," Meg said, a frown darkening her usually cheerful face. "Or forgot something."

"I'm not going to scold you," Becca said kindly. She gestured toward the stool and Meg perched on it, as tentatively as if she expected it to disappear at any second. "I wanted to speak to you about Trevelyan Fitzroy."

With an expression of dismay, Meg sat up even straighter. "I ain't done nothing unseemly!"

"I don't believe you have, but I wanted to warn you to take care. I'm sure he's a very persuasive and fascinating young man, but you're a servant, and he's not. He may want to take liberties because of that. If he does, you have my permission to refuse him as forcefully as necessary, and if he continues to bother you, I want you to tell me right away. We won't countenance any young man treating our servants with disrespect. I don't want you to share Hester's fate."

And she herself should remember the fearsome consequences of seduction.

"Of course I'd come to you, my lady, if he was bein'…like that. No honey-tongued squire who looks like the devil's own temptation is going to get far with me. Why, he'd just be after a quick tickle and tumble and—" She colored. "Beggin' your pardon, my lady."

"However you say it, you're right, and I'm relieved you're on your guard." As she should be, Becca reflected. "Now we'd best get below. If I'm late for chapel, my father won't be pleased."

Meg rose. "I'm grateful to you, my lady, for carin' enough to warn me."

Becca nodded as she headed for the door.

"My lady?"

She turned back. "Yes?"

Meg looked even more nervous than she had when Laelia was in high dudgeon. "I've been wondering…that is, you've got some pretty dresses. Why don't you ever wear 'em?"

Becca glanced down at her plain garments and simple leather girdle, which held her ring of keys to all the locks in the castle save her father's chest in his solar. "My woolen gowns are comfortable and I don't have to worry about getting them dirty. When I'm wearing an expensive dress, I always feel that if I move too much, I'll ruin it."

"I'd wager that if you wore such clothes more often, you wouldn't," Meg replied. "You'd soon be used to them and stop thinking about it so much."

"I don't think they suit me, either." Becca shrugged. "Besides, what does it matter how I look? I realized long ago I'd never be a beauty."

"But you're not homely, neither," Meg said eagerly. "You don't want to be a maiden all your life, do you? In a pretty dress and with your hair done like your sister's, I think you'd look very nice indeed."

Becca bristled. "I'm not about to hamstring myself trying to please some man. If someone wants me, he'll have to take me as I am, and if that's not good enough, I won't have *him*."

Meg blushed. "Yes, my lady. Sorry, my lady. I didn't mean no disrespect."

Becca let out her breath. "No, I'm sorry, Meg, for losing my temper. I know you meant well." She managed a grin. "Everybody who wants to see me married means well, I suppose."

"I do see what you're getting at," the maid replied. "About a man wanting you as you are. Maybe that'll happen sooner than you think."

"And one day, men will walk on the moon," Becca replied skeptically. "Now we had best be on our way. I've been chastised enough already today."

Although secretly fearing an indignant command to leave at once, Blaidd strode toward the chapel as if all were well in the world. He didn't want anybody watching—the servants, the soldiers, even Trev—to realize just how important it was that he stay. Last night he should have remembered his purpose and the ruse to support it, even if he chafed at the dishonesty.

In spite of his impetuous, foolhardy behavior, he couldn't help harboring the hope that Lady Rebecca would admit, if only to herself, that he hadn't forced his kiss upon her. Then he could also hope that her own guilty conscience would ensure that she keep what had happened between them a secret.

He shoved open the chapel door and saw both the lord of Throckton Castle and his beautiful daughter turn and smile at him. They also shifted aside, making room beside them. Obviously, he was not in disfavor.

He couldn't be completely relieved, however. Perhaps Lady Rebecca hadn't yet had the opportunity to tell her father what had happened.

He swiftly surveyed the rest of the people assembled for Mass and caught sight of that lady, half hid-

den by the gray-haired, but still robust, soldier Blaidd
had seen at the head of the guards at the gate. This
man had watched with interest, and with something
else in his eyes, when the lady spoke. With...
affection.

Judging by his position, he was probably the garrison commander, and it wasn't inconceivable, based
on his age, that he'd known Lady Rebecca all her life.
Perhaps he had that devotion some servants devel-
oped for the children of their masters.

Then Lady Rebecca realized Blaidd was looking at
them. Her expression grew as scornful as if he carried
a particularly loathsome, communicable disease.

Once more fearing his stay at Throckton Castle was
almost over, Blaidd made his way to the front of the
chapel.

"Good morning, Sir Blaidd!" Lord Throckton
cried with jovial geniality as Blaidd joined the nobleman and his beautiful daughter. "I'm delighted to discover that you aren't like so many young men now-
adays who have so little respect for our faith, unless
a Crusade be attached to it."

His friendly manner made Blaidd regret his actions
last night even more. "There are plenty of young men
more devout than I," he replied.

Somebody behind him sniffed with audible disdain,
and he wasn't hard-pressed to guess who it was.

The priest arrived to begin the Mass, sparing
Blaidd any further conversation. He paid little heed
to the words of the service, however. He kept envi-
sioning Lady Rebecca going to her father afterward

and telling him that Blaidd was an immoral, disgusting lout who should be sent packing without further delay.

By the time Mass concluded, this image was so vivid he wouldn't have been surprised if she walked up to the altar, faced the entire assembly and denounced him for a blackguard right then and there.

Steeling himself for that eventually, he turned around to look for her—and realized she'd already gone.

That was a relief in some ways, yet in another, he feared it was only delaying the inevitable. If he had to leave in disgrace, he'd rather get it over with at once.

Perhaps this was her idea of retribution, to drag out the wait and torment him with uncertainty. If so, she was going to learn the folly of that plan, for Sir Blaidd Morgan allowed himself to be played by no man, and no woman, either, he thought as he followed Lord Throckton and Lady Laelia from the chapel. He spotted Lady Rebecca talking with some soldiers outside the barracks, and decided to find out if he was in trouble or not. He told Lord Throckton and Laelia that he wanted to ask Lady Rebecca something about his baggage, then excused himself and headed toward her.

She looked only mildly surprised to see him. "If you'll pardon me, Dobbin," she said to the older soldier, "I believe our guest wishes to speak to me."

The man nodded and, after giving Blaidd the once-over, meandered away, his men with him, leaving them alone near the barracks door.

"I do wish to talk to you, my lady," Blaidd agreed as he came to a halt. He struggled not to sound impatient, although his nerves were taut as a ship's rigging in a gale. "Is there somewhere more private we can speak?"

She raised one brow in query. "Do you think I'll risk being alone with you again?" she asked quietly. "Whatever you have to say to me, you can do so here."

He subdued a scowl. "I'd like to know if you intend to tell your father about…" Rather than be specific, he gave her a look that she had to comprehend.

"Why wouldn't I?" she asked evenly, regarding him as steadily as Sir Urien Fitzroy on the training field after Blaidd had blundered.

"Because I give you my word that I won't do it again."

"It shouldn't have happened the first time."

She must like watching him twist in the wind, he decided, but she had the upper hand, and they both knew it. "I agree, and I'm sorry. Sometimes desire overrules the head."

She snorted in a most unladylike manner. Her glance darted below his belt before returning to his face. "*Something* overrules your rational mind, Sir Blaidd. In that, you are like many men. However, since you've apologized *again,* I'll be lenient." Her gaze hardened. "But don't take that as a sign that you may do as you please, with me or anyone else here.

And might I suggest that, in future, you avoid situations that later require apologies.''

He bowed and tried to make light of the situation. ''I'll try.''

''You'd better do more than try, or you won't get far in your wooing of my sister. Now if you'll excuse me, I must see to the day's meals.''

With that, she walked past him, her head high and her bearing as regal as a queen's.

Even if she limped.

Chapter Five

Several days of rainy weather passed, during which Blaidd did his best to avoid Lady Rebecca while everyone was more or less confined to the castle. It was rather obvious she was of the same mind about him, for although they were often in the hall at the same time during the day, they spoke only during meals, and only when it was necessary. She dutifully played her harp for dancing when her father made the request, and Blaidd dutifully danced.

He spent most of his time with Lady Laelia, as a man courting a woman should. Despite her outward beauty, however, this felt more and more like imprisonment. She asked very little about him personally, and didn't seem to want to talk about anything to do with her family or her home. If he tried to ask questions, she appeared bored and listless.

Finally, after several fruitless attempts to find a subject to spark her interest, he'd finally found one when he began to speak of the court. Then she grew more animated, asking questions about the king and queen, the lords and ladies, the entertainments, the royal apartments.

When he wasn't being interrogated by Laelia, he attempted to engage Lord Throckton in games of chess or draughts, hoping to sound the man out about his politics, to see if he could find any hint that Throckton was discontented enough with Henry's rule to foment actual rebellion. Unfortunately, Lord Throckton usually insisted Blaidd stay with Laelia, as if this was a great favor, and spoke only vague generalities when he did not.

In spite of these impediments and distractions, Blaidd kept an eye on the man as well as he could and discovered Throckton didn't appear to do anything remotely suspicious. If he was planning rebellion, he was being very careful about it.

Still, there were things that made it difficult for Blaidd to dismiss talk of traitorous plots completely. There was the man's astonishing fortress, for one thing, constructed with as much expense and care as if he was expecting a war any day. The garrison had to number a hundred at least, and they were well trained and well armed. Blaidd had spent years with fighting men, and these were some of the finest soldiers he'd ever seen. Men that skilled and well trained didn't come cheap.

A lord could, of course, plead the necessity of guarding his land, but few put so much of their resources into it. Where was the man getting the money to pay for his soldiers, their weapons, and this castle? To be sure, the estate looked moderately prosperous, but even so, it didn't seem possible that Throckton could afford such a fortress and provide for so many soldiers unless he had another source of income.

Yet the man himself was so friendly, so pleasant....

His father would tell him to utterly disregard that; nevertheless, Blaidd found it hard to accept that a man could be so hospitable and encouraging to a courtier of a king he despised and hoped to ruin.

The other thing Blaidd had come to realize, although it had nothing to do with his mission, was the unusual position of Lady Rebecca in the household. By rights, and as the eldest, Lady Laelia should be the chatelaine, overseeing the food and linen and everything else in and about the hall and apartments. However, those tasks seemed to fall solely to Lady Rebecca. Keys jingling as she moved, she went from the kitchen to the storeroom to the buttery with seemingly tireless energy. She gave orders to the servants and spoke with the merchants who came to sell their goods. She apparently organized everything.

Blaidd had yet to discover exactly what Lady Laelia did except look lovely and embroider.

He wasn't the only one getting restless here, either. Trev was clearly beginning to wish he had more to do than polish Blaidd's sword and shield. He'd been good about obeying Blaidd's admonitions concerning the serving women, but a bored youth and a pretty maidservant who always had a smile for him could find themselves in mischief soon, if the weather didn't clear.

Then, after a tedious evening during which Blaidd decided he and Trev would ride out the next day, rain or not, the morning dawned sunny and warm—a beautiful spring day. Blaidd felt years younger, and he was determined to get out for a gallop across a meadow.

Blaidd was in such a good humor, he whistled as they left the chapel after Mass and headed toward the hall to break the fast. Lord Throckton walked beside him on his left, Lady Laelia glided along on his right and Trev brought up the rear. Lady Rebecca had disappeared, probably into the kitchen.

"I feel as merry as your tune, Sir Blaidd," Lord Throckton said with a deep chuckle. "It looks to be an excellent day for hunting. Will you join me?"

"I'll be delighted to, my lord." Blaidd smiled at Lady Laelia. "Maybe you'll accompany us?"

He was surprised to see her dart an uneasy glance at her father.

"Of course she will!" he cried. "Have no fear, Laelia, I'm sure Sir Blaidd will keep a moderate pace if you ask him."

A moderate pace? Blaidd had to struggle not to betray any disappointment. But he'd been hoping for a wild gallop, and he was quite sure Aderyn Du would be wanting that, too.

Lady Laelia stared at him woefully with her big green eyes. "I'm afraid I'm a timid horsewomen, Sir

Blaidd. If you'd rather not ride with me, I'll understand.''

Being a gentleman, Blaidd battened down his frustration. He could always exercise Aderyn Du later. ''Of course I won't mind. Besides, how could I truly appreciate your beautiful countryside at a gallop? Or if you prefer, we could stay behind,'' he finished, remembering he was supposed to be courting her, although this meant losing an opportunity to speak with her father.

''That won't be necessary,'' Lord Throckton said. ''She'll ride, won't you, Laelia?''

''Yes, Father.'' She looked up at Blaidd. ''I'm sure you'll be considerate of my maidenly fears,'' she murmured.

Blaidd immediately thought of another young woman, one he couldn't imagine having ''maidenly fears.'' He could more easily picture Lady Rebecca glaring an opponent into submission.

He tried to put her, Throckton's other daughter, out of his mind. ''Naturally, my lady. My greatest pleasure will be your company.''

God's wounds, that was a bit much, but Laelia beamed, gazing at him with gratitude and admiration. One would think he'd offered to sacrifice his life for her.

A little while later, Blaidd stood near the stable beside a restless Aderyn Du, waiting for the rest of the hunting party to assemble. The beaters and other servants who would travel on foot were already assembled near the inner gate, talking and laughing among themselves. A groom had led out a fine brown gelding sporting an expensive looking saddle and bridle, and a white mare that was surely for Lady Laelia. Trev was still in the stables, saddling his horse and taking his own sweet time about it. Perhaps he'd gotten a bit lazy these past few days, and a reprimand would be in order. Or at least a pointed remark.

Blaidd's gaze roved over the buildings, and he noticed scaffolding on the eastern wall, which obviously still needed some work. There were no workmen there now. Perhaps they'd gone to work on another part of the castle. Lord Throckton had mentioned something about a gate the other evening.

Blaidd should have paid more attention to that and less to Lady Rebecca's playing.

Aderyn Du tossed his head and shifted his feet, obviously anxious to run. Blaidd wished he didn't have to keep a tight rein on him, but there didn't seem much help for it. Maybe after the noon meal they could go out again. Surely Lady Laelia and her father wouldn't miss him for a few hours.

Tapping his foot, Blaidd continued to watch the stable door, wondering if he'd have to go in and urge Trev to get a move on.

Then, to his surprise, Lady Rebecca appeared at the entrance to the stable, leading a remarkably fine roan. She was as plainly dressed as always, except that she wore a long gray cloak and gauntlet gloves of leather. Obviously, she was going riding. With them?

Why not?

Because she'd never appeared anxious to spend time with them before; her household duties seemed to occupy all her time.

She caught him watching, and his first impulse was to turn away, like a little boy caught with stolen sweetmeats.

He wasn't a little boy, though, so he didn't.

Then he expected her to ignore him.

She didn't.

"You look surprised, sir knight," she coolly noted as she led her horse near the excited Aderyn Du, who got more excited. It was as if he were anticipating a race. "Having one leg shorter than the other doesn't prevent me from riding."

"I'm sure, my lady, it would take a great deal to prevent you from doing whatever you set your mind to," he replied. "I didn't think you could spare the time from your many duties."

A smile twitched at the corner of her lips and her blue eyes sparkled. It struck him that she seemed as anxious to be out of the castle as he and Aderyn Du were. "I'm not indispensable. I've been cooped inside for long enough, and I think the servants will be happy to be rid of me for a little while."

"Command can be onerous," he agreed. "And the weather has been dismal."

"I thought the Welsh were used to rain," she replied, her intriguing smile growing a little wider. It was like seeing the sun peeking out from behind a storm cloud—just as lovely, just as welcome.

"Used to it we may be, for fine sunny days are

rarer in Wales than here. But that means we appreciate the sunny days even more. I'm anxious to enjoy this one.''

''Your horse seems anxious, too.''

Blaidd ran his hand down Aderyn Du's strong neck. ''Aye, he is. He needs a good gallop to calm him.''

She cocked her head and her smile altered to a rueful one. ''If you're riding with Laelia, that's not likely.''

''So I understand. I hope to have the chance later.''

She nodded and eyed his horse again. ''That's a very fine animal. May I?'' she inquired, moving forward to pet Aderyn Du's muzzle.

''He cost me a small fortune, I admit, but he's worth every ha'penny,'' Blaidd said proudly.

Aderyn Du didn't suffer the touch of strangers gladly, but he accepted her stroking with excellent grace. Meanwhile his master was mesmerized by the sight of Lady Rebecca's slender, strong gloved fingers moving slowly down his horse's smooth face.

''What's his name?''

Blaidd stopped staring and focused his attention on her gleaming, intelligent eyes. ''Aderyn Du.''

''That's Welsh, isn't it?''

''Aye. It means black bird. Because he flies when he runs, you see.''

She laughed, a merry sound even prettier than her eyes. ''It suits him.'' She nodded at her horse. ''This is Claudia. I didn't choose that mundane name,'' she hastened to explain, as if he would think the less of her. "She's fast, too."

"What would you have called her if you'd had the naming of her?"

Lady Rebecca pondered a moment, her brow wrinkled with concentration, her full lips pursed. Then a smile bloomed and her eyes lit up. "Firebrand."

Oh, God help him, as she smiled at him, so pleased and happy, he wanted to pull her into his arms and kiss her until neither of them had breath to whisper.

"Ready on time and waiting, too!"

As startled as if he'd kissed the man's daughter right there in the courtyard, Blaidd spun on his heel to see Lord Throckton trotting down the hall steps. The man was attired in his usual fine garments, and his cloak was lined with what looked like wolf's fur.

Blaidd immediately covered his discomfort with a genial grin. "Aye, my lord. I've been admiring your buildings, too."

Lord Throckton gestured for the groom holding the reins of the brown gelding to come toward him. Then he glanced up at the walls. "Not finished yet, but I haven't got the coin to complete it all. Not with this year's taxes being what they are, eh? I'm sure your father's noticed the increase."

"Yes, he has," Blaidd answered honestly.

"More money for the crown, less for me, and so I have to wait until next year to finish the postern gate and some of the merlons on the eastern wall. Pity, but what can you do?"

Blaidd shrugged. It seemed an odd thing to be glad

that the man might not be as prosperous as he appeared, but he was.

"Laelia will be along shortly," Lord Throckton said. He gave Blaidd a wink. "You know how women are."

Some women, Blaidd thought as he noticed Lady Rebecca move away toward the gate without speaking to her father.

"Where's your squire? Isn't he coming, too?"

"Here he is now, my lord," Blaidd said, nodding at Trev as he appeared at the stable door leading his horse. "He's as anxious for a ride as I am."

"His father's quite the famous fellow."

"Justly so."

"Did Urien Fitzroy train you?"

"Aye, my lord, and my brother, Kynan, and Trev, of course."

"Perhaps one of these days you'll have a chat with Dobbin, my garrison commander. Maybe you can teach that old dog some new tricks." Lord Throckton chortled at his joke.

"I'd be glad to, and in truth, I should have some practice myself, or my sword arm will be getting as rusty as a blade left out all winter."

That got another laugh from the lord. "Oh, I doubt that!"

More anxious than ever to be on his way, Blaidd glanced at the gate. Lady Rebecca was there, talking and laughing with the soldiers and servants, clearly in high spirits.

And yet there was something about her that simultaneously made her seem aloof and apart, as if try as she might to be one of them, she never would be. She was a woman, of course, but there was more to it than that. It was as if she had a maturity and wisdom they didn't share.

"I understand your other daughter will be joining us, too," he said, turning his attention back to Lord Throckton.

"Eh?" The man looked taken aback, until he followed Blaidd's glance. "Oh, she is, is she?" he said, sounding neither pleased nor otherwise. "She'll probably not stay with us for more than a little while. She'll go galloping off and return when she wills."

The man's matter-of-fact tone prompted Blaidd to say, "With an escort, I assume."

Lord Throckton frowned and shook his head. "She'll lose 'em before they know she's gone. Always has, always will."

"But surely, my lord, even if your lands are safe, a lone woman shouldn't—"

"She'll be safe," his host interrupted in a tone of finality. "She's been doing this for years, and there's not an outlaw who could catch her, anyway."

"My lord, surely there must be a soldier or two who could keep up with her," Blaidd persisted, appalled to think the man had so little concern for a daughter's safety.

"And *I* told *you*, she's been giving us the slip since she was a little girl," Lord Throckton replied, smiling but clearly losing his patience. "I've tried warning her, ordering her, frightening her, and she still won't listen. Short of tying her to her bed, I've run out of ideas. If you have any, young man, I'll listen—but I won't guarantee they'll work.''

Blaidd realized he'd protested too much, and sought to lessen the damage. After all, Lady Rebecca was her father's responsibility, not his. ''I'm sorry, my lord.''

Lord Throckton's annoyance fled as quickly as it had arisen, and he clapped Blaidd companionably on the shoulder. ''Well, in most cases, you'd be right about the risk, but this is the exception. Still, it says a lot that you felt concerned enough to speak out. Spare me the spineless stripling who says only what he thinks I want to hear.'' His hand fell as he turned. ''Now where in the name of the saints is Laelia? It'll be noon before we're gone at this rate. *Laelia!*'' he bellowed, the name echoing off the walls and drawing everyone's attention.

''Here, Father! There's no need to shout,'' the lady said as she appeared at the entrance to the hall, blushing and looking prettily upset. ''I was just putting on my cloak.''

And a beautiful cloak it was, of soft, dark blue wool trimmed with fox, with a hood that framed her beautiful face. Beneath the cloak, Blaidd spied a skirt of lighter blue wool.

The groom holding the white mare led it forward.

Blaidd immediately offered to help Lady Laelia, an offer she didn't decline.

As he held his hands for her to step into, he glanced

toward the gate again, to see Lady Rebecca swing into the saddle unaided.

He could just imagine the look she'd give him if he'd offered to assist her.

The pressure of Lady Laelia's foot in his palms reminded him of what he was supposed to be doing.

And that he should pay attention to her, not her sister.

Chapter Six

There was one good thing about the delay leaving Throckton Castle that morning: the road was much less muddy than it would have been earlier. Although there were plenty of puddles, the higher ground was quite dry.

It was damper in the wood the hunting party entered. The hounds sniffed at nearly everything, and the horses' hooves squelched in the mud. Several startled sparrows flew up into the cloudless sky and scattered. Occasionally a squirrel paused as it ran by on a branch, and stared at them as if wondering what they were doing there.

The beaters had gone on ahead, and the other servants, whose tasks were to transport the weapons, tend to the hounds and carry home the game, came behind, their voices hushed as they whispered together. Occasionally some of them laughed, and often in that burst of laughter, Blaidd distinguished the musical merriment of Lady Rebecca. She seemed to be having a wonderful time. He, meanwhile, was riding between a silent Lady Laelia, who looked a little pale as she gripped her reins, and her father.

Another burst of laughter sounded, and this time, in addition to Lady Rebecca's mirth, he recognized Trev's boisterous, youthful crow of delight. Blaidd twisted to look over his shoulder, and sure enough, Trev had joined the lady, and the men walking on foot beside her mount.

"You must forgive my younger daughter," Lord Throckton said, his lips a little thinned and his gray brows lowered in what was almost a scowl. "Becca spends too much time with the peasants. Always has. I can't break her of that any more than riding away from her escort."

Blaidd noticed that Laelia didn't look pleased by her sister's actions, either. "It's a rare lady who feels so at ease with her servants and tenants," he said, without indicating whether he approved or not.

In truth, though, he was reminded of some of the stories his father used to tell about his mother. She'd been delicately reared and had had, when they first married, a very firm and limited notion of what a lady did and what her relationship with those considered beneath her ought to be. Blaidd had always found that hard to believe, for the woman he knew cared for their tenants as if they were her family. He couldn't imagine living in a castle where the nobles treated their servants like slaves.

"Tell me, is it true the queen is with child at last?" Lord Throckton asked.

Blaidd tried not to look surprised at the unexpected question. Perhaps Lord Throckton was desperate to take attention from his seemingly impossible younger daughter. "Yes, she is."

The older man grinned. "From what I have heard of Henry's affection for the girl, I'm surprised she hasn't borne him an heir already. It's been what, nearly two years since he married her?"

Blaidd shrugged. "Who can say why such things happen, even in the happiest of marriages? And she was little more than a child when they wed."

"Too young," Lord Throckton murmured, glancing at Laelia, who didn't seem to hear.

"Already there have been several Masses of thanksgiving, and prayers for a son," Blaidd noted.

"Naturally," Throckton acknowledged with a nod. "Every man wants an heir."

Blaidd heard an undercurrent of bitterness and didn't begrudge the man. All noblemen hoped for a son to inherit their name and title and lands. So did Blaidd, although he wanted daughters, too. His father always said that with sons came grave responsibilities, while daughters gave a man joy.

"Or if God does not see fit to send a son, a man longs for a fine son-in-law to give him grandsons, if He wills," Lord Throckton continued.

Blaidd smiled at his host. "My mother can hardly wait for grandchildren." He looked woeful. "I'm afraid I've been a disappointment to her there."

"Surely that will soon be mended, once you take

a wife. I'm sure any woman you wed will be more than willing to do her duty in your bed.''

''Father!'' Laelia cried, scandalized and blushing. ''What a thing to say!''

''Take no offense, my lady, for I don't,'' Blaidd said, grinning. ''My father also says it's a parent's duty to embarrass his children, to pay them back for all those sleepless nights when they were infants.''

Lord Throckton roared with approving laughter, and the lady managed a little smile.

''Simon de Montfort continues to be a great favorite at court, especially among the ladies,'' Blaidd said in an offhand way, turning the conversation back to the king and his court. He should make the most of this opportunity while he had it, and he most certainly didn't want to discuss his failings as a son and heir.

''Who is that?'' Laelia asked, her smooth brow wrinkling with puzzlement. ''He's sounds French.''

Blaidd nodded. ''He was born there, but he's renounced his claim to his French land and titles in favor of his English ones. The king recently recognized him as the earl of Leicester.''

''So he's not one of the queen's relations?'' Lady Laelia asked.

''No. But many of the English barons were appalled by his marriage to the king's sister. They feel they should have been asked if they approved or not, especially since it required her to break the vow of chastity she took when her husband died.''

''She took a vow of chastity?'' Laelia cried in disbelief. ''Whatever for?''

"Out of respect for her late husband, of course," Lord Throckton answered. "That should have kept her well out of her brother's political machinations, too. I was shocked she agreed."

For a man who lived this far from London and never traveled to the king's court, Lord Throckton was very well informed. Still, that wasn't so very unusual. Blaidd's own father rarely ventured from home, but he listened closely whenever Blaidd or his brother returned from court and spoke of what was transpiring there. Hu Morgan's friends kept him informed, too. Who was to say Lord Throckton didn't have friends who did the same?

"You haven't met Simon de Montfort," Blaidd explained. "He's a very charming man of great abilities. Despite his birth, I think we can expect great things of him in the future. He believes in a permanent council, something he calls a parliament, to advise the king and administer the government. Many of the barons and knights like the idea."

Lord Throckton frowned. "De Montfort had better keep quiet about that, or brother-in-law or not, he risks upsetting Henry, who's got that Plantagenet temper—or so I've heard."

Blaidd couldn't disagree. "He does, but hopefully he'll listen to Simon and appreciate his wisdom."

"If he were really wise, he wouldn't give so many honors and estates to his wife's relatives," Lord Throckton said. He eyed Blaidd shrewdly. "How is it you, a Welshman, don't hate the man? His treatment of the Welsh has hardly been generous."

"No, it hasn't been, and I'm well aware of their just grievances. I've no liking for wars and battles, though, where so many can be killed for so little gain. I prefer diplomacy, so I try to represent the Welsh at court and speak for them whenever I can. Also, Henry is my lawful king, and I swore an oath of loyalty to him when I received my knighthood. I'm duty bound to honor it."

"An aversion to violence? That's an odd sentiment coming from a knight," Lady Rebecca declared.

Blaidd hadn't realized she and Trev had drawn so close.

He pulled Aderyn Du to a halt, letting Lady Laelia and her father ride ahead. When Lady Rebecca and Trev were beside him, he nudged Aderyn Du into a walk again. "Just because I'm trained to fight doesn't mean I'm anxious to do so. I've seen bloody death, my lady, and I would spare all whom I care about from it, including the peasants who farm my family's lands."

"What if talk avails nothing? Then men must fight."

"If all else fails, then yes, I agree it must be war. Yet I fear too many noblemen go to war for nothing more than personal power and greed, and don't care who dies for their ambition."

"A fine sentiment," Lord Throckton said with approval as he looked back over his shoulder. "I only wish the king shared it."

"I believe Henry *is* anxious to avoid war, my lord," Blaidd said. "He's a peaceable man by nature, and perhaps overly generous. But he's young and newly married. Hopefully, with age will come greater wisdom, and less of a desire to please his wife.''

"Yes, he's young and liable to err. I suppose we all must have patience and give the man a chance,'' Lord Throckton said as he faced forward again. ''After all, it's only natural to want to please your bride, even if she's French. Perhaps especially if she's French, eh?'' he finished with a deep chortle.

They reached a fork in the road, where a path veered off to the west, through deeper woods and underbrush.

"I've had enough talk of politics and the king and war,'' Lady Rebecca announced. ''Farewell.''

Without any further ado, she punched her heels into her horse's side and took off at a trot along the narrow path.

Nobody else seemed surprised, and Laelia even looked rather pleased. Blaidd was not. There might not be any outlaws on Lord Throckton's land, but what if she fell? What if she injured her other leg?

He dare not risk offending Lord Throckton or Laelia by abandoning them; nevertheless, he simply couldn't accept letting the lady ride alone. ''Trev, go with Lady Rebecca.''

Trev looked crestfallen. ''I'll miss the hunt—''

Blaidd gave him a stern look, and a blushing Trev immediately did as he was told.

"That really wasn't necessary,'' Lord Throckton growled. ''She'll go to a gallop the moment she hits the meadow on the other side of the wood, and he'll never catch her.''

"I hope you're right, my lord. It will do my squire good to discover that as excellent a rider as he may be, he can yet be bested by a woman,'' Blaidd said, silently congratulating himself on thinking of this excuse.

No matter what he said to his host, he was confident Trev could catch up to the lady. He wondered what Lady Rebecca would say to Trev when he did. She surely wouldn't be pleased, but it would likely do *her* good to realize she could be caught, and not necessarily by honest young men.

A man dressed in muddy tunic, breeches and boots came jogging toward the nobles. "The beaters are in place, my lord,'' he panted, tugging on his forelock.

"Excellent!'' Lord Throckton cried, his good humor apparently restored.

"If the hunt is going to begin in earnest, I should go back,'' Laelia said softly, moving her horse off the road to make way for the hunting party.

"Good hunting, my lord,'' Blaidd said as he dutifully did the same.

Lord Throckton called out to two brawny male servants, ordering them to return to the castle, too.

A wise move from a protective father, Blaidd reflected, taking no offense, as the hunting party rode off around them in a cacophony of hounds, hooves, excited voices and splattering mud.

"I'm sorry to keep you from joining them,'' Laelia

said, her green eyes full of remorse, when they returned to the road and headed back toward the castle.

Blaidd immediately wiped any regret from his face. "It's quite all right. I certainly don't mind the company of a beautiful woman instead of hounds and horses."

Laelia blushed and looked down demurely. "I suppose you've known many beautiful women at the king's court."

"A few, but none so lovely as you." Blaidd inwardly cringed at his lack of originality. Unfortunately, he was discovering that Lady Laelia never inspired anything more genuine in the way of a compliment. "It's a pity you've never been there."

"My father doesn't like to travel."

"It can be dangerous," Blaidd agreed.

"And uncomfortable, too, he says, staying at inns where you don't know who was in the bed before you, or if there are fleas. And the food would probably be terrible." She sighed sorrowfully. "I'd at least like the opportunity to see the king and the nobles and the fine ladies."

"The fine ladies might be sorry to see *you,* for your beauty would outshine them all."

She flushed very prettily. "I daresay there are few men as handsome or valiant as you at court."

"There are many more handsome than I, and bravery can be measured many ways, my lady."

She slid him a shy glance. "Tell me, do other men at court have hair as long as yours? Is this a new fashion?"

He laughed. "No, only a few. In this, I am woefully out of fashion."

"Then why don't you cut it?"

"Because I like it this way."

Her shapely nose wrinkled a little. "But if it's not the fashion at court…"

Keeping in mind the ostensible reason for his presence, he dropped his voice, but not so much to cause their two beefy escorts to come any closer. "Don't *you* like it?"

She blushed bright red and didn't meet his gaze. "It makes you look…uncouth. Like a savage."

"That doesn't appeal to you, my lady?"

She spoke with a decisiveness he hadn't expected. "No."

In the next moment, however, that brief vitality and surety had disappeared. "Of course, it isn't for me to criticize, Sir Blaidd."

"You are entitled to an opinion," he said, not at all upset by her dislike of his long hair. He was relieved that she'd finally said something sincere. "To be sure, I'm not happy to hear you don't approve of my hair, but if that's what you really think, so be it."

"You're not angry?"

"No."

"Or upset with me?"

He grinned. "Not a bit."

She looked as if she didn't really believe him.

"My lady, it's a poor fellow who doesn't care to know what a woman really thinks, about anything.

It's not always pleasant to hear an honest opinion, I grant you, but I prefer that to evasion.''

"You really mean that, don't you?" she asked incredulously, admiration shining in her eyes.

"Well, within reason, of course," he amended.

Her lips turned down in a peeved frown. "Yes, some women are far too outspoken and forward."

"I gather you're speaking of your sister?"

"She can be very trying at times." Laelia's tone softened, and it didn't seem she was being insincere when she said, "I try not to be too angry with her. It must hurt her terribly to think she'll never get a husband. Between her leg and her tongue, what man would want her? Still, it's a relief to know my father will have someone to look after him in his old age, after I am wed."

And thus her sister was disposed of. He shouldn't be so surprised that Laelia would speak with so much conviction of her sister's fate, for such would be the portion of any younger sister who didn't marry. In Lady Rebecca's case, though, it seemed a very great pity. The only thing less suited to her than nursemaid to her father would be life in a convent.

The reverend mother of the convent wouldn't know what had hit her—unless it be the devil in human form, refusing to obey, forgetting to be silent.

No, Rebecca would be much better suited running a man's household and controlling a boisterous family. He could easily picture her surrounded by happy servants and joyous, noisy dark-haired children, with a few puppies at her feet to complete the scene. Her loving husband would come sneaking up behind her and embrace her, making her start and curse, and then laugh as he turned her toward him for a searing kiss, regardless of servants, children and puppies—

Blaidd stopped picturing and surreptitiously glanced at the richly attired, beautiful woman riding beside him at a leisurely pace. She'd probably hate puppies. They'd be too noisy, too dirty. Maybe she'd think the same about children, too.

Not that it mattered. After all, he wasn't really here to woo her…or anybody else.

It was midafternoon when Becca and Trevelyan Fitzroy returned to the castle. What an impertinent young rascal he was, Becca reflected as she prepared to dismount.

Meanwhile, young Fitzroy leaped easily from his horse and in the next moment was beside hers, holding his hand out to assist her.

Who else but an impertinent young rascal would dare to shout out as she galloped away from him that she had to stop or he was going to throw up?

Afraid he was ill, she'd halted, only to have him immediately and merrily confess that was the only thing he could think of to say to get her to slow down. Then he'd told her he would die—"Absolutely perish of shame!"—if he came back without her. Not only that, but Sir Blaidd Morgan would reprimand him as only that knight could, without shouting but, "Oh, my lady, he can fairly flay the flesh from your bones with the look he gives you!''

Since she didn't want the boy to suffer on her account, she'd agreed to let him ride with her. She shared her refreshments with him, too. During the time they sat on the grassy verge of the river, Trevelyan had revealed some very interesting things about Sir Blaidd Morgan, not the least of which was the esteem in which he was held at court, by men as well as women.

''He's a trusted friend of the king,'' young Fitzroy had boasted.

She'd wondered how her father would react to that bit of information. It was certainly no secret that he didn't think much of Henry, or his method of government.

But she was not her father's spy, and after the conversation that morning, he would have some inkling of Sir Blaidd's political views without any help from her. Whether that would be enough to make him an unwelcome suitor for Laelia was far from certain, however. Laelia's opinion of him seemed to improve daily, and thus far, her father had voiced no objections.

Becca could understand why. The Welshman was a genial, interesting, very attractive man.

''You must allow me to assist you, my lady,'' Trevelyan Fitzroy declared, interrupting her reverie. ''Otherwise, Blaidd is going to have my head. See, here he comes now, in high dudgeon.''

She followed his gaze, to find Sir Blaidd stalking toward them like a man on a serious mission.

Now she could well believe he'd win any tournament he entered. She could even believe he would do so with nothing more than his bare hands.

"Very well," she conceded. She didn't want to admit that Sir Blaidd could inspire her to do anything, so she continued, "But only because you managed to beat me to the river by jumping that fallen log and the one right after it. I was sure you or your horse would balk."

"What, over a fallen log? Not likely. And how could we not, when you'd done it? I'd never be able to hold my head up."

"And a handsome head it is, too," she noted as he put his hands firmly around her waist. Still in his grasp, she slid to the ground.

Sir Blaidd Morgan came to a halt nearby, hands on his narrow hips, sword swinging because of his hasty pace. He crossed his arms and leaned his weight on one leg. "So, you both had a lovely time, did you?" he asked, his voice dripping honey but his eyes flashing fire. "You've been gone half the day."

Trevelyan stared at the ground and flushed.

At the man's arrogant sarcasm and the boy's shamed reaction, Becca's gloved hands balled into fists. "How dare you chastise him?" she demanded. "He was only heeding your orders when he followed me—orders that need not have been issued—and he stayed with me because he believed it was his duty to do so. If we're later returning than you expected, that's not his fault. Or would you rather I had scolded him thoroughly for presuming I need a keeper, and sent him back alone?''

Sir Blaidd continued to stare at her for a long moment, then, still glaring, addressed Trevelyan Fitzroy. ''Take the horses into the stable and see they're looked after.''

''Blaidd, I'm sorry but—''

''I don't want to hear any explanations or apologies. I've given you an order.''

''Yes, sir,'' Trev mumbled as he hurried to do as he was commanded.

Regardless of the grooms, stable boys and any servants currently crossing the courtyard, Becca marched up to Sir Blaidd and jabbed him in the chest. ''You arrogant bully! Why did you embarrass the boy like that? He was only obeying your unnecessary orders.''

Sir Blaidd grabbed her hand, his grasp warm and just tight enough to hold her still. ''How I treat my squire is none of your business, my lady,'' he retorted, his dark eyes still blazing. He released her hand and bowed with mocking courtesy. ''I humbly ask your forgiveness for caring about your welfare. I should, of course, allow you to be attacked, possibly raped or killed, if that is what you want, and forgo the oath I swore when I became a knight.''

She put her hands on her hips. ''Did I *ask* for your protection?''

Hands clenched at his sides, he leaned forward so that they were nearly nose to nose. ''My oath does not say, 'But only if she asks.' And I assure you, my lady, I take my oath to protect women as seriously as I do my vow to be loyal to my king.''

Becca wouldn't back down, not even if his nose came into contact with hers. ''Even if I refuse your protection outright?''

''You can try to do so, but it won't absolve me of my oath.''

As they stood glaring at each other like two angry bulls about to charge, it suddenly occurred to Becca that it had been a long time since anybody except her family had spoken to her that way, and even then, her father never got *that* angry. Sir Blaidd Morgan's fury made no allowance for her rank, her sex or disability. He treated her as if she were…his equal.

Another realization came hard upon that one. She remembered where she'd seen the expression on Sir Blaidd's face as he marched up to them. It was the sort of look two rivals for Laelia's attention gave each other.

Surely Sir Blaidd couldn't be *jealous?* Of that boy? Over her? The thought made her laugh before she could help herself.

Sir Blaidd frowned darkly. ''I amuse you, do I?''

She wasn't going to admit that the notion he might be jealous had ever crossed her mind, or he'd be the one laughing. Still, the slightest chance that it might be so gave her a certain measure of confidence.

''I find it delightful that you have no qualms about getting angry with me,'' she confessed evenly. ''A lot of men treat me as some sort of delicate child.''

"I'm very aware you're not a child, my lady," he growled in his velvety, deep voice.

Although she was sure seduction was not his intention, her body nevertheless responded as it had in the chapel. Desire, sly and overpowering, began to stir within her.

"I'm glad to hear it," she replied, attempting to subdue that wayward feeling. "Therefore, sir knight, if I choose to do a thing, you ought to let me do it."

"As tempting as that may be, given your lack of gratitude, I remind you that my sworn oath forbids it. If you insist upon risking your neck, I'll do all I can to protect you. Now, unless you're planning another ride, I bid you good day, my lady."

As she watched him stride away, Becca wondered if Laelia appreciated the sort of man who was courting her. Sir Blaidd was easily worth twenty of the fools who had come wooing before him.

Chapter Seven

Blaidd wiped the perspiration from his face with the back of his hand and bent again, swaying, preparing to strike with the broadsword clutched in both his hands. Blood oozed from the cut on his naked chest, made by Dobbin when he was a bit too slow to respond. He should have known better. Like his father and Sir Urien, Dobbin was still a strong and vigorous man, despite his age, and obviously skilled. He also possessed the wisdom of experience, and sure enough, none of Blaidd's usual tricks and feints had worked against the older man.

His breath visible in the chilly morning air, Dobbin circled Blaidd warily. Blaidd slowly swiveled, keeping his gaze firmly on his opponent. He watched the man's sword, waiting to see if it dipped, indicating fatigue. He noted Dobbin's shoulders, low and relaxed, not tensed up near his ears. This man had fought many, many times, and had confidence in his abilities. He moved with slow deliberation, too, not the jerky steps of a nervous fighter. All in all, Dobbin was an opponent to be reckoned with.

''What are you waiting for?'' Blaidd heard Trev mutter from the group of foot soldiers surrounding them in the inner ward, watching.

Blaidd's temper flared, but he quickly got it under control. He wasn't going to get angry and behave like an apoplectic ogre again, as he had four days ago when he'd confronted Lady Rebecca in the courtyard.

Trev was still sulking over what had happened that day. Blaidd understood why; he'd wounded the boy's pride with his public reprimand, especially because Lady Rebecca had been right—Trev had only been following his orders. Blaidd had apologized later, saying there was no excuse for him to lose his temper like that. He'd also pointed out that Lady Rebecca had reprimanded him in public, too, although in her case, she was quite justified. Trev had shrugged and tried to act as if nothing was wrong, but things hadn't been the same between them since.

Another error since arriving here.

At least Lady Rebecca seemed to forgive him, after she'd so soundly chastised him. Her attitude since had been exactly as it was before, neither better nor worse. Because of that, Blaidd hadn't told her he was sorry, especially considering what had happened the last time he'd done that.

The tip of Dobbin's sword moved slightly lower, but not with fatigue. Blaidd recognized the preparation to strike, and waited a necessary split second before raising his own sword to meet Dobbin's. Then, with a twist of the wrist that could be agonizing if not done properly, he finally managed to unsword Dobbin, catching the man's blade and sending it skittering along the grass to come to rest at...Lady Rebecca's feet.

"Well done, sir knight," she coolly said above the excited babble of the men. She bent down and effortlessly picked up the heavy weapon, then handed it to him.

She wore her usual gown of simple brown wool, and her thick, beautiful hair was covered by the sort of equally plain scarf servants wore.

Blaidd preferred such garments to fancy silks and velvets that limited their wearer's movements. She looked ready to meet any challenge or solve any problem, domestic or otherwise.

Sheathing his sword, he tried to speak without any obvious emotion. "Thank you, my lady."

"You're bleeding. It's not a serious wound, I hope?"

He glanced down at his chest, acutely aware that she was looking at him and that he was half-naked. "No. I've had worse."

"Lady Laelia sends her regrets, but she is unwell today and will not be able to join you in the hall."

"I'm very sorry to hear that."

Averting her eyes from his sweat-slicked torso, Becca studied Sir Blaidd's face. He appeared concerned that Laelia wasn't feeling well, as anyone might, but not overly so.

All this time, and she still couldn't tell how he

really felt about Laelia, or anything else. "It's a headache, nothing more. She gets them sometimes, and a day of rest should see her quite recovered."

Becca moved toward Dobbin, who was wiping his flushed, perspiring face with his tunic.

What Sir Blaidd was doing at that moment, she didn't know, because she didn't look. It had been enough to see him stripped to the waist, his lean, tautly muscled chest gleaming in the morning sunlight, while he wielded his heavy sword as if it weighed no more than a ball of wool. She'd been shocked by the cut, just as she had been to see who the combatants were, until she recalled Sir Blaidd's request to train with Dobbin and his men.

"God's wounds, I was sure I had him there at the end," Dobbin complained to the men gathered around him, their expressions as consoling as if he'd lost a favorite pet. "That Fitzroy must be as fine a trainer of fighting men as they say. I've never seen such a move." He raised his voice. "Can you show us how you did it, Sir Blaidd? Slowly?"

She glanced at the Welshman, to see that he had put on his tunic. Thank God.

Sir Blaidd's brows rose. "What, now?"

"Or later, if you prefer," Dobbin replied with deference.

Sir Blaidd grinned. "Now's as good a time as any," he said, once again drawing off his tunic, his movement smooth as silken fabric slipping over a merchant's arm.

Becca turned to go, until Dobbin's call made her

halt. "Stay a moment, my lady. After he shows us that move, maybe you can show him how you shoot." He smiled at Sir Blaidd. "I taught her, sir," he bragged, "and I reckon she's as fine an archer as any of those Welshmen we hear about. She can't shoot so far, because she's not got a man's strength, but she's dead accurate."

Although she was as proud of her skill as Dobbin was, Becca didn't feel the need to demonstrate that particular talent to Sir Blaidd Morgan. "I don't think that will be necessary. I'm sure he'll take your word for it."

"It so happens, Dobbin, that I'm considered a fine shot myself, my father insisting that all his sons be trained with every weapon, even if bows are considered fitting only for foot soldiers." Sir Blaidd's grin widened, but there was an unmistakable gleam of challenge in his eyes. "Perhaps a contest is in order?"

Taking up the bow had been Dobbin's suggestion, made when she was lying in bed while her leg healed. He would teach her as soon as she was able to get up, he'd promised, and she wouldn't feel so helpless then.

She'd seen the merit in his idea at once, and had been thankful for something to think about other than what she *wouldn't* be able to do anymore. Afraid her father wouldn't approve, they hadn't said anything to him about it for a long time, until she was as good as any of the garrison.

She'd harbored a faint hope he'd be pleased, but

he'd given them both a skeptical scowl. "If I need her to defend Throckton, I'll call," he'd sniffed.

Well, she was being called upon to defend Dobbin's skill as a teacher, and that was just as important.

She gave Sir Blaidd a patronizing smile. "How could I resist? I only hope your pride won't be seriously wounded when I win."

"I'll send a couple of the lads for butts and targets and the bows and quivers," Dobbin said eagerly, before Sir Blaidd could change his mind. "While they're preparing things, Sir Blaidd can show us that move."

Several minutes later, after Dobbin had perfected the technique of disarming his opponent with that particular twist of his blade, Blaidd and Becca prepared to shoot. Behind her, Becca heard a low murmur. Wagers were being made and she wondered who was the favorite. Dobbin would bet on her, she was certain, but she had no idea whether the other men might pick her or the Welshman.

Although Sir Blaidd was now properly clad in a tunic belted about the waist, Becca tried not to pay attention to her opponent as he tied the leather guard around his left forearm. One of the soldiers standing beside him held an unslung bow of yew, another a quiver.

Becca already had her guard on, and a soldier handed her a bow. Bracing the weapon against her foot, she quickly slid the string into place at the top and plucked an arrow fletched with goose feathers from the quiver the soldier held in his other hand.

"Best two out of three the winner?" Sir Blaidd suggested as he, too, strung his bow.

"If you wish," she said.

Now that they were ready, the soldiers who had been holding their accoutrements stepped back out of the way.

As Becca nocked her arrow on the bowstring and raised her bow, she put out of her mind everything except the bull's-eye painted on a cloth tacked to a butt of straw. She took aim and waited for Dobbin to give the signal to let fly.

He did, and the familiar twang of a bowstring sounded in her ear as it snapped. Her arrow flew through the air, straight and true, to hit the center of the target. Smiling with satisfaction, she looked at Sir Blaidd's target.

His arrow was likewise sticking out of the center of the bull's-eye. A roar of both approval and dismay went up from the men as Trev and Dobbin trotted down the ward to see who had made the better shot. Becca waited, her toe tapping, as they conferred for what seemed a very long time.

"We must be close," Sir Blaidd remarked.

"I suppose," she answered.

"Dobbin said you were naturally gifted. So you are, in both archery and the harp. You would almost be worshipped in Wales with those skills."

She wondered if that were really true, and how it

would feel to be approved of wholeheartedly, instead of being considered odd.

Dobbin held up his hand. "The lady wins!"

That got another roar of approval, as well as a few mutters, while the judges returned. Trevelyan Fitzroy looked as if he'd just been told the sun wasn't going to rise tomorrow.

She'd noticed signs of strain between Sir Blaidd and his squire ever since they'd returned from riding that day. She felt a small twinge of remorse for being the cause of any animosity between them, but not much. Sir Blaidd had rebuked the boy unjustly, and if things were not the same between them, it was Sir Blaidd's fault far more than hers.

At the moment, however, Sir Blaidd seemed to take everything in stride, including making the poorer shot. "I'll have to do better with the next one," he said evenly as he reached for another arrow.

Becca also selected another arrow. They raised their bows simultaneously, and again Dobbin's cry to let fly filled the expectant silence. Her bowstring twanged and her arrow struck the target.

Off center.

With a gasp, she looked at Sir Blaidd's target, to see his arrow in nearly the same place as the previous one. A curse flew from her lips, while several of the soldiers groaned. This time, no consultation was necessary. A delighted looking Trevelyan retrieved Sir Blaidd's arrow, while a glum Dobbin plucked hers free.

"Forgive my choice of words," she said through clenched teeth. "That wasn't a ladylike thing to say."

"You don't like to lose," Blaidd said, still as cool and calm as a pond on a windless summer day. "Neither do I. And as for being ladylike, many of the ladies at court could make a soldier blush with their language."

"And you've been intimately acquainted with many, no doubt."

"Quite a few," he calmly replied. "Certainly enough to know that being a lady isn't a state conferred by birth alone. Several women of lowly birth of my acquaintance are more ladylike in the best sense of the word—gentle, polite, generous, kind."

She obviously wouldn't fit his notion of being a lady. "Best two out of three, wasn't it?" she said as she grabbed another arrow.

"Aye, my lady."

He nocked his arrow and drew his bow, as did she. She pressed her lips together, determined to beat him.

"Let fly!" Dobbin cried again, and this time, to Becca's joy and relief, her arrow hit the very center of her target, an even better shot than her first, while Sir Blaidd's went wide.

She jumped for joy and nearly cheered, then settled down immediately. She didn't want to look as if she was gloating.

Trevelyan Fitzroy rushed to the target, looking ready to snarl, while Dobbin was all smiles.

"A clean win for my lady!" he shouted.

"Alas," Sir Blaidd said after a moment. "A poor shot. Trevelyan's father would be ashamed of me."

His lips twitched as if he was stifling a laugh, and another explanation, one that enraged her, came to mind.

"Maybe it was and maybe it wasn't!" she called back. She faced Sir Blaidd squarely, so angry she could spit. "Did you shoot wide on purpose?"

He looked taken aback and shook his head. "I assure you, my lady, I *never* lose on purpose. It was only that *alas* was not the first word to come to mind."

So firm was his denial that she believed him, but she needed to be certain he was not acting out of pity for her. "We'll shoot again, and this time, do the best you can."

"I did," he protested. His eyes flashed with warning. "And I did *not* lie when I told you I'd done so." After a tense moment, however, he shrugged his broad shoulders. "But very well. If you want, we'll shoot again."

"Good," she snapped, as a mystified Dobbin and a confused Trevelyan reached them.

"What's this about, my lady?" Dobbin asked.

"I fear Sir Blaidd thought it would be unchivalrous to let me lose. Perhaps you can assure him my pride will not shatter if I do."

Dobbin tugged at the collar of his tunic. "Well, Sir Blaidd, she don't *like* to lose, o' course, but you'd better do your best."

Sir Blaidd planted his feet. "I didn't *let* her win. I

made a bad shot. Trev will confirm that it's been known to happen before.''

Trev didn't look pleased. ''He's an excellent shot.''

''Not all the time,'' Blaidd insisted, which was the truth, and Trev should just admit it. This wasn't a tournament, after all. ''What about the time I shot your father in the leg?''

Becca's eyes widened, while Dobbin whistled and the other men listened in stunned silence. ''You shot Sir Urien Fitzroy?'' Dobbin asked in a whisper.

''Aye. Last year. He was too confident in my aim and stood too close to the target.''

All eyes turned to Trevelyan, who blushed in silent confirmation.

''You should have heard the words he used on that occasion,'' Blaidd added. ''Colorful, to say the least. Of course, I deserved everything he said.''

''Perhaps you're a bad shot, after all,'' Becca allowed.

''So do you wish to try again or will you accept your victory?''

''Since you are willing to confess that you hit the famous Sir Urien, I am willing to accept that I won fair and square.''

Blaidd relaxed, then their gazes met and held for a moment, until they both blinked and looked away.

Out of the corner of her eye, Becca saw Meg hurrying toward her.

She was glad for the interruption, she told herself, as the girl came to a halt. Meg cast a quick glance at young Fitzroy, and a longer one over Sir Blaidd, before addressing Becca. "The wine merchant's come, my lady."

"Oh. If you'll excuse me, Sir Blaidd, Dobbin." She surveyed the rest of the soldiers. "And you, too, men. I must see to ordering wine. Or I could stay here and try to get another bull's-eye—"

"No, no, my lady!" various voices called, some loud, some muted. "You won, fair and square."

"And nobody else gets the wine you do from that old snake!" another voice called from the back.

"Your soldiers have wine, not ale?" Sir Blaidd asked, obviously a bit surprised.

"Both. My father says men with full bellies and good drink are more apt to be grateful, and loyal. Treat them well and they'll protect you and your land as if they're family. But wine is served only on Sunday. The rest of the time they have ale." She raised her voice. "Or my father would be a pauper, the way they drink."

A chorus of cheerful denials filled the air, and Becca laughed, enjoying the easy camaraderie she shared with the soldiers, even though she knew that what they most appreciated about her was the food and drink she ensured was provided for them.

"Men come from all over England to serve Lord Throckton," Dobbin confirmed just as proudly. "We've got the best soldiers in the land here."

"Yes, I can tell he's got an excellent garrison," Sir Blaidd agreed. "And the wine I've enjoyed has been most excellent, too." He bowed. "I thank you, my lady." And then the impertinent fellow winked. "And

I trust I shall continue to enjoy fine wine, excellent food and good company for the rest of my stay here.''

"How long might that be, Sir Blaidd?" she asked without thinking.

His dark brows rose. "Are you suggesting I've overstayed my welcome?" he inquired, causing the men all around them to fall silent.

"Not at all," she hastened to assure him, anticipating what her father would say if he heard she'd asked such a direct question to a guest. "I simply need to know how much of the best wine to get."

"I hope you're not implying I drink too much?"

"No, no!" she protested, getting a little flustered. "We always keep a store of good wine, but I'm sure my father will want you to have the very best Bartram has, so I should know how much to purchase. I meant no criticism of you."

"I just wanted to be sure," he said, breaking into a wide smile.

She stared at him in disbelief. "Were you teasing me, Sir Blaidd?"

He gave her a rueful grin and his deep brown eyes fairly sparkled with good humor. "Forgive me again, my lady. I couldn't resist the temptation."

A man like him should never, ever speak of temptation to her.

She should be furious with him for getting her so upset despite his smiles and his eyes and his good-humored loss at archery.

She *was* furious with him. She *had* to be furious with him.

"Good day, then, sir knight," she said as she turned on her heel and limped quickly away, Meg scurrying along behind.

"She's something, isn't she?" Dobbin said as he joined Blaidd. Behind them, the soldiers began to remove the butts and targets, and make their way back to the castle.

Blaidd noticed that the disgruntled Trev didn't linger. "You taught her well."

Dobbin grinned. "It's easy when the pupil's eager to learn."

"Still, it's an unusual skill for a lady to acquire. I'm surprised her father allowed it."

Dobbin colored and shifted his feet. "Well, he didn't exactly know about it." The older man caught Blaidd's eye and hastened to explain. "It was after she hurt her leg. They was all weepin' and wailin' and sayin' she'd never walk again. She was that glum, lying abed, so I tried to think of something to help her." He spread his hands in a gesture of helplessness. "I'm just a soldier, sir, and could only think of soldierly things."

"Clearly it was a suggestion that met with her approval."

A shy smile lit the man's face. "Aye, it did."

Blaidd decided to take the opportunity to ask a few questions. "I gather she fell out of a tree?"

"Aye, sir, aye. Up to a bit of mischief, she was, like always. Oh, she was a one for capers and larks!"

"Wild, was she?"

Dobbin looked offended. "Spirited, more like."

"I suppose her father was often angry with her?"

A troubled expression flitted across Dobbin's face. "Aye, sir, and sometimes still gets right put out. Mind, I'm not saying he don't care about her. He was some upset when she fell, as we all were, what with her wee bones sticking out and all. Makes me ill just to think of it. I've heard grown men screaming from less, but not a sound did she make, not even when the apothecary set her leg as best he could."

Blaidd had seen plenty of broken bones himself, and he silently agreed that the ones where the bone pierced the skin were gruesome—and often deadly. "It's a wonder she lived at all."

"Take more than a broken leg to kill her, even one like that," Dobbin said, as proudly as if she were his own daughter. "And she was that determined to walk again, she wouldn't stay still."

"Perhaps because a kind man had offered to teach her something usually reserved for boys?"

Dobbin's blue eyes sparkled. "Well, that might have been one reason." He reached for the bow Blaidd still held. "I'll take that back to the keep for you, sir."

"Thank you."

As Dobbin joined the other soldiers heading into the inner ward, Blaidd suddenly realized that he should have questioned him about the garrison and fortifications, not Lady Rebecca, no matter how intriguing he found her.

Chapter Eight

Surveying the empty cot in their bedchamber, Blaidd swore under his breath. Where the devil had Trev got to? The lad had imbibed more ale than he should have, then stumbled out of the hall before Blaidd could speak to him. After that, Blaidd had excused himself as quickly as possible and left the hall. He'd hoped Trev had gone to bed, but obviously, he hadn't.

Maybe he'd gone to the barracks to spend some time with the friends he'd been making among the soldiers, including Dobbin. Maybe he'd gone to pay back a wager or two, for if he'd bet on the archery contest, he would have bet on Blaidd, and lost.

Maybe he'd gone to the stables to see the horses, perhaps even fallen asleep on a pile of hay. He'd looked drunk enough to pass out almost anywhere.

Blaidd turned to leave the chamber—and found himself face-to-face with Meg. He breathed a sigh of relief that Trev wasn't with her.

The girl blushed and wrung the end of her apron

in her hands as she stammered, "I—I've come…that is, I'd like a word with you, sir, if I may. Please."

Although he was curious to know what she wanted to talk about with him, he was more anxious to find Trev. "Can it wait until morning?"

She shook her head, and her expression grew truly desperate. "It's important."

He thought of a possible explanation for her presence, and her uneasiness. This wouldn't be the first time a lady had sent her maid to act as her envoy. "I'm sure Lady Laelia will appreciate that I can't…" He hesitated because Meg looked almost disgusted. "You weren't sent by Lady Laelia?"

"No!"

Another explanation gave him a very pleasant jolt. "Did Lady Rebecca send you?"

"God's wounds, no!"

So much for his ability to guess what was going on. "Meg, why exactly are you here?"

"I came to tell you…."

She looked even more nervous, as if she was about to reveal serious secrets.

God save him, maybe she was, secrets that had nothing to do with either Lady Laelia and Lady Rebecca. Maybe he'd been woefully neglecting a potential source of information. "Yes?" he prompted gently, not wanting to scare her off.

Meg took a deep breath and the words flowed out in a torrential whisper. "Lady Rebecca's the finest lady I know, and she likes you and I think you like her, and you *should*. She's a hundred times better than her sister, and a really clever man ought to want her instead. You do like her, don't you?''

This wasn't what he'd expected, and he wasn't sure how to answer. He couldn't risk telling this serving girl—or anyone else—that he preferred Lady Rebecca to Lady Laelia, whom he was supposedly still courting. ''I do, but—''

''But nothing, sir, begging your pardon!'' Meg persisted. ''I hope you ain't thinking that just because she's not a beauty like her sister, you don't think she'll do. Lady Laelia's spoiled and selfish and...'' Her whole body tense, she flung the last words at him as if daring him to deny it. ''She'll probably be barren, too!''

In her desperate words Blaidd heard a fierce loyalty. He could admire both the servant who expressed it and the woman who'd earned it. But he dare not reveal anything of his true feelings, especially not to a servant, and a loquacious one at that. ''I realize you are acting in what you think are your mistress's best interests—''

''I'm telling you, you ought to marry her and get her out of here!''

There was a different desperation in her voice now, one that roused his suspicions. ''Why do you think she has to get away from her home, her family?''

Meg's gaze faltered. ''Because they don't appreciate her as they ought. They treat her like a drudge.''

''There's no other reason?''

The girl raised her hazel eyes to regard him steadily. ''I want her to be happy, and I think you'd make her so. Otherwise, I'm afraid her father'll marry her off to somebody who'll make her miserable.''

''Nothing else?''

''What could be worse than that?''

He could think of one thing. A traitor wasn't the only one who suffered when he was caught. All his land and goods would be forfeit to the crown. If Throckton was guilty of treason, Lady Rebecca and Lady Laelia would be impoverished. He would be stripped of his title, and so would they. They would be left to fend for themselves in a world that had few choices for unmarried women with few skills. It would either be marriage to a merchant or someone from a lower class, or the convent.

That was if they were considered innocent of any involvement in their father's schemes. If such was not the case, it would be imprisonment and death for them, as well.

Blaidd told himself he mustn't think of that. His oath of loyalty and his duty were to the king. He was here to safeguard Henry, not Lord Throckton's daughters.

Nevertheless, Meg's assertion that there could be nothing worse for Lady Rebecca than an unhappy marriage gave him some relief, for if Meg thought a miserable marriage the worst fate that could befall her mistress, she must not be aware of any more serious danger.

He put a smile on his face. ''I should point out, Meg, that in spite of your fervent belief she'd be better off married to me than living here, the lady herself might disagree.''

"She might at first, but I'm thinking you could persuade her.''

"What of love, Meg? Shouldn't I love her?''

"You don't?''

Her demand took him completely aback. But then, Meg was a loyal servant who obviously cared a great deal for her mistress. Otherwise, what would make her think that he loved Lady Rebecca? "As I said, I like her, Meg, but that doesn't mean I love her.''

Meg eyed him with what looked surprisingly like skepticism. "If you say so, but that's a start, at least. If you spent more time with her, you'd see she's deserving of a better life.''

"What if she decides I'm not the man for her?''

To his further surprise, Meg grinned, as if he'd just asked a very silly question. "Oh, I don't think that'll be a bother. She likes you, too. I can tell. And she respects you. There aren't many men beside her father and Dobbin she respects.''

Meg started to sidle away. "You won't tell her I said anything, will you, sir? I don't think she'd like it.''

"No, I daresay she wouldn't. Nevertheless, I shall definitely bear in mind all that you've told me.''

With a nod, the maid scurried away like a mouse, leaving Blaidd with much to occupy his thoughts as he left his quarters to find Trev.

He headed first for the stables. Above, a few clouds hid parts of the night sky, but there was no rain upon the breeze. Tomorrow would likely be a fine day. Perhaps he would take Aderyn Du out for another gallop. Maybe Lady Rebecca would likewise decide a ride was in order. Maybe he could catch her, as Trev had, and this time he would be the one she laughed and joked with. She would let him help her dismount. He'd put his hands about her slender waist and let her body slide along his to the ground.

As he pushed open the stable doors, Aderyn Du whinnied as if in greeting. Blaidd went to his horse and patted his muzzle, then searched the stalls and the loft, sneezing from the chaff.

Sneezing again, he stepped back out into the courtyard and wondered where the young scamp had got to. He doubted it was far—but then again, Trev was young, and the worse for ale. Blaidd could recall a few nocturnal adventures of his own when he was sixteen and in his cups—

"Damn!" he muttered as an explanation came to him. Sir Urien would never forgive him if his son got a disease, or was beaten and robbed.

Blaidd strode toward the gate and up to the guards, who were leaning on their spears. "Is this the way you protect this courtyard, leaning about like old fishwives gossiping?"

The men hastily straightened. "Sorry, sir," the younger one muttered.

"Did my squire come this way?"

The men exchanged looks. "Aye, my lord, he did."

Blaidd addressed the older one, who was likely to

be senior in rank. "Couldn't you see the lad was in no fit state to be wandering about?"

"He seemed all right to us, sir. Polite as could be."

"He was drunk!"

"A bit wobbly," the younger one admitted, "but not too bad, sir. He could talk clear enough."

Discussing Trev's condition was hardly helpful. "Did he go into the village?"

The two guards nodded, and the oldest pointed with his spear tip. "That way, sir."

Of course.

"You won't...you won't report us to his lordship, will you, sir?" the youngest one asked worriedly.

"Not this time," Blaidd growled as he hurried through the gate. He broke into a trot as he crossed the outer ward, and then slowed to a more dignified pace as he reached the outer gatehouse, where he'd first encountered Lady Rebecca. Dobbin was talking to the guards there, and when he saw who was approaching, came to meet him.

"It'll be your squire you're after, I expect?" Dobbin inquired, grinning.

"Yes."

"Bit in his cups, eh?"

"Definitely."

"And looking for sport?"

"I expect so, yes," Blaidd answered grimly, fearing he knew exactly what kind of sport had tempted Trev, and where.

"Well, sir, if you don't mind me asking, why not leave him to it?"

"Because I'm responsible for him, and we both know what can happen in a whorehouse."

Dobbin nodded, but made no move to get out of the way. "A proud, high-spirited lad like that, he might not take it kindly if you come after him," he observed, as one mentor to another. "Maybe it's best to let him have a taste. He's a bit old to be tied to anybody's apron strings, isn't he?"

"How would you feel if it were Lady Rebecca going to visit a young man?"

"Well, that's different, ain't it? He's a lad, she's a woman."

"Not to me, it's not. Trevelyan's father is counting on me to take care of his son, and that means keeping him out of trouble—and a whorehouse spells trouble, in a host of ways."

He didn't wait to hear Dobbin's answer, if he made one, before he hurried through the gatehouse, then broke into a jog.

Maybe the boy was in one of the inns, just talking or drinking, Blaidd thought hopefully. Or getting in a brawl. That would be slightly better than the whorehouse.

Cursing himself for not keeping a tighter rein on his squire, Blaidd decided to go to the whorehouse first. If Trev wasn't there, he'd go to the inns next.

He burst through the door of the stew and came to a halt, hands on his hips. Half-dressed whores stared, while a few men obviously waiting a turn jumped to their feet. The blond girl wasn't there.

The one he recalled as the boldest among them,

plump and dark-haired, was standing at the bottom of the stairs. She sashayed forward now, and he realized she must be the madam.

"Well, well, well, my man, impatient, are we?" she purred, a greedy gleam in her black eyes.

"Is my squire here?"

"Who?"

"You know who I mean. Is he with that blond girl?"

"Maybe they're upstairs and maybe they're not. What's it to you if he pays his own way?"

Blaidd faced her, feet planted, arms akimbo. "Woman, I've come to fetch him, and you'd better tell me which room he's in, or so help me, I'll tear this place apart until I find him!"

The woman scowled and nodded toward the stairs. "First one on the right." As he dashed up the rickety steps, she bellowed a warning. "Hester!"

Blaidd threw his shoulder against the door and stumbled into the room. The girl was fully clothed and so was Trev, who was lying facedown on the filthy bed.

"He passed out," Hester said, obviously afraid, as Blaidd strode forward. "I didn't do nothing to him, I swear."

"Did he do anything *with* you?" Blaidd demanded as he yanked Trev up to a sitting position and put his shoulder under Trev's arm. He didn't see any cuts, bruises or blood, thank God.

She shook her head. Judging from the state of their respective garments, he believed her, and relief flooded through him as he hoisted the unconscious boy to his feet. He'd have to half drag, half carry him back to the castle. "Where's his money?"

She pointed at the pouch still tied to Trev's belt.

"If any's missing, I'll be back," Blaidd vowed as he started toward the door. Trev muttered something, but didn't wake up.

"Why don't you come back, anyway?" the girl said, her voice smooth as honey. "By yourself."

"I don't use whores," he growled.

"Too good for us, are you?" she charged. "Well, aren't you the exception, then."

He paused on his progress to the door. "If your name is Hester, Lady Rebecca told me about your plight. I'm sorry."

Her eyes widened, and he could see what a pretty, innocent girl she must have been.

"I'm going to ask you a favor, Hester. If Trev comes here again, send him back. His first time with a woman shouldn't be...well, not like this."

The innocent transformed into hard-edged practicality. "I won't make much money sending customers away."

Blaidd reached into his own purse and tossed her a silver coin. "Then I'll make it worth your while. And again, I'm sorry for what happened to you, and ashamed of any man who debases his rank by such behavior."

She stared at the coin, then him, then wordlessly went to hold the door open for him. A few of the women had gathered at the top of the stairs.

As he passed her, Hester caressed his chest and let loose a throaty laugh. "Do come back, sir, without the baggage. I'll make it worth *your* while." As the other women laughed raucously, Hester's expression changed again, to something serious and sincere. "For Lady Rebecca's sake, come back," she whispered. "I've got something important to tell you."

Then she laughed as coldly as the most hardened prostitute imaginable. "By all means, sir, come again," she said, "and bring your friends, but only if they can hold their ale."

Blaidd wondered if the girl really had something important to tell him, or if she saw him merely as a customer who needed a little more persuading.

Yet if so, why would she mention Lady Rebecca?

First Meg was worried about her mistress, and now this girl seemed worried about her, too.

Perhaps there were indeed secrets in Throckton Castle.

"How could you do it?" Laelia complained the moment Becca entered their bedchamber. Even though Laelia lay in bed, where she'd been all day, her body fairly quaked with rage.

Without waiting for her sister to respond, Laelia launched into a litany of Becca's latest sins. "Going to the outer ward and mingling with the soldiers! Interrupting their practice! And then challenging Sir Blaidd to an archery contest!"

"How's your head? Better, I hope?"

"Don't try to change the subject! How could you act with so little regard for your dignity and station?"

"I went to the outer ward to tell Sir Blaidd that you were ill. Forgive me if I shouldn't have. As for the archery contest, that was Sir Blaidd's idea. Wouldn't I have offended him if I'd refused?"

Laelia's eyes narrowed and her lips thinned. "How did he discover you could shoot? You told him, didn't you?"

Becca put a shocked expression on her face. "What, me mention such an unladylike accomplishment? Of course I didn't."

"Then it was Dobbin! I'm going to speak to Father about him—"

"Don't you dare!" Becca cried, glaring at her. "You leave Dobbin out of your complaints! I accepted the challenge, not him."

A timid knock at the door interrupted them. The door opened and Meg sidled inside.

"You're late!" Laelia snapped.

"Yes, my lady. I'm sorry." She scurried to the table and got the brush. "I'll do your hair first, shall I?"

"Yes." Laelia eased herself out of the bed and put on her thick robe. She slid her feet into her fur-lined slippers and went to sit on the stool by the dressing table.

Becca hoped that was going to be the end of her tirade, but alas, it wasn't.

"Making Sir Blaidd send his poor squire after you—"

''He didn't have to do that,'' Becca interrupted. ''There was no need, and I'm sure Father made that perfectly clear.''

Obviously she'd been wrong to think that hadn't bothered Laelia, even if she hadn't mentioned it in the interim.

''He did because he's a *gentleman*. When will you ever behave like a *lady?*'' Laelia demanded.

Becca pulled off her scarf and shook out her hair. ''I don't know why you're so upset. Sir Blaidd didn't come after me. You had all that time to be with him on your *leisurely* ride back to the castle. You wouldn't have wanted his squire with you, would you? You ought to be grateful to me.''

''Well, I'm not! Riding off like a bandit, dressing like a servant, shooting weapons like a soldier. It's a wonder you're not the laughingstock of Throckton!''

''Dobbin wanted to show—''

''*Dobbin* wanted?'' Laelia replied incredulously. ''What does it matter what *Dobbin* wanted?''

As Meg gave her a sympathetic look over the top of Laelia's head, Becca regretted bringing her friend Dobbin into it, especially when she didn't have to agree to shoot. The truth was, *she'd* wanted to show Blaidd her skill. ''You're right,'' she said after tossing her scarf on her bed. ''It was my choice, not his. But I'm not sorry for it.''

''You should be! What an undignified thing to do!''

''You're forgetting that I limp, too. All in all, I'm a sad disappointment to my noble blood.''

Laelia swiveled to regard her sister, leaving Meg holding the brush in midair. "You don't have to be," Laelia retorted. "If only you'd behave properly."

"If I behaved the way you consider *proper,* I'd be bored out of my head," Becca replied honestly. "Father doesn't seem to mind—much." She hesitated a moment. "Or not often anymore, so there's no need for you to get so upset."

"Father simply got tired of trying to stop you," Laelia charged. "He's given up, but I won't. It's not too late for you, Becca, to change and make yourself more…more…"

"Marriageable?" Becca suggested.

"Yes!"

"You should stop worrying about my chances of getting married, Laelia. I don't."

"You're my sister, Becca. Of course I'm going to worry about you."

"I do appreciate that you care, Laelia, really I do," she replied, "but I don't want to change. And if that means I don't get married, so be it." Becca headed to the door. "I've just remembered something I forgot to tell the cook for tomorrow."

She went out and made her way down the steps. In truth, she hadn't forgotten anything, and Rowan was probably fast asleep. She just didn't want to be around Laelia anymore. Not for a little while.

She didn't want to talk about Sir Blaidd, or her deficiencies or marriage. She wanted to be alone.

She continued through the dim hall, lit only by the fire still glowing in the hearth. Some of the hounds slumbering there stirred and growled low in their throat, until they realized who it was.

She paused at the door and peered into the courtyard. Nobody stirred except the sentries on the wall walk and the guards at the gate.

She hurried on toward the chapel as swiftly as she could. Once inside, she wondered for a moment if Sir Blaidd would appear again, then dismissed that thought. She'd do better not to think of him at all, ever again. Or remember how he'd looked that afternoon, half-naked with a broadsword in his hand, circling Dobbin.

Or later, during their little contest, when he hadn't seemed to mind losing to a woman.

He really wasn't like any other knight she'd ever met.

Apparently, however, he'd found just as much favor with Laelia. Her father certainly enjoyed his company, too. It seemed that, of all the men who'd come here, Sir Blaidd had the best chance of winning Laelia. That meant Becca would have to look on as they married. Visit them at their home. Dandle their children on her lap....

As she envisioned all these things, Becca realized that she'd been lying—lying terribly—when she'd told Laelia that she didn't care about getting married. She hadn't before, when it seemed better to live a life unwed than to marry any of the samples of young manhood who came to court Laelia. But her feelings had changed with the arrival of Sir Blaidd. If she could marry him...or someone like him...

There was no one like him. She felt that in her bones, and as a vision of her future spread before her, she realized she'd never really known true loneliness before.

Her life could be worse, of course. Much worse. She was the daughter of a wealthy lord, so she would never go hungry or be cold. She had friends here, especially Dobbin, who was like a second father to her. She would always have a home here.

She said a silent prayer of thanksgiving for all that she had, and of hope that she wouldn't begrudge Laelia her husband, if it came to pass that it was indeed Sir Blaidd.

Rising, Becca made the sign of the cross and went to the door. As she went into the courtyard, she glanced at the gate to see who was on guard tonight, and spotted two men, one helping the other, who seemed to be unconscious.

The one who was not unconscious had very long hair. Sir Blaidd…and his squire?

Fearing the lad was hurt, Becca broke into the sort of half gallop that was the closest to a run she could manage. "Sir Blaidd," she cried when she was closer. "Is he injured?"

Sir Blaidd came to a halt. "He's not hurt. I regret to say, my lady, that he's passed out from too much drink."

The lad raised his head as if his neck were made of twine. "I'mmmm na' drunk," he slurred. "Jus' sleepy."

Sir Blaidd grimaced and raised a brow, as if to say, "You see?"

She didn't want to add to the tension she'd already inadvertently caused between them by sounding upset or dismayed, or even disappointed. "He's young, and young people sometimes do very foolish things. Here, let me help."

She went to his other side and slid her shoulder under Trevelyan's right arm.

"You don't have to do that," Sir Blaidd protested. "I can manage."

"If you've had to get him all the way here from the village in this condition, I imagine you're tired. Despite my leg, I'm perfectly capable of lending a hand, or a shoulder, in this instance."

She spoke in a tone that brooked no dissent, and this time, Sir Blaidd wisely didn't protest.

As they made their way toward the apartments, she said, "I thought he looked a little ragged at dinner. I should have asked Meg to stop serving him."

"I should have told him to stop drinking," Sir Blaidd said. "He's my responsibility."

She couldn't deny that. "Where did you find him?"

Sir Blaidd's expression hardened, and she guessed his answer before he gave it. "The brothel. He hadn't had time to do anything truly stupid, I'm glad to say."

She was rather surprised by the note of disdain in Sir Blaidd's voice.

He caught her look. "They're desperate places for desperate men, and even more desperate women."

"I've been suggesting to my father for years that he find a way to close it down, but he never does. He's of the opinion that men must have their sport."

"Then it's very unhealthy sport, for the whores as well as their customers." Sir Blaidd sounded quite firm in that opinion, and she couldn't help being impressed.

And yet... "A poor woman may have no choice."

"I know." The knight sighed with resignation.

It was only when they reached the entrance to the apartments that it occurred to her that it was very unladylike to be discussing prostitution.

However, getting the limp Trevelyan up the stairs in the dark was enough of an effort that they had no more conversation, about anything. They got to the second level and started down the corridor that ran along the outside of the building. Narrow, arched windows allowed light in during the day, and since it was a clear, moonlit night, no torches burned in the sconces.

Once at their chamber, she helped Sir Blaidd get Trevelyan onto the bed. The knight grabbed one of the boy's boots, and she the other, and together they tugged them off. After dropping the boot, Sir Blaidd tossed a blanket over the youth, who began to snore.

Blaidd turned toward her then, his face illuminated by the silvery light of the full moon. He gestured for her to leave the room, following her when she did.

After shutting the door behind him, so that they were alone in the corridor, he whispered, "Thank you for your help. Those stairs would have been difficult without you.''

She couldn't think of a thing to say to that.

Nor could she think of a thing, period, as he moved a little closer. His eyes were in shadow, but she could feel the intensity of his gaze nonetheless. ''My lady, are you in any danger here?'' he asked in an urgent whisper.

She hadn't expected *that*. ''No, of course not. This is my home.''

''There is nothing to make you fear for your future well-being?''

There was, and she was looking at him, but she'd never admit that to his face. ''No. Why do you ask?''

''Meg said something to me today that makes me fear all isn't well for you here.''

''She's wrong!'' And she would have a few words with Meg about the error of a servant discussing her mistress with a guest.

''Is she? She says they don't appreciate you here as you deserve, and I don't disagree.'' He reached out and caressed Becca's cheek. Her whole body seemed to tingle at the contact. She should make him stop, but she…simply…couldn't. ''Are you happy here, my lady?''

''Yes,'' she sighed. Then she came to her senses and abruptly stepped back. ''Don't do that.''

''I'm sorry.''

''You're courting Laelia.''

''I did come here with the notion of courting her, and she's a fine young woman in her way, but…''

But what? Becca wanted to shout. She felt as if she might explode as she waited for him to continue.

"But she may not be the woman for me."

As a wild hope and conflicting doubt warred within her, all Becca could manage to reply was a very feeble, "Oh?"

"Indeed, I'm beginning to think I should be courting her sister instead."

Thrilled and confused, aghast and delighted, Becca couldn't speak.

Then he put his arms around her, drew her into his embrace and kissed her.

Chapter Nine

Sir Blaidd Morgan had kissed many women, but no other woman's embrace ever inspired such a fierce longing within him.

For a long time he'd dreaded that he was doomed to a series of shallow relationships. That he would wind up marrying simply to satisfy duty and the need to provide an heir. That he would never have a truly loving marriage like his parents.

The hope that he might escape that fate with Becca was his final coherent thought before he surrendered to the passion she created within him. He thought no more about his parents, or Laelia, or the king, or Lord Throckton, or Trev slumbering in the chamber nearby. All Blaidd was aware of was her, warm and soft and welcoming, as she returned his kiss. Her fingers wound through his long hair as she pressed her body close. And closer.

Her limbs relaxed, soft and supple as a willow bending in the wind.

His desire exploding, he slipped his tongue between her lips, to touch and dance with hers. As their kiss deepened, he eased her back against the wall.

Becca didn't feel the coldness of the stones behind her, or their roughness. She was glad of their solid support as his right hand slipped along her ribs and up toward the curve of her breast.

While he stroked and kneaded gently, she relaxed, soft as melted wax, her whole body hot with need in a way completely new, completely wonderful. Her arms entwined about his waist, her hands moving up his back and over the taut muscles. She clutched him tightly and swayed, leaning into him more.

He began to undo the lacing of her bodice, beneath her collarbone. Too overwhelmed by the sensations he was creating, she made no protest. When her bodice was loose, he insinuated his hand into the woolen garment.

Over her linen shift, his thumb brushed the hard peak of her nipple, making her gasp with surprise at the unexpected pleasure.

He broke their kiss to trail his lips along her cheek, her jaw and down her neck as she arched back, her head grazing the stone walls ever so slightly. Panting, she felt him nuzzle her bodice and shift lower, so that his mouth pressed against the naked flesh of the rounded tops of her breasts.

She put her hands on his head, supporting herself, as he licked and nibbled. Then, regardless of the fabric, he drew her nipple between his lips, and his tongue swirled over and around the taut tip.

She moaned softly. He raised his head and again kissed her mouth—not softly this time, or delicately, but with a warrior's fierce, unbridled need.

And she, a warrior, too, in her own way, met his need with just as much intensity. There was no tenderness, no gentle yielding. It was an equal give and take, of need and lust and yearning.

His hips ground against hers, telling her more strongly than words what his body craved.

She pulled him closer, rubbing against him with savage urgency. Never in her life had she felt this way, needed this way, wanted anything as much as she wanted to be with him, completely.

His knee slipped between her legs and she pushed her center against the firmness of his thigh. A new hunger arose, primal and desperate, as she repeated and repeated the action, rocking against him with wild abandon. Again he pleasured her breasts, first one, then the other.

An anxiety unlike anything she had ever felt surged through her body, propelling her beyond thought to a place where only feelings and this burning, driving need existed. Until the tension snapped, replaced by a clenching, throbbing release.

He stilled and drew back, nearly as limp as she was without his support. He was panting so hard he could barely speak. "Becca...my lady...I...forgot myself."

With her own ragged breathing filling her ears, she stared at him. His hair was a tousled mess. At some point, she must have undone his tunic, as he had un-

tied her laces. Her lips felt swollen and so did…
somewhere else.

God save her, she'd acted no better than a whore
in an alley! She had forgotten who and what she was:
a high-born lady who should conduct herself with dignity.

And yet she still wanted to throw herself in his
arms and beg him to make love with her.

His hands slipped to her bare shoulders, then he
slowly raised her bodice back into place. He took her
cheeks gently in his hands, and it was all she could
do not to turn her face to kiss his palm. "I shouldn't
have done that."

"I should have stopped you," she whispered.

"I should never kiss you."

"I should slap you if you try."

He smiled wistfully. "I think, my lady, we're both
besotted. We know better, and yet—"

"And yet we can't help ourselves."

He nodded. "Obviously, we have a dilemma, unless I cease courting your sister."

"Do you…do you want to do that?"

His smile grew slowly. "I'm quite certain I don't
want to court your sister anymore. I'd rather court
Lord Throckton's younger daughter."

Happiness stole over Becca. And yet she didn't
want to cause her sister any unnecessary pain. "I
think both she and my father may be upset about
that."

Blaidd's hand meandered slowly up her back. "She
may be upset, but I don't think it'll last. I'm sure

another man will be along to court her soon. As for your father, he likes me, does he not?"

"Yes."

"Then why should he care which of his daughters I choose?"

"I suppose you're right. Still, I don't want our...us...to cause a lot trouble if we can avoid it. It would be better if you first made it known that you didn't think you and Laelia would suit, and took your leave. After a little while, you could come back on another visit. Since you and my father get along so well, that shouldn't seem suspicious." Becca smiled merrily as she toyed with the dangling lace of his tunic. "Then, lo and behold, you discover *me*. Perhaps by then, as you say, there'll be somebody else already courting Laelia. That way, there'll be no hard feelings."

Blaidd grew thoughtful. "You seem to have this all planned out."

"I can think very quickly sometimes."

"And well, too. Therefore, I'll do as you say. I don't think I should leave too soon, though. It might look suspicious if I suddenly depart."

"You're right again. In about a week, perhaps."

"That will give me time to let Laelia realize on her own that my feelings for her are not what they should be. Even better, I can use the time to get to know you more, my lady, although my *feelings* for you," he whispered, bending toward her, "are already turning into something quite amazing."

They kissed again, losing all track of time or place, until a sound in the room behind them interrupted them.

''God's wounds, I think Trev's fallen out of bed,'' Blaidd said, letting go of her.

''And I should leave before somebody sees us,'' Becca said, suddenly realizing how it would look if that happened.

She had no real idea how long she'd been there. Had Laelia gone to sleep, or was her sister waiting up for her, wondering where she was and what she was doing?

Not that she'd ever guess, not in a thousand years. Still, Becca didn't want to have to come up with an explanation.

''Until tomorrow, then,'' Blaidd whispered, kissing her quickly once more.

''Until tomorrow,'' she said softly as he went inside the chamber.

As Becca hobbled away, she felt as if she were dancing with happiness.

Which, in a way, she was.

Trev had not fallen out of bed. He'd knocked the candlestick off the table beside it.

Once Blaidd realized what had made the noise, he relaxed against the closed door and slowly let out his breath.

God's wounds, what the devil was he doing?

Despite how he felt about the astonishing Becca, he'd come here on a mission for the king, not himself.

He shouldn't be falling in love. But he was. He felt that in his heart, in the marrow of his bones.

Worse, he was falling in love with a woman who might be the daughter of a traitor.

What if her father was guilty? Lord Throckton would be arrested, charged with treason and be-headed—because of *him*.

What would Becca think of him if he were the instrument of her father's conviction? Would she be able to love him then?

And what would Henry and Blaidd's own parents say when he declared his intention to marry a traitor's daughter? No nobleman should want such a woman for a wife.

Blaidd ran his hand through his hair, then sat heavily on his bed. Perhaps he was getting worried over nothing. It was still very possible that the king's suspicions regarding Lord Throckton were un-founded. In all their conversations, Throckton had said nothing many other, loyal nobles hadn't ex-pressed concerning the king and the power and re-wards he was giving to his wife's relatives. Even Blaidd had voiced some reservations in that regard. If Becca were not here, he might already be heading back to Westminster to assure the king his fears were groundless.

And yet…there were things that still didn't make sense here. Not just what he'd noticed at the first, about the fortress and Lord Throckton's wealth. Meg seemed so fervent in her need to have Becca married and away from here. That harlot had something to tell him—for Lady Rebecca's sake, she'd said. He sensed that there were many secrets in this place. Whatever else was happening, it was his duty to ensure that those secrets didn't include a conspiracy against Henry.

How long should he stay here? Blaidd wondered. How long would it take him to be sure, one way or another?

He pulled off his boots, then yanked his tunic over his head. Trev moaned and shifted, smacking his lips.

Blaidd looked outside at the moon and decided on a course of action. He'd stay for another fortnight. If he couldn't find evidence of a rebellious conspiracy by then, he could be relatively certain there wasn't one to find.

Trev opened his eyes a crack. Thankfully, and although he knew not how, he was in his bedchamber at Throckton Castle, the windows shuttered with linen so that the room was blessedly dim. His head ached like the devil, his mouth was as dry as old leather and his stomach... He'd barely thought of his stomach before he leaned over the bed and emptied its contents into a bucket somebody was holding for him.

When he was finished, he flopped back and squinted at Blaidd, who was shoving the bucket out the door with his foot. "Oh, God save me," he groaned. "I'm dying."

"No, you're not," Blaidd replied as he sat on the end of the bed. "You were drunk and now you're paying for it."

Trev rolled on his side so he faced the wall, away from the stern visage of Blaidd Morgan, who couldn't possibly understand what he was feeling. How could he? Every woman Blaidd wanted, wanted him more. Trev's brothers always spoke of that with awe and respect, and not a little envy.

"Why don't you go away until I feel more myself?" he muttered. "Then you can lecture me all you want about the evils of too much ale, as I'm sure you're anxious to do."

"I think you're learning about the evils of too much ale all by yourself. It's the evils of going to a whorehouse that you apparently need to hear again."

Trev pressed his eyes shut as his stomach rolled. Those weren't just dreams? He'd really gone there and done…something. Try as he might now, he couldn't remember much beyond stumbling up the steps behind that blond beauty who smiled so invitingly, crooking her finger for him to follow.

"Don't you remember?"

Trev wished Blaidd would go away and leave him to his torment.

For tormented he was, in a way that had nothing to do with his physical ailments. Now, in the harsh light of day—or what would be the harsh light of day if the windows weren't shuttered—he was horrified to think that his first time with a woman had been nothing more than a cold business transaction. What should have been a pleasant memory instead filled him with disgust and shame. And dread. What if Blaidd was right, and the girl was diseased? What if he got sores—or worse? What if it fell off? After all, what did he know of such illnesses?

He rolled over so that he could see Blaidd, then struggled to sit up. "I made love with her, didn't I?" he demanded, a note of panic in his voice. "Is she diseased, do you think?"

"I have no way of knowing if she's diseased or not—and neither would you, so it's a damn good thing you didn't get very far."

Trev fell back against the sweat-soaked pillow. "I didn't?"

"No. You were still fully clothed when I found you, and so was she."

Reprieved. Relief flooded through Trev, taking the edge off his shame.

"So although I'm going to give you a lecture you won't soon forget, it won't be as bad as the lecture you would have gotten if you'd rutted with her."

Trev stared at Blaidd with surprise, and not because he was going to be lectured. That wasn't unexpected. It was the word Blaidd used. Unlike many knights, Blaidd rarely used such words for anything to do with women and lovemaking.

"I'm not going to dignify what men do with a whore by calling it making love."

"Oh, God, Blaidd, I don't know what I was thinking...."

"Try. I'd like to believe you had some reason for behaving in such a manner, even a poor one."

Trev felt even more foolish as he attempted to explain what had motivated him to go to the brothel. "I was angry at you."

"I apologized for scolding you in the courtyard, and I don't think I destroyed the honor of Wales by losing to Lady Rebecca yesterday. At any rate, I fail to see how being angry at me prompted you to get drunk and go to the stew. There may be a fleeting pleasure in such a thing, but no man I respect would find his self-esteem between the sheets of a whore's bed."

Trev plucked at his bedclothes. "I wasn't angry about that."

Blaidd's brow furrowed with puzzlement. "What then?"

The lad shrugged and looked away.

"What got the son of Sir Urien Fitzroy so upset he'd act like an idiot?" Blaidd asked in a tone that demanded an answer.

The suffering Trev turned as red as holly berries. "Meg," he mumbled. "She…she hardly even notices me when you're around." He shrugged again.

Blaidd was about to tell him that was a stupid reason for what he'd done when he recalled a certain period of irrational jealousy when he was fifteen, over a milkmaid whose name he could barely remember now. "So you were trying to drown your sorrows, and then decided to redeem your wounded pride by finding a woman who wouldn't say no to you. Oh, Trev, my lad, you should have come to me. If the girl's paying attention to me, it's not because she's interested in me herself—and I wouldn't respond if she was. I'm a guest here, too, so I wouldn't dally with my host's servants even if she threw herself in my arms, which she won't because she thinks I should marry her mistress.''

Trev's mouth fell open.

''Meg likes me only insofar as she thinks I'd make a good husband for her mistress,'' Blaidd clarified. He wondered how much he should tell Trev, then decided that Meg might say something to his squire about her views if she thought it would help her cause. ''She wasn't speaking about Lady Laelia, either. She thinks I should marry Lady Rebecca.''

Trev frowned. ''But Lady Rebecca's crippled.''

Blaidd got to his feet and looked down at the young man with an expression Trev had never seen before. ''I see I'll also have to lecture you on how ignorant it is to judge a person by such things.''

Blaidd turned on his heel and headed to the table across the room. He poured some water into a goblet there, using the activity to get his temper back under control. The lad was only saying what other people would, expressing the surprise they would feel about his choice. He should be able to subdue his temper better. After all, he wasn't new to prejudice. Men at court had whispered unflattering things about Welshmen behind his back. Some still did, although never the ones he'd faced in a tournament.

But this was different, because they would be talking about Becca.

He went back to the bed and handed the goblet to Trev. "Sip, don't gulp," he cautioned.

As the boy did as he was told, Blaidd said, "Lady Rebecca may not be as outwardly beautiful as her sister, but she has many other qualities. She's good and clever and kind, plays the harp like an angel, runs this castle as well as either of our mothers could and…" He was, perhaps, revealing too much of his affection for her too soon. "You should respect and admire her for those things, even if she walks with a limp."

"I do admire and respect her—a great deal," Trev said as he set the goblet down on the small table beside the bed. Between the bucket and the water, he was already looking much better. "I didn't realize you liked her so much, that's all."

Blaidd didn't answer as he went to back to the larger table and pulled a linen cover off a tray. The aroma of fresh bread wafted toward Trev. "Can you eat anything?"

"I don't know," he answered warily. "What do you think?"

"It's been a very long time since I've been dead drunk. Once was enough for me—and I trust it will be for you, too. That's hardly a way to earn respect."

Trev eyed the loaf. "Maybe a bite will help settle my stomach."

Blaidd nodded and brought the tray to him. As the lad broke off a piece and began to nibble as delicately as any novice nun, Blaidd settled back down on the end of the bed. "Now, which lecture will it be first—

the folly of sleeping with whores, or the stupidity of judging a person by outward appearances?''

Trev sighed. It was going to be a long morning.

Smiling at the contrariness of life, Becca hummed softly to herself as she drew out the pretty blue velvet gown her father had given her last Christmastide. Now that she didn't have to dress well to attract a man's notice, she wanted to.

"You're very cheerful this morning," Laelia noted as Meg tied the lacings at the back of her own emerald-green-and-gold damask gown.

"It's a beautiful day," Becca answered brightly, which was true. The sun shone like a day in Eden, the air was warm, the scent of herbs from the kitchen garden wafted in their window—and best of all, Blaidd Morgan liked her. He liked her better than Laelia. He liked her enough to kiss her with passion and desire. He liked her enough to want to court her, and perhaps—oh, joyous, exciting thought—perhaps soon his affection would turn into love.

She'd lain awake for hours after she'd returned last night and found, to her relief, that Laelia was already fast asleep. She'd snuggled under the covers and remembered his kisses, his embrace, the excitement, the need, and all the words he'd said. She couldn't have been happier if her leg had been miraculously made normal again.

She looked back at the dress and frowned. If she didn't want to arouse any suspicions, she shouldn't act as if anything was different, or dress in a way that would cause people to wonder what had changed. Besides, riding was definitely in order today and the velvet dress wouldn't do for that.

"I should think you'd be too tired to be cheerful after you were so late coming to bed last night," Laelia said.

Becca glanced at her and her gaze met Meg's, whose eyes were wide with barely suppressed curiosity. "Yes, well, I had to remind the cook to get some eels. Father was saying how much he'd relish a dish today."

That wasn't strictly a lie. She had reminded Rowan about the eels, but before the evening meal.

When she went to return the blue gown to the chest, Laelia caught sight of it. "Are you finally going to dress like a lady today?"

"I thought I noticed a tear, that's all. Fortunately, I was wrong." Becca replaced it and pulled out her dark blue gown. It was made of light wool, and while certainly not as luxurious as the velvet, it was pretty in its own way, and fit to perfection.

"Then I suppose it's also too much to hope that you'll act more like a lady today and not decide to joust, or wield a blade?" Laelia sighed with exasperation as her hands fell limply to her sides. "I know you're proud of your skill with a bow, Becca, but I don't know how we're ever going to find a man who'll want to marry you if you do masculine things like shoot a bow."

Laelia walked toward her, and Becca was surprised

to see the sincere concern in her eyes. "I do care about your happiness, Becca. I truly do."

Becca took hold of her sister's hands and spoke just as sincerely. "It's not that I don't want to be married, Laelia. It's just that if I *do* marry, I want to be loved, and cherished, and respected. Otherwise, I'd rather not be married at all."

"I suppose we're not so very different," Laelia wistfully replied. "I want to be loved, too, Becca, and for more than my beauty. I think with Sir Blaidd, I may finally have found a man who truly sees beyond that."

For the first time in her life, Becca realized that she wasn't the only daughter of Lord Throckton who was judged for one characteristic. She'd always assumed it would be wonderful to be as lovely as her sister, but now she realized beauty could be a curse as much as her own crippled leg.

Yet as sorry as she felt for her sister, she hoped Laelia wouldn't begrudge her any happiness when she learned about her relationship with Blaidd. After all, Laelia's beauty gave Laelia an advantage Becca would never possess: a greater chance of finding a loving husband among the many men who came to court her.

Laelia headed for the door without pursuing the subject. "Don't be late for Mass," she said before she swept out of the room.

The moment she was gone, Meg stopped tidying the dressing table and turned toward Becca with barely suppressed excitement. Her eyes sparkled and she clasped her hands expectantly. "Well, my lady?" she whispered, as if she feared somebody might overhear.

Becca suddenly felt shy and embarrassed. "Well, my lady, what?"

Meg took a step toward her, and her eyes shone even more. "Well, Sir Blaidd...that is, did he say...anything?"

How well could Meg keep a secret? Becca wondered. Maybe she already guessed too much. If her father and sister found out what had happened, and from a servant's gossip...!

Becca forced herself to look stern. "I understand you have forgotten your place. It is not for a servant to discuss her mistress with one of our guests."

Meg's face reddened. "I was only trying—"

"I didn't ask for an explanation, did I?"

Meg hung her head. "I'm sorry, my lady."

"So am I. You could have caused some serious discord with your assumptions, Meg. Need I say, we couldn't keep a servant who did something like that, could we?"

"N-no, my lady."

Remorse gnawed at Becca, but she gave no indication that she was anything but annoyed. "If you give me your word you won't do something so foolish again, I won't tell my father. This can stay between us. Now go about your duties."

"Aye, my lady," Meg murmured before she hurried from the room.

Becca followed after, her steps slow, as she told herself that as much as she regretted upsetting Meg, there'd been no help for it. She couldn't risk letting Meg's loose tongue spoil her chance for happiness.

The Harlequin Reader Service® — Here's how it works:

If offer card is missing write to: The Harlequin Reader Service, 3010 Walden Ave., P.O. Box 1867, Buffalo, NY 14240-1867

NO POSTAGE
NECESSARY
IF MAILED
IN THE
UNITED STATES

BUSINESS REPLY MAIL
FIRST-CLASS MAIL   PERMIT NO. 717-003   BUFFALO, NY

POSTAGE WILL BE PAID BY ADDRESSEE

HARLEQUIN READER SERVICE
3010 WALDEN AVE
PO BOX 1867
BUFFALO NY 14240-9952

Chapter Ten

On the top of the rise, Aderyn Du restlessly shifted. Blaidd tried to steady his mount as he watched Becca gallop across the meadow by the river. She was easily the finest horsewoman Blaidd had ever seen; it was as if she and her horse were one creature.

His competitive spirit and Aderyn Du's evident yearning to gallop prompted him to kick his heels against his horse's sides. Down the hill the gelding charged, and soon they were racing across the meadow and drawing close to Becca and her mare.

Becca looked back over her shoulder and spotted them. He thought she might slow, but wasn't really surprised when she instead let out a whoop of glee and bent over her horse's neck, urging her on.

With an answering shout, Blaidd dug his heels into Aderyn Du, spurring him forward. His gelding didn't let him down. The wind whistled past Blaidd's ears as they flew, and his hair streamed out behind him like a banner in the breeze.

Blaidd laughed as they gained on their quarry. This was just what he'd hoped for.

That morning after breaking the fast, Becca had mentioned going for a ride through the river meadow and the wood upon leaving the high table, and he'd thought he'd finally found an opportunity to be alone with her.

After he'd spent some time boring Laelia with tales of training, he mentioned—with every appearance of remorse—that his gelding needed exercise, preferably a good gallop. As he expected, Laelia was only too happy to stay in the castle. He'd strolled to the stable, saddled his own horse and ridden out as casually as you please. It had taken him some time to find the river meadow, since he hadn't wanted to ask directions or look as if he had a particular route in mind.

As he'd passed through the village, he'd thought of Hester and what she'd hinted at. Could she really know something important? Perhaps one of Lord Throckton's men had thought to gain respect and importance by telling her something he'd learned—or only made up.

Becca and her horse suddenly made a hard left turn into the wood, a forest of oak and chestnut and hazel. Blaidd pulled hard on his reins, and Aderyn Du nearly sat back on his haunches before making the turn. In the next moment, they had plunged into the dimmer light filtered through the branches and leaves, moving along a path barely wide enough for horse and rider.

He saw the rump of Becca's horse disappear down another path and followed—and then couldn't see them, or any sign they'd even gone that way. He pulled Aderyn Du to a halt and listened.

He could hear only the birds in the trees and the rustling of branches as a squirrel dashed overhead.

She couldn't have simply disappeared. Rising in his stirrups, he slowly surveyed the bushes lining the path. He saw a gap in one, with the ends of some branches recently broken. She'd either left the path voluntarily there, or been forced that way. Aderyn Du's flanks quivered as if he, too, sensed that something was amiss.

Alert, with every sense heightened, Blaidd drew his sword and slipped from the back of his horse.

"I'm quite unarmed, sir knight," Becca called out from somewhere on the other side of the bushes.

Sighing with relief, he sheathed his blade. "Where are you?"

"Can't you see me?"

"Obviously not," he answered, grabbing his horse's reins and leading him through the break in the bushes. "Are you hiding?"

"Not particularly."

He looked around, but still didn't see her. "What does that mean, 'not particularly?'"

"It means I'm standing where you should be able to see me. Claudia is not so visible."

Wondering why Becca was being so mysterious, he followed the sound of her voice. "You wish to play a game, do you, my lady? What's the prize?"

"I wish for us to spend some time together where we won't be seen," she replied, closer now and on his right. "I thought you understood that when I said I'd be riding out today."

"I hoped that was what you meant. I also hope nobody finds it odd that I decided Aderyn Du needed a good gallop on the same day you went riding." As quietly as he could, he tied his horse's rein to a bush and crept forward slowly.

"I go out riding all the time, and even if they think we might encounter one another, they'll surely believe I'll treat you as I would anyone else by riding away from you as fast as Claudia will take me," she answered pertly. "They'd never imagine that I would stop and let you catch me."

He caught sight of the hem of her gown and lunged. "And so I have," he said as he pulled her into his arms.

She struggled halfheartedly for a moment. "I made it too easy!" she cried with mock annoyance. "I should have laid down so you wouldn't see me!"

"What, and get muddy?" he said as she relaxed.

While her arms encircled him, she glanced at the soft ground covered with ancient leaves. "Perhaps not."

"Definitely not, or what would you tell people when you got back?" he asked as his lips gently brushed over hers.

"That I fell. I do sometimes," she murmured, enjoying the sensation of being in his arms, and his featherlight kisses.

His mouth trailed along her cheek toward her ear. "Where's your horse?"

She tilted her head toward the sound of a stream, incidentally presenting the side of her jaw for him to kiss. "There's a little valley there."

"Ah. You know this wood well, I see."

"I've spent many an hour here."

"Alone?"

"Usually."

He drew back and looked at her with what she was fast coming to think of as his "warrior look." "Should I be jealous?"

"Absolutely not. I used to come here with Dobbin sometimes to practice my archery."

Blaidd's slow smile made her heart pound even harder. "That's all right, then."

He kissed her again, passionately—so passionately that she could immediately envision the back of her gown covered in mud.

She regretfully broke away. If she didn't, she wasn't sure she would be able to prevent things from going too far. But there could be very serious consequences if she made love with Blaidd Morgan here and now. The first would be that she'd never be able to keep their relationship a secret, because she was quite certain she'd want to spend every waking moment with him, either intimately or not.

"Why don't you fetch your horse and join me in the gully?" she proposed. "There's a log there we can sit on. I brought my harp, too. I can play for you, if you'd like."

He grinned. "I'd like that very much. I won't be a moment."

Blaidd was as good as his word, and soon they were seated side by side on a large fallen log, the trunk of an oak.

Becca found it wasn't nearly so easy to initiate a conversation with him as she'd imagined. For one thing, just the fact that such a man was sitting beside her, such a man who wanted her and kissed her so very thoroughly, was extremely distracting. Plus, he just sat there, smiling at her, as if he'd like to do nothing more than that.

"You know my family. Tell me about yours," she finally ventured.

"Gladly. Where should I start?"

"Wherever you like."

"Well, then, I'll tell you that my father was a shepherd in his boyhood, then a squire, then a knight. His marriage to my mother was not her idea, to put it mildly, but nevertheless they fell in love—passionately so. I have a brother, Kynan, and two sisters, Meridyth and Gwyneth. We generally get along, although there are times we don't."

"You all have such unusual names."

He laughed. "Well, mine is unusual even for the Welsh. It's not really a name at all. *Blaidd* means 'wolf' in my native tongue. My father thought his firstborn son should have a fierce name, you see, and he chose it. Not that I'm complaining," he added. "My mother was all for Bartholomew."

"I think Blaidd suits you better," Becca agreed. She ran a saucy gaze over him. "Between that name and your hair, you're very fierce indeed."

He held out a strand of his long dark hair. "You don't think I should cut it?"

"Not unless you want to," she answered honestly. "I really can't imagine you without it, though."

That brought another slow, seductive smile to his face, and she hastily thought of a question before she melted in a pool of desperate desire. "If your father was a shepherd, how did he ever get to be a squire?"

"Emryss DeLanyea, my father's overlord, saw his merit and didn't hold his birth against him. Mind you," Blaidd continued with a laugh, "Lady Roanna—that's Emryss's wife—says my father was so like a little shadow there was nothing else to do but put him to work, so a squire he became."

"He was very fortunate to have such a kind and generous overlord."

"Aye, he was. Emryss DeLanyea's one of the best men I've ever met. I hope that when I am in charge of an estate, I can be as fine a leader, as fair a judge and as good a husband as he, and my father, are."

Becca slipped her hand in his. "I think you will be. You're very good with your squire—just the right combination of commander and friend, I think."

He beamed. "You do?"

"Yes, and so does Dobbin."

"That's high praise indeed, although I can't take too much credit. Trev's a good lad. He's a bit brash and full of himself and prone to sulk, but that's a sixteen-year-old boy for you."

Becca toyed with a lock of his hair. "Were you that way when you were sixteen?" she asked, picturing his face younger, without all the lean angles. His lips likely hadn't changed much, though, or his wonderful eyes, except for the little crinkles that appeared at their corners when he smiled.

Blaidd gave her a look of mock offense. "Didn't you know, my lady, I was the greatest sixteen-year-old anybody in Britain had ever seen? Why, I was even going to show Sir Urien a thing or two about swordplay when I first went to his estate to train." He shook his head at the folly of youth. "The man damn near sliced my arm off, and that was in the first five minutes. I got over myself pretty quickly, I can tell you."

"I wish I'd been there."

"What, to see my utter humiliation?"

"To see you at sixteen." She nestled against his strong shoulder. "I'd wager all the girls were quite enamored of you. No wonder you thought you were something."

"I'm glad you didn't see me then, or you'd no doubt still be thinking I'm a vain, spoiled puppy." He caressed her cheek with his index finger. "What were you like at sixteen? Not vain or spoiled, I'm sure."

She sighed and looked away. "If you thought I was a shrew the first day you met me, then I'm very glad you didn't meet me then. I was very bitter."

"With just cause, I think."

She shrugged and didn't meet his gaze. "Laelia can't help being beautiful any more than I can help being crippled. I know that, but sometimes even now

I forget.'' She raised her eyes to look at him. ''That's why I'm hoping to avoid hurting her when she finds out about us.''

He regarded her steadily, and the air about them seemed to tremble with a new tension. ''She may be upset, no matter what we do. Are you prepared to accept that?''

She nodded. ''I'm not about to give you up because Laelia might be angry. Besides, there are plenty of other men for her.''

Blaidd smiled wryly. ''I'm delighted to know I can be replaced so easily.''

''I didn't mean it like that.''

''I know that, my darling,'' he said, kissing the tip of her nose. ''I'm not that sixteen-year-old peacock anymore. Thank God.''

He slipped his arm about her and drew her to him for a long, soft kiss. Then another, until she felt the passion build to the danger point, and pulled back. ''I hope your mother likes me.''

He kissed her forehead. ''I'm sure she will. And my father, too. And Kynan and the girls.''

Becca smiled wistfully. ''I never knew my own mother. She died when I was a babe.''

''I'm sorry.''

Becca shrugged. ''It's my father you should feel sorry for. She was his second wife. Laelia's mother was his first, and she died giving birth to Laelia. That's why we don't look much alike. He married a third time, but she died, too, also in childbirth. That baby—another girl—died, as well. My father once said God must not want him to have sons, so he would be content with his daughters." She made a wry little laugh. "Well, Laelia, anyway. I'm harder to appreciate."

"Not for me," Blaidd said firmly. "You're an excellent daughter."

She couldn't resist kissing his jaw. "You want sons, I suppose?"

"Yes, and daughters, too, with bright eyes and pink cheeks, who can ride and shoot and play the harp."

"That seems a long list, sir knight," she said gravely, although inwardly, she was absolutely delighted. She smiled as she envisioned the children they might have—strong, sturdy, handsome, chivalrous sons who would be welcome in any hall. Bold, happy daughters who didn't have to hide their opinions and who could walk without limping.

"It is quite a list," Blaidd agreed, "but I'm hopeful I'll succeed. That will mostly depend upon the wife I choose, of course. I do have a promising candidate in mind—and in my arms."

He was such a marvelous, attractive, virile man—and then another thought came to her mind. "Do you…" She took a deep breath. "Do you have any children already?"

"No," he answered without hesitation. "Or at least, none that I know of. I won't pretend I haven't made love to other women, Becca, but so far, none have come forth to claim I got them with child." He regarded her gravely. "If that should happen, I'll acknowledge any child I was responsible for bringing into the world.''

''I wouldn't expect anything less from an honorable man,'' she said, stroking his cheek and admiring his honesty, even as she subdued a stab of jealousy for any woman fortunate enough to bear his child.

''Your father seems to have made his peace with a lack of sons,'' Blaidd noted. ''Many a man would keep trying.''

''He has accepted it, or found it too painful to consider marrying again. I didn't know my stepmother well, but I think he cared a great deal for her. I know he loved Laelia's mother very much. He's told her so many times.''

''And your mother?''

Becca looked away. ''Not so much, perhaps. He never speaks of her.''

''Perhaps he loved her most of all, then?'' Blaidd proposed. ''Maybe he can't bear to talk about her because of the pain he felt at her loss.''

Becca looked at Blaidd with wonder and gratitude. She'd never thought of this explanation, but perhaps it was true. It was an unlooked-for comfort, and she blessed Blaidd for suggesting it.

His expression grew more grave. ''Since we are speaking of your father, I can't help noticing he doesn't think much of the king. He should, perhaps, not voice his frustration quite so often, or in public.''

Becca sighed and played with the lace of Blaidd's tunic, subduing the urge to slip her hand inside and stroke his naked chest. ''It's not the king himself he hates. It's the way Henry's rewarded his wife's relations, for nothing more than being his wife's relations. From what I've heard about the court, my father has a point."

"Whether his opinion is valid or not, a wiser man might think twice about announcing such views to all and sundry."

"Then you don't agree that Henry's filling our government with Frenchmen who don't have the welfare of England at heart? You think they aren't lining their own pockets and giving him bad advice?"

Blaidd sighed and loosened his hold. "I can't say I agree that the king makes wise decisions every day. I think he's a good, devout man who'll do well with wise counsel—perhaps this parliament that Simon de Montfort suggests. However, when all is said and done, and whether I agree with every decision or appointment he makes, Henry's my rightful sovereign, to whom I've sworn an oath of loyalty—as has your father."

As Blaidd gazed at her, she was taken aback by the intensity in his brown eyes. "Do you believe he will abide by that oath?" he asked.

"Of course!" she assured him. "To do otherwise would be treason."

Blaidd nodded. "Yes, it would," he said grimly. "And the consequences could be disastrous, for him and for you."

She stared at him, incredulous. "Are you saying my father may be betraying that oath just because he dares to suggest that Henry's making some mistakes?''

Blaidd rose and took hold of her hands, his grip strong and warm as he pulled her to her feet. "I'm saying that unless your father wants people to wonder about his loyalty, he should be careful about what he says."

She cocked her head to regard him studiously. "Do *you* doubt his loyalty?"

"No. No, I don't," Blaidd said, without hesitation. His lips twitched in a little smile. "Praise God, I don't."

Her ire disappeared as quickly as it had arisen. "I'm sorry. You startled me. I thought you were accusing him, and you're a friend of the king. If you were to repeat what you said at court..." She didn't have to finish.

"I'm not accusing him," he assured her. "I'm just warning you, and I'm hoping you can warn him in a way that won't make him angry, either."

"I'll do my best," she vowed, seeing the wisdom of his words.

He smiled that slow, devastating smile again. "Why, my lady, we're standing very close together again. You know what that means, don't you?"

She shook her head.

"I'm going to have to kiss you."

She let him. Well, truth be told, she kissed him, too. For quite some time. She kept kissing him as he inched back and sat on the log, drawing her down until she was cradled on his lap.

"Blaidd?" she murmured as he nibbled her ear-lobe, sending the most delicious ripples of pleasure through her body.

"Yes?"

She managed to move away and get up. "I'm discovering I'm not as strong as I thought I was," she said. "If we don't stop, I'm going to want to make love with you here and now, muddy ground or not. I think I should fetch my harp."

"I think you're right," he replied. "And I appreciate both your wisdom and your self-control. I seem to have left both those qualities somewhere back in the meadow."

She laughed as she went to Claudia and took her well-wrapped harp out of the leather pouch tied to her saddle. Despite her care, the strings were woefully out of tune when she sat down and began to strum it. She tightened the pegs, and saw the way Blaidd watched her.

"Can you play?" she asked as she sat beside him.

Resting one foot casually on his other knee, looking completely at ease, he gave her a rueful grin. "A bit. You're much better."

"Is that really true, or are you just being modest?"

"Alas, my lady, it's true."

"I'd still love to hear you. Please?" She held out her harp to him.

Placing his feet flat on the ground, he accepted it. The instrument wasn't worth much, except to her, yet he handled it as if it were made of gold and precious stones, and that pleased her.

"I'm beginning to realize I'm going to have a difficult time ever saying no to you, my lady," he said as he started to tune the instrument.

"Perhaps it would help if you quit calling me 'my lady.'"

"Perhaps it would...Becca...but I doubt it." He lifted her hand and kissed it. "Indeed, I think you're going to be able to twist me 'round this little finger of yours the rest of my life."

His action thrilled her, but not so much as his words. The rest of his life?

As for the way he said her name in that deep, soft, baritone voice... "I fear you'll be able to get me to do anything you want, sir knight, if you simply ask me."

He got the most devilishly seductive gleam in his eye. "Really?"

She gulped and her hands trembled as she folded them in her lap. "Perhaps you should sing now."

He thought a moment, idly stroking the strings. Then he paused to let them grow still before he began to play and sing. In Welsh.

She had no idea what the words meant, but as the music of the harp and his low, crooning voice filled the wood, she didn't have to understand them. She felt the meaning, and knew he was singing a love song.

To her.

Her eyes focused on his strong, lean fingers, capable of so much more than wielding sword or lance or mace. His hands weren't smooth and soft, either, as so many noblemen's were. They were a man's hands, and when they touched her…

Her breathing quickening, she studied his head as he bent over the harp. Sir Blaidd Morgan was a curious, thrilling mixture of the civilized and the untamed, courteous yet primitive in his passion. He could sing and play, ride well, use a bow, dance…. Was there anything he *couldn't* do?

The strings stilled and his voice fell silent. He looked at her expectantly.

"That was wonderful, even if I didn't understand a word."

"It's about a man far from home, thinking about the woman he loves. He wonders what she's doing, and if she's missing him as much as he's missing her. He remembers all the little things about her—the way she brushes the hair from her cheek, the crease at the corner of her eyes when she smiles, the warmth of their bed."

"I thought it was a love song," she said happily.

"What else would I be singing to you, Becca?" he asked in a whisper as he set the harp down carefully on the log.

She couldn't think of an answer to that, especially when he drew her close. "I would sing love songs to you all day, if I could."

She had to smile at that. "Somehow, I think a man as vigorous as you would get tired of that."

He tucked an errant strand of hair behind her ear. "You're probably right. I might decide some activity was in order."

She tucked his own hair back. Even his ears were attractive. "What activity might that be, sir knight? Riding, hunting, a tournament?"

"Kissing, caressing, making love," he countered, leaning close to do the first.

Before he could, the harp slipped and he twisted to catch it before it fell.

Sighing, she rose and reached for it, glancing up at the sun. "I fear that's a sign we should be on our way. We've been here quite some time already."

"Not that long, considering I've rarely had a chance to talk to you alone."

"I wanted to be with you, too, Blaidd, but we have to be careful," she said as she began to wrap the harp again.

"I'm doing my best to change Laelia's opinion of me," he said as he fetched their horses.

"That's not going to be easy. You're a very fascinating man, after all, so she may be willing to overlook any flaws she may discover."

He muttered a curse as Becca put the harp in the leather pouch cushioned with fleece.

"You can't help being so handsome, but perhaps you could try a little harder not to be so charming."

"I did my best to bore Laelia this morning," he protested as he stepped behind Becca and wrapped his arms around her. "I can't be too disagreeable, though. I want your father to like me, or he might refuse to give me his permission to court his *other* daughter."

She leaned back against his hard chest. "What would you do if he did?"

"I suppose I'd have to steal you away under cover of darkness."

"That sounds exciting."

"Does it?" he murmured, his breath warm as he nuzzled her neck. "Perhaps I should do it, then."

She turned so that she was facing him, still encircled in his arms. "I wouldn't mind, but I doubt my father or a judge of the king's court would listen to me."

"I have plenty of friends there. They'd be on our side."

She cocked her head and regarded him quizzically. "You're not serious, are you?"

He didn't smile. "Actually, I am. If we were desperate enough, I'd risk it."

She kissed him lightly on the cheek. "That's for offering, but let's hope it doesn't come to that. Now, you must go back to the castle. I'll wait here awhile, then return."

"I'll wait. You ride back. I don't want you here all by yourself."

"Blaidd, haven't I made it clear that—?"

"Becca, my dearest, most stubborn woman, please indulge my male urge to protect the things I cherish."

She saw an unmistakably obstinate glint in his eyes, as well as sincere concern. "Since you put it that way, very well, sir knight, I concede—on one condition."

"What's that?" he asked warily.

"Another kiss before I go."

The warmth of his smile enveloped her. "Gladly, my lady, gladly."

Chapter Eleven

The cook threw up his hands in exasperation. "Boys these days!" he cried, turning from Becca to glare at the two downcast scullions standing near the large stone sink set in the wall. "Lazy things, the pair of them! My pots haven't been properly cleaned in a week. And that one—" he jabbed his plump finger at the smaller of the two "—used my best ladle to kill a mouse!"

Becca was used to Rowan complaining about the kitchen boys; he did it twice a week at least. But the news about the ladle and the mouse made her feel a little sick.

"I had to use the ladle as kindling, didn't I?" Rowan shouted, gesturing wildly toward the largest hearth, which could hold a whole cow for roasting.

Becca felt better. In spite of that, she continued to regard Rowan as if his trouble was nothing short of a catastrophe. "A great pity, Rowan."

Rowan slammed his broad hands down on the long,

scarred oak table where all the food was prepared. "These two have *got* to go!"

He shoved off from the table and crossed his arms. Behind his bulky body, Becca spotted a mouse running across the floor toward the pantry. "Perhaps if you'd allow the cat into the pantry—" she began.

"It's not about the mice!" Rowan roared. "He broke my best ladle."

When he was in this sort of state, Rowan reminded her of nothing so much as a big baby. Her lips started to twitch as she imagined him in a giant cradle, rubbing his eyes with his fists like a tired, cranky infant.

Doing her best to look serious, she said, "I understand that, and I agree that some punishment is in order. I'll speak to them and—"

"Speak? What good will that do? I've spoken to them till I'm blue in the face, but they won't listen! Brats, the pair of them!" Rowan bellowed.

Becca was no longer amused. They had enough trouble keeping maidservants; all too often, once they were properly trained, they left Throckton for other towns, or got married. "Rowan, I can appreciate that you feel your property was wantonly destroyed, but the hiring and letting go of servants is not your province. It's mine. Now I suggest you get to the bread, and leave me to deal with the scullions."

Rowan scowled, but he wisely realized she was in no humor to hear more. Nodding, he turned and headed to the pantry, where the flour was kept.

"Come with me, boys," Becca said, leading them out into the courtyard, where a brisk breeze made her skirts whip around her ankles. It tugged at the cloaks of the sentries on the wall, as well.

A quick scan revealed that Blaidd wasn't there. He and his squire—who seemed to have gotten over his anger with Blaidd—were likely in the outer ward with Dobbin and his men, training.

The friendship that had sprung up between Dobbin and Blaidd pleased her immensely. They were very alike in some ways: strong, confident, skilled. It would upset her terribly if Dobbin didn't like Blaidd, or vice versa, because there was no doubt in her mind about how she felt about Blaidd. It had to be love, a love that had grown in the past several days, as they'd shared a few more very pleasant moments alone, talking quietly when they could manage it, and exchanging a few brief, surreptitious kisses, too.

Laelia didn't seem quite so eager to be with him now, while her father still clearly enjoyed his company. They'd played chess more than once, and spent a few hours talking politics just last night.

Becca pushed thoughts of Blaidd to the back of her mind in order to concentrate on the domestic crisis. "Now, boys," she said when they reached the well. "What are your names?"

"I'm Bert," mumbled the one who'd used Rowan's ladle as a bludgeon. He was a tanned, brown-haired boy of about ten. "He's Robbie, my lady."

Robbie looked to be about a year older and had vibrant red hair, slightly dusted with flour. His skin was pale, almost translucent, where it wasn't covered with freckles.

"Very well, Bert and Robbie," Becca said gently, "I'd like to hear your side of things. Why haven't you been doing your work properly?"

"We 'ave, my lady!" Bert cried defensively. "But he was always sayin' it wasn't right, so we…so we…"

"So you gave up working as well as you could?"

Neither boy said anything. Bert's toe traced the circumference of a cobblestone.

"Can you see that using Rowan's best ladle to kill a mouse wasn't the wisest idea?" Becca asked.

"He was getting away," Bert protested. "I just grabbed the first thing to hand, my lady."

She studied them a moment. "Tell me, do you like working in the kitchen?"

The boys exchanged wary glances. No doubt they liked the pay and the fact that they would never go hungry working there. It was always easy to slice off a bit of meat or nick an apple.

"I'm not sure I can persuade Rowan to give you another chance," she said. "If I can't, you'll have to go home, or I'll have to find something else for you to do."

"I like horses, my lady!" Bert piped up immediately. "I'd rather be a stable boy than a scullion."

"Me, too!" Robbie echoed.

Becca considered a moment. One of the stable boys had recently left the village to go to London. A groom had spoken to her just the other day about wanting to marry and become a farmer, which meant a stable boy would become a groom. There would be room for two more boys. "Here's what we'll do. If you can find me two likely lads among your friends in the village to take your place in the kitchen, I'll think about putting you to work in the stable."

"Thank you, my lady!" Bert said, grinning from ear to ear.

"Now, give me your aprons and be off."

They quickly divested themselves of the white cloth aprons and handed them to her, all bunched up. As they dashed toward the gate, she smiled at their enthusiasm, although not for long. Now she'd have to find somebody else to wash the cauldrons, bowls, ladles, brushes, and clean the spits. Maybe Bran or Tom—

"Becca!"

She turned to see her father trotting down the steps of the hall and come hurrying toward her. He held a rolled parchment in his hand, which he tapped against his leg when he halted.

"Yes, Father?" she said, wondering what message had brought that air of expectant excitement to him.

"We're going to have guests arriving after the noon today. A Danish prince, in fact, and his entourage of fifty *herremaend*—lords of that country. I wasn't sure when they'd arrive, but this message says they're nearly here."

Becca stared at her father, completely flabbergasted. "A Danish prince? With fifty men?" she repeated as if in a daze. "Why are they coming *here?*"

"He wants to trade, or so he says. Perhaps tales of your sister's beauty have reached as far away as that. Wouldn't it be something if Laelia were to become a princess?"

Becca looked around swiftly, wondering who else had heard the news. "But a Dane, Father!" she quietly protested. "Prince or not, his people have been our enemies for centuries. Have you forgotten?"

Her father didn't look at all troubled. "That was long ago, Becca. We're not at war with them now. So if a Danish prince wants to buy our wool or court my daughter, I'm not going to refuse."

"But what will the king think of—?"

Her father made a sweeping motion with the parchment, as if sweeping Henry himself out of the way. "Henry won't give a damn, as long as I pay my taxes so he can give presents to his French relatives and friends."

Remembering Blaidd's warning, Becca opened her mouth to offer more objections, but her father held up his hand to silence her. "I'm not going to debate this with you, Becca. See that there are sufficient quarters prepared for Valdemar and his men, and that there's plenty of good food at table. And the best wine."

"Sir Blaidd Morgan is still here," she reminded him, wondering what her father was going to say to that. "I gather he's a good friend of the king."

"Of course he is! And he's welcome to tell Henry all about Valdemar, if he thinks it's important. It might be good for Henry to hear that there's a world out there beyond France and the pope." He winked, as mischievous as a boy. "And there's nothing wrong with a little competition for Laelia, either, eh?"

Chuckling, he headed off to the stables, likely to have the grooms start preparing for the arrival of the Danish horses.

As Becca watched him jauntily walk away, she had her doubts that even if Blaidd wanted Laelia, he'd ever be chosen over a prince, by either her father or her sister.

On the other hand, if Laelia was to be offered to a Danish prince, Blaidd would be free to court Becca as he willed, which was a very pleasant, exciting thought. And surely Laelia wouldn't begrudge her sister's relationship with Blaidd if she herself became a princess.

Yet what would her family's alliance with a Danish prince mean to Henry?

They were minor nobility, as her father said and Laelia complained. Perhaps her father was right, and the king wouldn't care, as long as Lord Throckton paid his taxes.

She should ask Blaidd, Becca decided. He would have a better idea of the king's possible reaction, and if he thought the visit was risky, she could try to dissuade her father from doing business with the Danes.

Unfortunately, before she'd even gone a step, a guard shouted from the wall walk that a large party was approaching.

Almost immediately, an entourage fit for a prince entered the inner gate, as if the guards had been forewarned to let them pass. Their banners waved in the breeze and the air was filled with the jingling of mail and harnesses, the babble of foreign words and the creaking of the baggage cart rumbling over the cobblestones.

A blond giant of a man—obviously the prince—rode at the head of the band of armed and armored men. His blue cloak, held with a huge golden broach, was thrown over his broad shoulder. His mail gleamed in the sun and he surveyed the courtyard as if he were a returning hero.

Becca watched, dumbfounded and worried, while the guards positioned on the wall walk and at the gate stared, and servants peered out of doors and windows. Moments later her father hastened out of the stable like a merchant spotting a customer with a large purse.

Becca moved closer to the steps. Dobbin and Blaidd, followed by a panting Trevelyan Fitzroy, came through the gate behind the last of the Danes. Both older men were perspiring and breathless, as if they'd run there. Dobbin looked shocked and confused; Blaidd's expression was a masterpiece of non-revelation, but she could see the tension in his shoulders and the interrogative lift of his brows.

Blaidd began making his way through the company of scornful Danes, heading straight for her father and the prince, while Dobbin stayed by the gate with his men.

The Dane swung out of his saddle and landed lightly on his feet, which was rather unexpected considering he had to be over six feet tall and had shoulders like an ox. He strode toward Lord Throckton, who came to a halt at the bottom of the stairs leading to the hall.

"Greetings, Prince Valdemar!" her father began.

Before he could continue, the Danish prince checked his steps—not because of her father's salutation, but because he'd seen Laelia, who appeared at the door of the hall.

For once when under a man's scrutiny, Becca's sister didn't immediately soften like a half-wilted flower and look at the ground with every appearance of demure modesty. She stared at the Dane as if she'd never seen a man before.

He stared right back at her, completely ignoring everyone else.

Lord Throckton gestured for Laelia to come forward. "Prince Valdemar, allow me to present my daughter Laelia."

She smiled and bowed with an energy and eagerness that made Becca's eyes grow as wide as the wheels of the baggage cart.

The Dane bowed low and elegantly. "I am honored, my lady," he said in a deep, accented voice.

Laelia's smile widened. This was not the false-friendly smile she so often gave a man. This was a genuine smile of a sort Becca hadn't seen on her sister's face in years. "I'm delighted, Prince Valdemar," she said, her voice clearly audible above the crowd.

"You must not call me prince, lovely lady," he replied. "Lord Valdemar will do."

Laelia looked confused, and so was she, and their father.

"I am the offspring of the king of Denmark, but not the queen," Valdemar explained.

A bastard prince, then. Her father suddenly didn't look quite so impressed. "And this is my younger daughter, Rebecca," he snapped, gesturing at her.

At her father's unexpected and brusque introduction, Becca bowed, stumbling a bit as she lost her balance.

Lord Valdemar's scrutiny was distinctly scornful. But she was used to that sort of regard from handsome, arrogant men.

Then Blaidd reached the steps. The Danish prince ran a scornful gaze over him, too, taking in Blaidd's leather jerkin worn over his naked chest that exposed his lean, muscular arms, his plain, muddy breeches and his worn leather boots.

"Who is this?" Valdemar haughtily demanded.

A fierce expression crossed Blaidd's features for a brief moment and she feared he was going to draw his sword, but he didn't.

Instead Blaidd put a genial smile on his face—which didn't reach his dark eyes—and bowed just as elegantly as Valdemar had. "I am Sir Blaidd Morgan of Wales."

The Dane smirked. "A Welshman? I thought all Welshmen were dwarves."

Blaidd's smile chilled her. "Obviously, we're

not," he replied, "any more than all Danes are pirates."

Valdemar glanced at Laelia, who was still watching him as if he was made of solid gold, and then he laughed, a low, deep rumble of good cheer that echoed off the stone walls of the courtyard. "Well, once we were, but those days are over. Now we trade for what we want."

"Exactly!" her father cried, hurrying to come between them. "Lord Valdemar is here to purchase some wool—and honor us with his presence, of course!" He steered Valdemar and Blaidd toward the hall. Laelia, for once forgotten, hurried after them like a puppy at their heels.

"Sir Blaidd is a friend of our king, my lord," he continued, "and a fine fighter. Now come, and we'll have refreshments."

Her father's last words brought Becca to her senses with a snap. Nothing had been prepared for these guests, who couldn't be turned away now. Rowan would have a fit. How much wine did they have? And was there hay and straw for the horses? They'd have to find clean linens for the bedding....

Although all she really wanted to do was talk to Blaidd about this unexpected visitation, she had too much to do now to try to find a quiet moment with him.

Unfortunately, she couldn't snatch a quiet moment alone with him that night, or the next day, or the one after that.

Chapter Twelve

In the dim light of the waning moon, Blaidd slipped like a spider down the rope he had slung from one of the merlons. He'd found a spot shadowed by a tower, out of the nearest guard's line of sight. Blaidd wanted to get to the village, and the brothel, without being seen.

The arrival of that arrogant Dane had been like a clarion call. Even if he was falling in love, he should have been doing more to find out if Lord Throckton was harmless or not. He should have questioned Meg more closely; he should have gone to see Hester sooner. Now Meg was too busy with the extra work the Danes required, and he'd been trying to stay as close to Valdemar and Lord Throckton as possible, to discover if their alliance was merely for trade, or another, darker reason. So far, trade seemed to be the only purpose for this visit, and as far as Blaidd could ascertain, this was the first time any Danes had come to Throckton. Every servant he asked said so, although he had learned that Lord Throckton often had guests from various places, and not all of them came to court the lovely Laelia.

This wasn't necessarily a sign of treachery, though. It could be evidence to suggest that Throckton's income was derived from canny trading with a host of foreigners.

Blaidd hadn't had a chance to speak with Becca, either, to hear her views on the Danes. She was likewise busy with her household duties.

He doubted she would see anything suspicious, anyway. That day in the wood she'd made it clear that she believed her father was completely loyal to Henry. As for Laelia, although she was definitely fascinated by the Dane, Blaidd was sure her disinterest in politics wasn't feigned.

Lord Throckton continued to be the genial host, yet he skillfully managed to evade any question Blaidd ventured about his dealings with foreigners, claiming, when Blaidd was able to pose a query, that such visits were solely about trade, which wasn't treasonous.

He should have been more diligent nevertheless, Blaidd had realized. He shouldn't have allowed himself to be blinded by his emotions and the good cheer of his host, and put his own happiness above his duty.

Reaching the ground, he slid down the side of the dry moat, then climbed up the opposite embankment. Keeping to the shadows of the buildings, creeping along like a housebreaker, he made his way to the brothel.

Once at the whorehouse, he made sure no one was

watching, then ducked inside. His arrival was greeted with gasps of surprise and smirks from the few women waiting below, and low, sultry laughter from the large, dark-haired madam. She sauntered toward him, her black, beady eyes gleaming with triumph and greed. "I figured it was only a matter o' time before you come again."

"I find myself unable to stay away." He scanned the women gathered there. "Where's the fair one?"

"Ah, I thought she'd be your choice. She told me how you was looking at her when you dragged that boy off. And of course, if her high and mightiness there in the castle won't let you touch her, our Hester's enough like her to make it easy to pretend, eh?" The woman leered and cackled. "You wouldn't be the first."

Blaidd felt soiled, but he continued the ruse regardless. "How much?"

"Five pennies."

"Five seems excessive."

"Not for her, as you'll find out soon enough."

He reached in his purse, which was purposefully nearly empty, and handed her the coins, which she slipped into her stained bodice. "Where is she, then?" he asked.

The woman jerked her head toward the stairs. "Same as before. You might have to wait a bit, though. She's a busy one, our Hester."

The woman's grin was like a death mask, and it was all Blaidd could do to keep the disgust off his face.

"I'll keep ya company while ya wait," one of the other whores offered, sidling closer.

"I don't want to wait." He eyed the madam. "What'll it take to get rid of whoever's with her now?"

Again, that greedy gleam came to the woman's eyes. "Another five pennies."

Blaidd scowled, but paid. He'd already wasted enough time.

The woman waddled toward the steps, then heaved herself upward. He didn't wait to be invited; he followed her at once.

The other whores laughed and jeered. "What, not good enough for ya, are we? We could show you a thing or two!"

He thought they probably could, but it would be nothing he would care to learn from them.

The madam reached the familiar door and Blaidd tried to ignore the noises coming through the flimsy barrier—the creaking of the bed ropes and what sounded like the grunting of a pig at the trough.

The madam pounded on the door with her beefy fist until he thought she'd shatter it. "Oy, miller, time's up!"

The sounds inside abruptly ceased. "So soon?" a man's voice querulously demanded.

"Aye!" the woman bellowed back.

They could hear the man's grumbling, his bare feet hitting the floorboards and the rustle of fabric.

"Hurry up!" the madam demanded as she glanced

at Blaidd, who was making no secret of his impatience, if not for the reason she supposed.

The door flew open, and a large, red-faced man appeared, his yoked shirt unlaced. He was holding his breeches and boots. ''You old cow, what the devil—''

He saw Blaidd and went even redder. Without another word, he pushed past the madam and hurried down the stairs.

She cackled again and shoved open the door for Blaidd to enter. ''Here you go. Enjoy!''

He had to push his way past her bulk to get inside. When he did, the woman pulled the door closed, and he could hear her laughing as she made her way down the stairs.

The young blond woman was still in the bed, sitting up with the filthy sheet held to her breasts. She gave him a come-hither smile. ''Oh, it's you, is it?''

Blaidd walked toward the bed, getting as far away from the rickety door as possible. ''When I was here before, you implied you had something to tell me, something to do with Lady Rebecca. What is it?''

Hester slid out of the bed, leaving the sheet behind. ''Is that all you want?'' she asked, her voice sultry as she strolled, unabashedly naked, toward a rickety table bearing two dented bronze goblets and a wineskin.

''Yes.''

She poured herself some wine, then leaned back against the table as she sipped it slowly, giving him ample time to look at her slender, shapely body and the golden mane of hair that was her only covering. She set down the goblet and smiled. "Are you sure?"

"Absolutely. So if that was a lie intended only to get me here, I will not stay." He turned on his heel. "You may keep whatever profit you've made from my visit and give whatever reason you like for my early departure."

"Even if I say you couldn't get it up?"

His hand on the latch, Blaidd looked back at her over his shoulder and gave her a cool smile. "If you think anybody will believe that, go ahead."

She ran to the door and covered his hand with hers. She gazed up at him, and this time, he saw sincerity in her green eyes. "Don't go. I wasn't lying. I got something important to tell you."

He removed his hand, so that hers fell away, too. "Then why the game?"

She shrugged. "Men expect it, and you're a man, aren't you?"

"Not that kind."

"So you're the exception, not the rule," she said grimly as she went to the pile of clothing near the table. She drew on a soiled shift, then sat on the bed. "I hear you're a friend of the king."

"Yes."

"A good friend?"

"Some would say."

"He'd listen to you? If you vouched for somebody, he'd believe you?"

"Probably," Blaidd answered warily.

She nodded in acceptance. "Good, because you've got to help Lady Rebecca."

Dread skittered down Blaidd's spine. "You think she's in danger?"

"I think she could be, but not through anything she's done, and you've got to tell the king that, if things get…bad."

Blaidd's eyes narrowed. "What do you mean, bad?"

Hester swung her feet, and didn't answer him directly. "I hear there's more visitors to the castle."

Valdemar's entourage would have been hard to miss as it passed through the village. "Aye."

"This ain't the first time Danes have come here, but they didn't say they was Danes then. They said they was Germans. One of 'em that come here for a bit o' fun let it slip they wasn't." She made a face. "Seems I reminded him of a girl back home."

More apprehension filled Blaidd. If this was true, why the secrecy, unless Lord Throckton's meeting with the Danes was for more than trading?

But if there was a conspiracy, why would Valdemar be proclaiming his nationality so openly? "There's nothing illegal about Danes trading with an English lord."

He'd said that to Trev, too, and Hester's expression was just as skeptical as his squire's had been.

"You think that's all he wants, to trade?" Hester demanded as she jerked her thumb in the direction of the castle. "You think that old spider up there doesn't have other plans? Why, that Throckton's planning to make an alliance with the Danes, all right, 'cept wool ain't got much to do with it. Between his army and theirs, and with some of the barons who don't like Henry, they could march on London and overthrow the king.''

She was absolutely right, and if that was Throckton's scheme, that would be open rebellion. But how would a whore know what a lord was planning? ''I've been here for weeks now,'' Blaidd said, ''and while he's discontented with the king's rule, that's a far cry from treason.''

Hester smirked. ''I wager you think he's got no ambition at all. That he's perfectly content here in Throckton, with his castle and his wealth? That he's not jealous of them with more power at court?''

''He's given no indication that he cares about power at all,'' Blaidd replied.

''Then he's fooled you, too, with his smiles and lies. Why do you think he hasn't let Laelia marry? He's waiting for somebody with real power and influence to ask for her.''

''Or he may be wanting the best marriage possible for his daughter.''

''You think he really gives a damn about his daughters? My mother was a servant in the castle, and she was there when all three of his wives lived and died. He made it plain as the sun on a summer's day that he wanted sons. He didn't mourn for long after they died. My mother heard him *curse* his last wife for giving him another useless female.''

"He treats his daughters well," Blaidd protested, unwilling to believe her.

"Because they're useful—Laelia to make a marriage to his advantage, and Rebecca because she runs the castle. He's nothing but a lying, scheming hypocrite. He plays the kindly, generous host, 'cept he's not kind or generous. He's an ambitious, selfish lout without a drop o' pity or charity."

"I can understand why you might believe that. I know he didn't help you when you got with child."

"Damn right he didn't," she retorted, her slender hands balling into fists. "He called me a whore and threw me out of the castle. If I could have stayed there, my baby might have lived. Instead, he was born here, in this...this place." She gestured at the filthy room and her voice grew stronger. "Throckton as good as killed his own grandson!"

Blaidd stared in stunned disbelief. "Lord Throckton—?"

"Is my father." She stood and slowly turned completely around, a mockingly coy smile on her face. "Can't you see my resemblance to the beauteous Lady Laelia? Didn't that old hag below point it out?"

God's wounds, he *could* see a resemblance. It was slight, but there, in her green eyes and blond hair, and the shape of her jaw. "Is that why Bec—Lady Rebecca—tried to help you?"

Hester stopped smiling. "She doesn't know," she said grimly. "Nobody does, 'cept him, and me, and now you. My mother was paid well to keep the secret. She did, until she was on her deathbed, then she made me swear to keep it, too.'' Hester frowned. ''What, you think only lords and ladies can keep their word?''

''I'm surprised you didn't reveal the truth when he treated you as he did.''

''That made me *ashamed* to think he'd fathered me.'' She gave Blaidd a sour smile. ''Aye, we peasant folk can be ashamed of our noble blood, when it's like his. But it was for Rebecca's sake I didn't say anything. She was the only one ever treated me decent after that, and she loves her father, not that the bastard deserves it. Why do you think that even though he treats her like a drudge, she's still here, running the castle and sparing her sister the effort? There's nobody more loyal and loving, and I reckon the truth'd just about break her heart. That's why I ain't shouted his true nature from the top of the village church. Aye, and there's more. Do you think because he's not got a wife he's living like a monk? No girl over fifteen 'cept his own escapes his notice.

''He don't rape them, if that's what you're thinking,'' Hester continued. ''But he's a master at seducing, and he's rich. He gets most of the ones he wants, then pays 'em to keep quiet. Either they leave Throckton altogether, or use the money for a dowry. He squeezes every penny out of the poor he can manage, too, threatening 'em and bullying. Lady Rebecca don't know the half of it.''

Blaidd's heart twisted and ached as he listened. Becca *was* loving and loyal; she wouldn't want to believe her father capable of such things—if indeed, he was, and these weren't lies or exaggerations told by a bitter, angry woman.

"So when I say these Danes ain't here to trade, you should believe me." She flipped a lock of hair over her shoulder with a return to her coy, yet brazen, manner. "Some of 'em like to brag, and one of 'em who was more drunk than the others told me that one day they'd be living here for good."

"It's fairly obvious, Hester, that you have no love for Lord Throckton," Blaidd said. "How can I believe anything you say about him?"

"How can you trust a whore, eh?" she asked as she sat and crossed her legs. "Well, Sir Blaidd, I guess you can't. So maybe I'm telling you nothing but lies because I'm bitter about what he did to me. Maybe I ain't telling you this because I care about the one person who treated me decent after that bastard of a knight got me with child, and I don't want to see her suffer for her father's doings. If that's what you think, then I'm sorry I told you." She raised her hand and pointed. "And there's the door."

Blaidd stayed where he was. "Hester, I'm willing to accept that Lord Throckton may not be quite as he seems, but if I'm to believe anything more, I'll need proof."

She shrugged. "Believe me or not as you will, Sir Blaidd. But if I'm right and Throckton's up to no good, I want you to know that Lady Rebecca's innocent. I want a friend of the king's to know the truth."

"I give you my word, Hester, that if the man's a

traitor, I'll do everything in my power to ensure that Lady Rebecca doesn't suffer for it.''

Hester got to her feet. "Good. Now go, and tell that sow I won't be earnin' any more money for her tonight. I wager she got enough out of you, anyway.''

Blaidd went to the door, then paused before opening it to look back at her, standing so stiff and defiant in that squalid room. A lord's daughter? He could well believe it now.

He bowed as if she were the queen. "I appreciate why you've told me all this, Hester. I thank you, and it may be that one day, Lady Rebecca will thank you, too.''

Hester nodded regally as he went out and closed the door.

Then she sat on the filthy bed and covered her face with her hands.

The next morning, Becca hesitated on the stairway leading from the apartments to the courtyard. Dobbin was waiting at the bottom, leaning against the wall, his head down and his arms folded across his chest, in an attitude that looked so like despair, she shivered.

She tried to think of what could account for both his presence and condition. "What's happened?" she asked as she continued her slow progress downward. "Is there trouble with the men?"

Straightening, Dobbin uncrossed his arms. "With *a* man," he clarified.

"Which one?" she queried, assuming it was one of the soldiers. "What's he done?"

Instead of answering immediately, Dobbin put his hand on her upper arm and steered her outside, then into an alley between the apartments and the hall, as if he didn't want anyone to overhear what he was about to tell her.

"What's the matter?" she asked urgently, dread growing with every moment.

Dobbin ran his hand over his chin, and she realized how tired he looked, as if he hadn't slept all night.

"Dobbin, tell me!"

His eyes full of remorse, he said, "I'm sorry, my lady, but last night, Sir Blaidd Morgan went to the village. To the brothel."

Becca slumped back against the stone wall. Blaidd had gone to the *brothel?* Blaidd, who had seemed so disgusted when his squire had done that very thing? Who had spoken with such distaste about the existence of such things, and even with sympathy and dismay for the women who worked in them? "Are you *sure?*"

Dobbin nodded. "Aye. Charlie was on sentry patrol on the wall walk and he saw him start over the wall. He was sure who it was because of his hair, you see, so he didn't raise the alarm. After all, the man's a guest, and he was one man going out, not a bunch coming in. I told Charlie to go after him and tell me where he went."

Charlie was the one archer in the garrison Becca could never beat. He'd once hit an apple hanging on a tree more than seventy feet away. So if he believed he'd seen Sir Blaidd Morgan—so distinctive with his long, savage hair—climbing over the wall, he probably had.

"He was even more certain who it was when Sir Blaidd come out of the brothel. Got a good look at 'im then." Dobbin reached out to touch her arm. "I'm sorry," he repeated. "I misjudged him, too. I never thought he'd be the sort."

Becca took a deep breath and tried not to let disappointment overwhelm her. "I was sure he wasn't."

"Aye, and that's why I thought you had to know. I've seen what's going on between you, and I was glad, for your sake. But now…" He paused a moment, then continued, his voice stronger. "But while it might break your heart to hear it now, I've seen the misery a man like that can cause a woman, and I won't have that happen to you."

It did break her heart, for Dobbin's words had destroyed the honorable, moral Blaidd she'd believed in. She'd been right that first night in the chapel: he was a lascivious scoundrel. Even worse, he was a hypocritical lascivious scoundrel. He'd tricked her with his soft words and passionate kisses, and played her for a fool. As for other things they'd done… She could only be grateful she hadn't gotten into his bed.

"Becca—Lady Rebecca, maybe it's time he left," Dobbin gently suggested.

"Oh, yes, he'll be leaving. Today," she declared, her voice gruff. Despite her growing anger, there was a lump in her throat that wouldn't go away.

"What reason will you give your father?"

"Hopefully I won't have to give him any, after I

speak to Sir Blaidd alone and make it clear his true nature has been discovered. If he goes to my father, and Father allows him to stay, at least Laelia will know what she's letting herself in for if she marries him, and I'll have done all I could to prevent it.''

''On the attack, eh, my girl? I should have guessed. After you're done talking to the lout, I doubt he'll stay. Want me and a few of the lads to follow him and make sure he knows he won't be welcome back?''

''As well as give him a scar or two to remember us by?'' She shook her head. ''No, Dobbin. Don't waste your time. The less we have to do with him, the better.''

''As you wish, my lady,'' Dobbin replied, with an undertone of regret.

She patted his arm. ''I do appreciate how hard it was for you to do this, Dobbin, and I'm grateful. Now I'd better get to Mass. Sir Blaidd Morgan, hypocrite that he is, will surely be there, and afterward, I can send him on his way.''

Dobbin watched her as she headed slowly toward the chapel, her head high. She was a lady of dignity and worthy of the utmost respect, loyalty and love. More than that, she was her mother's daughter, and a woman any man but Throckton would be proud and blessed to call his daughter.

Chapter Thirteen

Blaidd knew something was wrong the minute he saw Becca in the chapel. She was deathly pale, and she looked at him as if he'd hurt her terribly and roused her formidable ire at the same time.

What the devil had happened? Had she guessed he'd lied about his motive for coming there? Or was it something else? Had he been seen going into the brothel? That would certainly account for her indignant mouth and disappointed eyes.

How could he explain what he'd been doing there without telling her what Hester had said, and the reason he'd come to Throckton in the first place? He'd have to think of something. He'd have to make things right between them, somehow.

Standing to his right, Lord Throckton gave him a questioning glance, and Blaidd realized he was fidgeting. To his left, Trev had apparently noticed that, too, for he was regarding him quizzically.

Lady Laelia, on Lord Throckton's right, and Valdemar beside her, didn't seem to be paying much attention to anything except each other.

"Itch," Blaidd muttered in explanation to Trev, reaching around to scratch his lower back, and incidentally glancing at Becca again.

She was still staring at him as if he'd betrayed her utterly.

He faced forward again, and tried to stand still and be patient. It was torture, though, feeling her looking at him, yet unable to do anything about it until the Mass was over—unless he wanted to make a scene, which he certainly did not. He wanted to take her hand and lead her someplace where he could speak to her alone, where he could find out exactly what she was thinking and try to make amends.

He didn't dare excuse himself and rush from the chapel when the service finally ended, either. He dare not reveal any impatience as he waited for Lord Throckton, Lady Laelia and Valdemar to lead the way out.

Becca was standing by the chapel door. She didn't speak; she just gave him a significant look, and headed toward the keep.

"Trev, you go ahead and break the fast," he said to his squire. "I'll be along shortly. I want to get a whetstone to polish my blade."

Trev nodded and walked away with the other people headed toward the hall, leaving Blaidd free to casually saunter after Becca, who was unlocking the armory with a key from the ring she wore on her belt. She disappeared inside.

He continued to stroll toward the keep as if in no great hurry. When he neared the round stone structure, he checked to see if anyone was watching. The sentries were all looking outward over the walls and not into the courtyard, and everyone else was in the hall, breaking their fast.

He slipped into the ancient tower. Lances leaned against the curved walls to his left. To his right were racks of plain swords. Beside them were pegs holding quivers. Unslung bows lay on wooden shelves, and there were smaller shelves for arrows. In the center of the room was a large empty hearth and a workbench where the armorer must do his repairs. Buckets, rags and some iron tools lay on its surface.

"Becca?" Blaidd called out quietly, his words echoing in the stillness.

"Down here."

He followed her voice and discovered a set of narrow steps leading to a level below, to what must be a storehouse, or perhaps cells for prisoners.

When he went down, he was relieved to find that the lower level was not cells, but a large and virtually empty chamber. A single small window provided a little light, enough to make the walls shimmer where water dripped down.

Becca stood in the center of the chamber, her arms crossed, her attitude one of anger and defiance.

"Where were you last night?" she demanded, stern and majestic.

He wondered if perhaps she'd thought he'd signaled her or somehow arranged a rendezvous—that she was upset over that, and nothing more serious. "Were we supposed to meet?"

"If you're going to try to play the ignorant innocent with me, it won't work!" she charged.

Obviously, he was wrong. This was much more serious a matter than forgetting a rendezvous.

"You've tricked me into believing you're an honorable, noble man, but you're not," she said. "I was right that first night you kissed me in the chapel. You're nothing but a lascivious, immoral hypocrite!"

There could be but one explanation for those particular words. "Somebody told you I went to the brothel," he guessed.

"Yes," she hissed, glaring.

"Who?"

"Someone I trust, the way I *thought* I could trust you."

"Did this informant also tell you I didn't stay long?"

"How much time does such business take?" she retorted. "I'm sure you're fast when it suits your purpose."

"Becca, I didn't go there for that."

She raised one brow skeptically. "Oh, you just wanted to *talk?*"

He regarded her angry features for a long moment as he decided what to do. He could hide his suspicions about her father, although that would mean agreeing that his visit to the brothel had been for his pleasure. Or he could be honest with her. He could trust her enough to tell her the truth, and warn her of her potential danger if her father was plotting against the crown.

And that was what he would do. "When I went after Trev that night and found him in the brothel, Hester said she had something important to tell me, something about you. I went to find out what."

Becca's eyes narrowed. "And you forgot this until last night?"

"I agree I shouldn't have left it so long."

"How wonderful to hear that you should have taken yourself to a stew sooner," she mocked.

"I'm being honest with you, Becca," he said firmly.

Her eyes flickered, but her lips remained thinned. "Let's say you're *not* lying. What thing of import did Hester have to impart?"

"Danes have come here before."

"They have not," Becca asserted. "I'd have known if they did."

"She said they claimed to be Germans."

Becca's angry gaze faltered for the briefest of moments, but in the next, defiance kindled again in her brilliant eyes. "Danes, Germans, what does it matter?"

"If it didn't, why would they keep their true nationality a secret?" he countered.

"That's assuming Hester's right. How did she come to have this alleged knowledge?"

"One of them told her where they were really from."

The defiant disbelief dwindled a bit, but her voice

didn't betray anything except absolute faith in Lord Throckton. "You would have me question my father's business based on what a man tells a *harlot*, one my father cast out of the household? She probably just wants to make trouble for us. And why would she tell you this, and not me?"

"Because she's heard I'm a friend of the king. She wants to protect you—and so do I. You could be in grave danger." Regretting what he had to say, but determined to tell her everything, he spoke with both sympathy and grim resolution. "Becca, your father may be plotting treason."

"Treason?" she gasped, too stunned even to be angry. "What madness is this? My father's as loyal to the king as you are! I won't stand here and listen to such nonsense!"

She made to go past him, but he grabbed her arm and looked intently into her agitated face. "Is he loyal, Becca? Are you absolutely certain?"

She wrenched her arm free. "Of course! How dare you suggest otherwise?"

"He complains about Henry and his rewards to his wife's relations."

"So do many men! So do *you!*"

"But I'm not entertaining Danes, or entering into alliances with them, or building a huge fortress with vast wealth that cannot come from the income of this estate. I haven't raised a personal army of well-armed fighting men with superior skills."

Becca backed away from him as if he were contagious. "Why shouldn't my father entertain a Danish prince? We're not at war with them. Why not enter a trade alliance? As for his wealth…I have no idea about my father's finances, but I'm sure he's come by every ha'penny honestly. And what man of wealth wouldn't want it well protected?"

"Becca, there's more," Blaidd said, his tone commanding, demanding that she listen. "Your father's loyalty was already suspect. Why, exactly, I don't know, but Henry sent me here to find evidence of a plot, or to reassure him that his suspicions were groundless."

"You're a *spy?*" Incredulity gave way to revulsion as she stared at him. "Oh, God—that's why you asked me about his loyalty! You were trying to get me to incriminate my own father!"

Her lip curled with scorn as she backed toward the steps. "You disgusting, despicable rogue! Is that why you kissed me, too? And made me believe you cared for me? So that I would tell you anything you wanted to know about him? Did you think that if I loved you, you could make me say whatever you wanted? That I would turn against my father and lie, the way you do?"

She tried to run to the door, but her legs were trembling, and her weaker one gave way. She fell to the floor of hard-packed earth.

He crouched beside her and put his arm around her to help her stand. "Listen to me, Becca! Please!"

She pushed his arm away and struggled to her feet.

"Leave me alone, you liar! I'd rather lie on this floor and die than take any help from you!"

"I love you!" Blaidd cried desperately. "That's why I'm telling you all this."

Although her whole body trembled, she managed to get to her feet and regain her balance. "I'm sure you love me," she sneered. "You love me so much, you suspect my father is a traitor and you want me to provide evidence of his guilt. You know what will happen to your beloved if he's found guilty, don't you? All my father's lands will be forfeit to the crown. Laelia and I will be penniless—and that's if we live. The king might accuse us, too. It won't matter if we're innocent or not. A Dane has come and a whore tells Sir Blaidd Morgan that he and my father are scheming to overthrow the king, so our fate is sealed." Her eyes narrowed. "What do you stand to gain if my father's convicted? Land? An earldom? Power? Wealth?"

"I'm trying to save you! How do you know he's *not* a traitor? If you have proof, tell me," Blaidd pleaded.

"I don't need proof that he's innocent. He's my father!"

"How well do you know him?" Blaidd demanded as frustration overwhelmed him. "Enough to know that Hester is his child?"

"What? You *are* insane—or she is!"

"She looks like Laelia. Haven't you ever noticed the resemblance?"

"Of course not, because it isn't there! And don't

you think I'd know if that were true? A thing like that could hardly be kept a secret.''

''She says her mother was sworn to secrecy as part of the bargain she made with your father when she discovered she was with child. He paid her for her silence. She made Hester swear not to reveal it, too.''

''Until now,'' Becca demanded scornfully, ''when a man comes seeking proof of duplicitous acts. What a convenient morality she has!''

''Until she guessed that the time had come to protect a person she truly does care about. Because of your kindness, she wants you safe, and because of what she knows about your father and his dealings, she fears that you're in danger, just as I do.'' Blaidd went to her and grasped her careworn hands in his, willing her to listen. To believe. To trust him. ''Becca, I came here because the king asked me to, for the reason I told you. I did lie about courting your sister, and I regret that. But what's happened between us is not false. I love you, and I want to marry you. If I didn't care about you, I wouldn't be trying to warn you. I've already heard enough to have your father arrested. I could have kept what I know to myself, and left for London without saying anything to you of my suspicions.''

She yanked her hands from his. She was calmer now—too calm. Calm in a way that told him she couldn't or wouldn't believe him. ''Whatever you say or think, my father is loyal to Henry. If it be treason to suggest that the king favors his wife's relatives at some cost to his kingdom, the dungeons of England would be filled to capacity. I suggest, Sir Blaidd, that you return to court at once and tell the king whatever you *think* you know. But be prepared, because if you accuse my father, I'm going to tell everyone that you found your reasons in a whore's bed, and that you tried to take advantage of your host's daughter for your own ambitious ends.''

''Are you going to tell your father what I've told you?''

He saw her struggle, and waited tensely for her answer. If she told her father, he and Trev might find out if there *were* cells in Throckton Castle.

Blaidd couldn't risk that. He'd have to keep her down here until they could get away.

''No,'' she said at last. ''Because I think you're wrong and nothing will come of your suspicions. *You have no proof.* I'll tell him you left because—''

''Tell him I realized the woman I loved was not going to return my affections, and I saw no need to linger.''

She nodded curtly. ''Very well.''

She went up the steps without a backward glance.

As he watched her go, he prayed to God that someday she would understand what he'd done, and why, and believe that he did love her.

He still loved her. He'd finally found a love that could last forever, but it wasn't going to bring him happiness.

Only the despair of knowing what might have been, and was forever lost.

* * *

Blinking back tears, Becca crossed the courtyard as quickly as she could. Sir Blaidd Morgan had to be wrong! Her father wasn't a traitor. He couldn't be.

Blaidd had come there under false pretenses. He was a liar, a sly, deceitful rogue who'd used her loneliness and vulnerability to further his own schemes.

She'd be happy when he was gone. Very happy!

She entered the hall and realized everyone had finished eating. "Where's my father?" she asked Bran.

The man's eyes widened at her harsh tone, and he pointed toward the stairs leading to her father's solar.

Without another word, she went to the stairs and began to make her way up. Her leg ached and she paused, rubbing it, before starting up again.

She was determined to tell him that Sir Blaidd Morgan was leaving. That was the only reason she was going there....

She paused again near the landing and leaned against the cool stone wall. No, it wasn't. She wanted to see her father's face, to compare it to Hester's. To see if there could be any truth at all to Hester's claim.

Because even as she'd denied what Hester had said, bits and pieces, words and phrases, kept coming to Becca, like colored threads of wool forming a tapestry. A little snatch of overheard conversation about her father and a maidservant here, other conversations cut short there. Glances exchanged when nobody thought she was looking. The maidservants who always seemed to leave so suddenly and so soon. His tolerance for men's "sport."

Dobbin's expression when he spoke of the misery a man like Sir Blaidd could cause a woman. Dobbin had been at Throckton for years and years. Was he speaking of her mother, and her father's other wives?

"You expect me to marry that *cripple?* I won't, not for that pitiful dowry."

Lord Valdemar's words, issuing from her father's solar, yanked her out of her reverie.

There was only one cripple in Throckton Castle.

Even more stunned than when Blaidd had made his startling announcements, Becca inched her way forward. The door to the solar was open just a crack, but it was enough for her to put her eye to the door. Her father sat behind the large trestle table covered with scrolls, quills, a vessel of ink and one of sand, as well as wax for seals. His sword, its jeweled hilt sparkling in the sunlight, also lay on the table. Valdemar, obviously angry, was pacing in front of it, and the tapestries moved in the breeze from his agitated steps.

"Be quiet," her father ordered, "and sit down. Let's discuss this like civilized men—or are you a pirate, as Sir Blaidd suggested?"

"I am the son of the king of Denmark!"

"And I will increase the dowry to thirty thousand marks."

Becca gasped at the sum. For him to marry *her?* She couldn't believe it. She had no notion... What was her father doing?

Valdemar sat, in a chair she couldn't see. She could only watch his feet, which shifted and moved restlessly. "And that's another thing," he said, still angry but somewhat mollified. "What's that Welshman doing here?"

"Another suitor for Laelia's hand, who would have been gone if you'd sent me word you were coming sooner than you did."

Valdemar's hand came into view, waving dismissively. "There is nothing to prevent me from coming here. Our countries are not at war. Or at least, not yet, and then it will be the Danes and you and your allies against Henry and his French friends."

Becca shoved her fist in her mouth to stifle the moan rising in her throat. God help her, Blaidd was right! She should have believed him, trusted him.

Was he right about *everything?*

"He's no fool, Valdemar."

She inched closer to hear what they thought of Blaidd. If they suspected him of knowing the truth, he might be in danger.

"And Morgan's a friend of Henry's. You'd better hope to heaven he believes that all we're interested in is trade, or the plans your father and I have made won't be worth a hangman's noose."

Valdemar slouched lower in his chair. "He believed you."

"So far, anyway," her father agreed. "And Laelia's not inclined to favor him, so he'll probably leave within the week. If not, I'll see that he does. As for my other daughter, crippled she may be, and with the tongue of an adder, but the agreement between your father the king and me includes an alliance by marriage."

Becca felt sick and too weak to move. Her own father was a traitor, and planning to use her to further his schemes.

"I would prefer your other daughter. I would take her for half that dowry."

"Laelia is not part of the bargain."

"Not even for a quarter of the dowry?"

They were haggling over them as if they were fish lying in a stall in the marketplace!

"Valdemar, if you don't wish to marry Rebecca, so be it," Lord Throckton said, his patience obviously wearing thin. "Your father the king has plenty of other sons. One of them will do just as well, and he will get these lands when I am a duke and the power in London, where Laelia will be queen."

How was Laelia going to be queen? Who did he think was going to be ruling England?

"That's assuming Henry will accept her."

He wasn't going to murder the king? Perhaps, somehow, she'd misunderstood and he wasn't planning rebellion, Becca thought hopefully. That hope was snuffed out with his next words.

"Once we've gotten rid of Eleanor and her blood-sucking relations, I'm sure my daughter's beauty will help convince Henry to accept the inevitable."

Any move against any member of the royal family was treason. There could be no denying now that her father was a traitor. He was planning on allying with the Danes to bring about a change in government, one that would see Eleanor dead or banished, and Laelia on the throne instead, while their father...their father would be the power behind the king, making Henry march to his tune.

"Why not kill the man?" Valdemar asked.

"Because he's my lawful king, anointed before God."

Becca listened carefully, her dismay turning to confusion.

"His wife was anointed, too."

"She's French." Rage burned in her father's eyes, with a fierceness she'd never seen before. It was as if he were another person. A stranger.

Perhaps he was. Perhaps she'd never really known him at all. Maybe nobody in Throckton had.

The fierceness diminished, as if he were putting on a mask, although there was still steel in his voice when he spoke. "We might have been able to overlook that because Henry was pleased with her, except that she brought those leeches with her."

"You might lose and wind up dead," Valdemar pointed out, obviously not nearly as confident of their success. "And I'll still be married to your homely daughter."

After everything Becca had heard that day, his barb couldn't hurt her.

What should she do? Tell Blaidd that he was right? Accuse her own father of disloyalty to the crown? What would happen then, to him, to her sister and to her? If he were convicted, he would be hanged, drawn and quartered. Yet that was the fate he was willing to bring down upon himself. Henry was their lawful king, and if he'd made a poor choice of wife, surely there had to be ways to neutralize her, and her relatives. War meant pain, deprivation and death.

The lives of a traitor's family were in danger, too, even if they were ignorant. Would Henry be merciful to them or would he see only that they were to be part of their father's scheme, however unwilling?

Even if the king spared their lives, their family's estate and money would be forfeit to the crown. She and Laelia would be penniless, the pauper daughters of a traitor.

"We won't lose if your father keeps his word. There are many other lords and barons who detest what Henry's doing." Her father gave Valdemar a slight, patronizing smile. "And it's not as if I'm going to be riding into battle myself. I'll leave that to the young hotheads. Have no fear, my Danish prince. If it seems things are going awry, I will ensure that my family survives unscathed. We'll have to flee England, perhaps, but I've plenty of money in coin and jewels, gifts from those who support my cause. You'll return to your homeland a very wealthy man. And as for still being married to my daughter..." He shrugged. "Take a mistress."

So cold, so callous. As if he weren't her father at all.

"You don't seem overly fond of the girl yourself," Valdemar noted.

Throckton regarded him steadily. "She's been a thorn in my side all her life, just like her mother. I shed no tears when that woman died, and if you want to shut your wife up in a convent after she's given you a son or two, and carry on as you please, you'll get no complaint from me.''

His words about her mother added to Becca's agony, and enraged her, too.

''Then why insist we marry?''

''Because, my dear Valdemar, bastard though you may be, you're a king's son, and I will have royal blood in my grandchildren's veins—and an alliance with your father that goes beyond mere words. Now, is there anything more you wish to discuss or have explained?''

''No.''

She heard the sound of chairs scraping against the stone floor.

Becca knew what she had to do now: she had to tell Blaidd that he was right. If she didn't, how could she expect mercy from Henry for her people, or her sister, or herself? Their father had chosen his course; the rest of them had not. And if it came down to a choice between her guilty father's life, or those of innocent people, was there really any decision to be made?

She turned and tried to move, then bit back a cry as excruciating pain shot through her weak limb. She stumbled, grabbing the handrail for support.

''How long have you been listening?''

Becca looked back over her shoulder, to see her father looming about her like a great bird of prey. Behind him stood Valdemar.

Chapter Fourteen

Her father's voice, his stance, everything about him seemed harsh, unfamiliar, as foreign as Valdemar.

As she straightened and faced her father, marshaling her tumultuous thoughts and even more tumultuous feelings, it was as if she were looking at a complete stranger. Pressing her lips together to keep from crying out as another searing pain shot through her aching leg, she tried to regain some measure of self-control and *think*.

"I said, how long have you been listening?" her father repeated sternly.

What should she say to him now? Should she admit what she'd heard? What would come of it if she did? What could she hope to achieve?

What should she do?

Gain more time. Time to think, to absorb all that she'd heard, and come up with a plan of her own, about what to do with this horrible knowledge.

"I wasn't listening," she lied. "I was coming to

ask you about rations for the garrison. I realized you weren't alone, so I decided to come back later.'' She forced herself to smile at Valdemar. ''I hope you weren't complaining about your quarters or the food.''

''Not at all,'' he said with a smile more bogus than her own. ''I was telling your father how much I admire you.''

A child could tell he was lying, and it was all she could do not to reveal her real reaction. ''Indeed? I thank you, my lord, for the compliment.''

Her father watched her closely, studying her face, and she fought to betray nothing.

At last, he relaxed. ''You seem to be in some pain, Rebecca,'' he said, smiling as he usually did.

She'd never be able to trust him, or his smiles, again.

''Perhaps Valdemar will lend you his arm?'' he continued. ''I've got some tithe rolls to examine right now.''

She nodded, glad that she didn't have to come up with a story to support her lie, even if she would rather have a snake about her than Valdemar's arm.

However, she had no choice, so she allowed the Dane that liberty, and they started down the steps. She leaned most of her weight on the handrail, so that she could keep some small distance between them.

''Are you sure you weren't looking for me, Lady Rebecca?'' Valdemar said slyly, his breath hot on her ear, his arm tightening about her.

''No, I wasn't looking for you,'' she retorted, trying to pretend that his proximity and his vanity didn't fill her with revulsion. "I told you, I had business with my father."

He halted.

"What is it?"

"I thought you were not nearly so pleasing as your sister," he said, touching her cheek as his gaze raked her body, "but perhaps I was mistaken."

"You certainly are mistaken if you think you flatter me by saying such things."

"Aren't you pleased that a prince wants to spend time with you?" he asked, edging her back against the wall.

No longer could she pretend that he didn't revolt her, that she didn't loathe his presence, his touch, everything about him. "No," she retorted, her voice stern and imperious. She shoved him back. "Get out of my way, my lord."

"Your father said you were tempestuous. Perhaps marriage to you will be interesting, after all," he said, and before she could open her mouth to tell him she'd never marry him, he tugged her to him and covered her mouth with his.

Horrified by his wet, unwanted kiss, ignoring the pain in her leg, she struggled to get free, twisting and kicking and punching. Nothing worked. His arms tightened about her like tongs and he forced his tongue into her mouth.

She bit down as hard as she could.

Swearing in his native language, he jumped back. She stood panting, trying to regain her breath and her strength, ready to thrust him down the stairs if he tried to touch her again.

"You should be delighted a prince of Denmark wants to kiss you, wench," he snarled as he wiped the blood from his lips with the back of his hand.

"I'd rather kiss a goat!"

"So would I! But it seems our fathers have other plans."

Upset, distraught, overwhelmed by all she'd learned, Becca lost the last of her self-control. "If you were as wonderful as you think you are, you'd reconsider anything that might rouse the might of England against you and your country!"

He stared at her.

What had she done?

She heard a noise behind her. She wheeled around, sucking in her breath at the pain from the sudden movement. Her father charged down the stairs toward her, his face scarlet with rage.

She'd thought he'd looked like a stranger before; that was nothing compared to the shock she felt now as he grabbed her arm, so tight she cried out in pain. "Father, let go! You're hurting me!"

He ignored her plea and gripped her tighter still. "Leave us, Valdemar," he growled as he began to drag her back up the stone steps.

Valdemar turned and fled down the stairs.

"Father, stop! You're hurting my arm!"

He didn't. He pulled even harder. "Shut up, you stupid girl!"

She tried to brace her feet, but her weak leg

wouldn't hold. It hurt worse than ever for her efforts. "Father, please, my leg!"

"I don't give a damn about your bloody crippled leg, except that it makes you nearly worthless." He shoved open the door to the solar and pushed her inside. She fell hard on her hands and knees on the stone floor, nearly striking the table.

Before she could get to her feet, he came in and closed the door. "So you *were* listening, you sneaking, sniveling little spy."

Panting and in pain, she crawled to the table and, holding tight to its edge, got to her feet. She turned, measuring the distance between her father and the door. "I didn't," she lied.

He lifted his hand and struck her hard across her face. Her cheek stung and she tasted blood.

"I should have packed you off to a convent the moment I could, you useless cripple," he sneered. "You're just like your mother. She was useless, too, birthing another useless girl before she died."

In that moment, the respect and love for the man who had sired her died within Becca. As he heaped scorn on her and her late mother, harsh, invigorating, righteous anger consumed her and burned the last of her love away.

"How dare you speak of my mother like that!" she cried, glaring at him. "And how dare you call me useless? Who's been running your household these past ten years? Paid the merchants, supervised the servants—and all the while watched as you exalted Laelia over me? She should have been in charge, not me.

And I berated myself for being bitter and jealous, thinking I was at fault to have such feelings about the people who loved me.''

Disregarding her pain, she limped toward him. She jabbed his chest with her finger, forcing him back. ''I was a fool, Father. A stupid, love-starved fool, trying to get your attention any way I could. By God, I wish you *had* sent me to a convent! At least there I wouldn't have had to watch you pamper and pet Laelia. I wouldn't have had my *deficiency* rubbed in my face every day. But I'm not the deficient one, Father. You are, for you're willing to break a sacred oath and dishonor yourself and your family, to start a war that will lead to destruction and death, because you're jealous of the power of a *woman*.''

She stared at him with disgust and shame to think that she'd once thought he was the most wonderful man in the world. ''How could you? How could you betray the oath you swore to the king? How could you use Laelia and me to further your despicable schemes?''

''You *are* a fool!'' he retorted, circling around to the other side of his table, so it was between them. ''You don't know anything about politics or the court! That French harlot spreads her legs for the king and her arrogant relatives become rich and powerful. If Henry can't see that they're ruining the country, he must be *made* to see it!'' He brought his fist down on the table with a crash, making the scrolls, ink vessel and sword hilt rattle.

''But not by war and rebellion!'' Becca cried.

"What you plan is treason, and men will die because of it. And you'll make our land vulnerable to the Danes again. You're giving them a foothold in this country. Have you forgotten what havoc the Vikings wrought in the past? And do you really trust that they'll be content with Throckton? I've listened to Dobbin and some of the others tell tales their fathers and grandfathers told them, of the time of the Viking raids in this part of England. Perhaps you should, too, and stop this insanity while you've got the chance."

"The day I listen to a whining, sniveling spy—"

She faced him squarely, shoulders back and eyes blazing. "Unless you send Valdemar away and stop this scheming, you stand in danger of being arrested for high treason."

He splayed his hands on the table. "I wouldn't try to betray me to the king, girl. It won't go well for you, or Laelia, if I'm accused. You're my children, after all. Laelia is to marry Henry after we've disposed of Eleanor. You are the means to assure my ties to the Danish king. Do you think they'll care if you agreed or not? By God, they won't! Henry's a boy, a scared little boy pretending to be king.

"If you're as clever as you think you are, you'll stand by me and do as I say and marry Valdemar." He took a deep breath and straightened, and she watched as the genial mask again fall into place. "You'll be able to stay here, if you're so worried about the peasants. You could keep them safe. And Valdemar's a handsome fellow."

She curled her lip. "What, you would try to buy

me off, too, and with Valdemar?'' she scoffed. ''Oh,
Father, how little you know me!''

''Damn you, girl, you'll be the wife of a prince!''
he shouted, bringing his fists down again. The ink
vessel fell over, and the thick black liquid spread over
the table, its pungent odor filling the air.

''I'll be a traitor's daughter, married to a man who
doesn't want me,'' Becca answered. ''I refuse to be
part of that. I'll see that Laelia isn't, either.''

He looked at her as if she were a servant who disgusted him. ''How do you intend to do that? You're
my property, Rebecca. My chattel. I can do with you
what I will.''

''If I have to be the one to give evidence against
you, I will, because I won't put England and everyone
I care about at risk.''

''You think you can bring me down, Rebecca?
You, a woman? A woman who's been unnatural from
birth, more like a boy than a girl.'' He stepped toward
the table and drew his sword, then let the empty scabbard drop as he came around the end. ''This is your
last chance.''

Trembling, her crippled leg weak and aching, she
couldn't move fast enough. Motionless, she kept her
gaze on his face as he pointed the tip of his sword at
her throat. ''Will you kill me, Father? Are you that
degenerate that you'd murder your own child?''

''You're not my child.''

She gasped as another shock rushed through her.

His blade flicked, cutting her cheek. ''I told you
your mother was useless. She was worse than useless

in my bed, so I sought another. That's how I knew the brat she bore couldn't be mine. I made her tell me who she'd been with. You're the bastard spawn of a woman no better than a whore, and a common soldier.''

Becca stared at him, eyes wide with disbelief. Yet that would explain so much. But who...?

The answer came to her in a flash of sudden understanding. There was one man who'd been a better father to her than her own. ''Dobbin,'' she murmured.

''Yes, Dobbin, that uncouth lout! Are you proud of your heritage now, my dear? You belong in the gutter, not at a lord's table. You should be grateful I didn't leave you out to die in a ditch.''

Memories came flooding to her, of Dobbin's gentle kindness, the look of longing in his eyes, the thing he'd said about a woman miserably married. And the realization that his eyes and hers were the same shade of blue. And yet... ''If that's true, why is he still here? Why didn't you send him away?''

''Do you think I was going to have it known that my wife had rutted with a soldier?''

Her eyes narrowed. ''And perhaps you enjoyed his torture, letting him watch you claim me for your own, just as you surely made my mother suffer with your womanizing.'' She smiled at the shock that appeared on *his* face. ''I know about that, too, Father—at last. No wonder she sought comfort elsewhere.''

He closed on her again, and she backed toward the door.

''What explanation will you give for my death, Father?'' she demanded, wondering if she could get close enough to the door and move fast enough to elude him if he struck. "It'll have to be a credible tale to excuse my murder, or you could have more trouble than you expect. The people like me, Father. While you were spoiling Laelia, I was enjoying their company, and I have many friends."

"You're mad," he said, smiling cruelly. "You've always been a little mad, but I excused you and tried to hide it. Then today, you attacked me. You tried to kill me, your own father. I promise you, I'll shed plenty of tears of regret and remorse that I had to defend myself against you, and kill you doing it."

"Sir Blaidd Morgan might have his suspicions that you're lying, no matter how much you weep," she said. "Between the arrival of Valdemar and my death, who can say what he might surmise?"

She'd tried not to speak of him, lest her father guess why he was here. Then Blaidd would be in danger, too. But she was desperate, trying to save her life.

Her father paused in his progress. "Morgan? Ah! I see which way your mind is tending. You plan to go to him and tell him what you've heard, thinking he'll believe you, and protect you." He laughed scornfully. "What good will that Welshman do you when you're dead? And he can say what he likes. I have friends at court, too, and I'll have more when I march on London with my army and Valdemar's at my back."

Becca risked a glance over her shoulder, to see if she was close enough to reach the latch.

"Too late, Rebecca. And you couldn't run fast enough, anyway," he said, his eyes gleaming with determination. "I'd catch you on the stairs."

He lunged, but she twisted away from him. Panting with the effort, she sidled as fast as she could along the wall. If she could reach the window...call for help...

He raised his sword to strike. With all that remained of her energy and determination, Becca threw herself at the window. She clutched the sill, holding on to it as if the very stones could save her life. "Help me!" she screamed.

A host of shocked faces turned toward the window. One, handsome and framed with long dark hair, stood out among them.

Then Throckton grabbed Becca's gown and hauled her back into the room.

Chapter Fifteen

The instant Blaidd heard Becca scream, he yanked his sword from its scabbard and tore through the courtyard. He took the circular stairs leading to Lord Throckton's solar three at a time and, using his shoulder, burst through the door.

A bloody sword in his hand, Lord Throckton stood over Becca, who was slumped on the floor beside the window. She clutched her side and blood—bright red and shining—oozed between her fingers. Her face was white as newly fallen snow. She looked...dead.

"Becca!" Blaidd gasped, his own blood pounding in his ears as he ran toward her limp, motionless body.

"Guards!" Lord Throckton shouted. *"Guards!"*

Savage, primal rage exploded within Blaidd, overpowering his pain as he whirled around to face the murderer. "You bloody, traitorous dog! All the soldiers in England won't help you now."

The color drained from Throckton's face as Blaidd closed on him.

Dobbin and two other soldiers appeared on the threshold, panting and staring in horror at the sight of Becca's body.

"What are you waiting for?" Throckton shouted at them, his eyes gleaming with triumph. "Kill him! Can't you see he's attacking me? He's already killed Lady Rebecca!"

"Your blade is bloody, not mine," Blaidd said through clenched teeth as he struggled to control the blood lust throbbing through his veins. A quick death was too easy for Throckton.

With fear and panic in his eyes, Throckton raised his weapon. "I had to do it. I was defending myself. She's in league with this Welshman! She came here and made all sorts of accusations, then tried to kill me! They're plotting against me, them and the king! They want to kill me and take over my lands."

"Where's her weapon?" Blaidd demanded.

Throckton's eyes flared. "She...she tried to strangle me."

Blaidd began to circle him, ready to strike if the man didn't lay down his sword. "Liar! And you dishonor her memory with that accusation."

His eyes full of hate, Dobbin slowly drew his sword. "So it wasn't enough that you tried to marry your way into power, first with Lady Laelia's mother, then Rebecca's, and finally that poor silly girl. I thought you'd given up your ambitions, that getting rich with your foreign trading would content you, and this fortress would give you what your pride required. A better man would have realized he had jewels in his daughters, especially Rebecca, and taken pride in them, too. But no, you're the same scheming, lecherous lout you've always been. I won't lift a finger to help you. And if Sir Blaidd gives the word, I'll gladly run you through.''

''I tell you, this man's in league with the king, and Henry's out to destroy me!'' Throckton bellowed at the two soldiers, his whole body quaking. ''You're paid to protect me! Do as I say or I'll have you executed!''

''I wouldn't speak of execution if I were you,'' Blaidd said as he halted and glared at his enemy. ''Throckton, I arrest you in the name of the king. The charges are murder and high treason.''

Before Throckton could protest, Blaidd addressed the soldiers. ''I represent King Henry, and if you help him, you'll be assisting a murderer and a traitor. Do you want to help the man who's killed Lady Rebecca, especially when the evidence of his guilt is before you?''

With disgust written on their faces, the guards held their hands away from their weapons.

''You're right in one thing, Throckton,'' Blaidd continued, his voice coldly, terrifyingly deliberate. ''I was sent by the king, although not to assassinate you. Henry already suspected you of plotting against your rightful king. I was sent here to find evidence of either your innocence or your guilt. I've discovered that Henry was right to be suspicious. And now you've even murdered your own child.''

''I'm not a traitor! You oafs, he's lying!'' Throckton shrieked at the soldiers. "Take this man and imprison him in the dungeon. And Rebecca tried to kill *me*."

"No, I didn't." Her whisper was barely loud enough to be heard, but pure joy filled Blaidd as he turned and stared, wonder and relief overwhelming him. She lived! Oh, sweet merciful God, she lived!

Blaidd hurried toward her, but Dobbin reached her first. The garrison commander cradled her in his arms as Blaidd knelt on one knee in front of her, his anxious gaze studying her pale face.

"He always was a poor aim," Dobbin muttered while examining her wound. "The blade must have slid along her ribs. It's bad, but I've seen worse."

Blaidd bowed his head in silent, thankful prayer. Then, as he raised his eyes to look at the woman he adored, he saw her blue eyes widen with horror.

With instincts honed from years of training and tournaments, Blaidd twisted, turned and, still kneeling, thrust his blade through Lord Throckton's chest.

The man's upraised sword fell to the ground.

Gulping for air, Lord Throckton stumbled backward. He fell over his table, sending scrolls tumbling to the floor. Trying to push himself upright, he began to cough as blood filled his throat and mouth.

But it was too late. His life ebbing, he slipped from the table to the floor, then fell sideways, dead.

Becca's strangled sob broke the silence.

Blaidd's heart churned with anguish as he turned back to her. "Becca, I had no choice."

She didn't answer. She turned away and buried her face against Dobbin's chest.

"Death would have been his fate, anyway," Blaidd pleaded, trying to make her see he'd been forced to kill the man. "This was a more merciful end than he would have received if he'd been convicted of treason."

Dobbin fixed Blaidd with a cold glare. "That's enough talk, Sir Blaidd. She needs tending, not words. I'll take care of her. I've got some skills looking after wounds."

"V-very well," Blaidd stammered as he rose.

A feeling of utter helplessness stole over him. Couldn't a soldier understand that he'd acted in self-defense? And if Dobbin couldn't, would Becca ever be able to forgive him for killing her father, even if he was a traitor?

What if everyone here reacted like Dobbin, with anger and hostility? Blaidd and Trev might be in danger. They might have to flee. He should find Trev at once.

The two silent, grave soldiers still stood on the threshold. Blaidd's hand gripped his sword; if they tried to stop him, they'd regret it.

Before he got to the door, Valdemar shoved his way past the soldiers and strode into the room. He halted abruptly when he saw Lord Throckton's bloody body, and Becca, and a gasp of surprise escaped his lips.

Roused by the sight of the Dane, Blaidd remembered he was the king's representative and must act like it. Taking command of the situation, he grabbed Valdemar's arm and pulled him toward the door. "We'll talk outside. Where's Lady Laelia?"

Valdemar flushed. "I don't know."

Blaidd didn't believe him, but it was better that she wasn't here to see her father's body and Becca's wound.

He discovered the stairs were crowded with curious and concerned soldiers and servants. He ordered them to go, all except Meg, whom he sent to the solar to help tend her mistress.

When everyone had gone, he faced Valdemar, who finally managed to wrench his arm free of Blaidd's grip.

"How dare you hold me as if I were a common criminal," the Dane growled as he rubbed his arm.

"How dare you plot to overthrow my king?" Blaidd demanded in return.

Valdemar stopped rubbing. "I don't know what you're talking about."

"Of course you do, and your erstwhile ally in a conspiracy against the king of England now lies dead in the solar. Your alliance is over."

His gaze flicking to Blaidd's sword, Valdemar took a nervous step backward. "There was no conspiracy, and our alliance was only for trade," he said, although his words lacked their former haughty certainty.

Blaidd regarded the man with a long, measuring, critical glare. "I don't believe that, and I doubt Henry will, either. He's not likely to look kindly on foreigners who are implicated in a plot against the English crown, so I suggest, my lord prince, that you flee while I give you the chance. If you stay, you risk imprisonment on suspicion of being involved in Lord Throckton's schemes."

Valdemar put his hand on his sword hilt and spoke with more confidence. "Your accusations are utterly unfounded. Where is your proof?"

"Henry is going to hear about what happened here, and who was involved," Blaidd replied, not the least bit intimidated. After what had happened in the solar, nothing this man said or did could upset him. "He already had his suspicions about Throckton, and now he'll have them about you, and your father, too. I'd stay away from England in future, if I were you, unless you wish to start a war."

Valdemar's face reddened. "This talk of war is ridiculous and you wouldn't dare imprison me!" he spluttered. "I'm the son of the king of Denmark!" He managed to regain some self-control. "Besides, you have no authority here."

"Since this isn't Denmark, I've got more authority than you do," Blaidd retorted. "And it's because of your father that I'm willing to let you leave. I don't want a war with Denmark started over the likes of *you*."

Valdemar's mouth moved but no words came out, and his face grew so red it was nearly purple. Then he turned on his heel and fled, leaving Blaidd to follow with slow, deliberate steps.

* * *

Becca slowly opened her eyes. She was in bed, in her father's—Lord Throckton's—luxurious bedchamber. Meg stood at a table across the room, washing something in the basin. The linen shutter on the window was half-closed and the only light came in through the remaining opening, dim and weak. That window faced east, so it must be early morning.

What was she doing here? What had happened?

The memories came flooding back: of what she had heard, the attack that had left her wounded, and the fatal, justified thrust of Blaidd's sword.

The man she'd believed was her father had tried to kill her. Instead, he'd died in this room, struck down by the man she loved as he defended himself.

Her side ached, but her physical pain was not important, except perhaps as a fitting punishment for not listening to Blaidd. She should have had faith in his words and not proudly, arrogantly refused to believe him. She should have trusted him.

She had to see Blaidd as soon as possible, to ask his forgiveness for doubting him. She hoped he would understand how difficult it had been to hear such things about her fa—about Lord Throckton.

She tried to sit up, but pain as fierce as a hot poker laid against her side made her gasp and fall back.

"Don't try to move," Dobbin said from somewhere beside her. "You'll tear the stitches."

She hadn't seen him sitting in the shadows beside the head of the bed. He leaned forward now and gave her a small smile as he took her hand in his callused ones and held it tightly.

This was her father. Her *real* father. How proud she was, and yet how foolish she felt for not realizing it sooner. How could she not have noticed that their eyes were the same shade of blue, or the way his nose sloped just like hers?

How could she not have noticed that Hester looked more like Laelia than she did? How could she have been so blind about so much?

Meg turned around, a dripping piece of pink linen in her hand, her eyes red rimmed. A relieved smile lit her face. "You're awake!"

"And you're dripping bloody water on the floor," Dobbin charged.

Dobbin was always brusque with the maidservants, so Meg paid him no heed. She continued to smile as she approached the bed, wiping her hands on her skirt. "Can I get you anything, my lady? Rowan made some broth special when he heard…" She chewed her lip and swallowed hard. "When he heard you were hurt. He claims it'll make you feel better in no time."

Becca nodded. "If Dobbin has no objections."

"Bit o' broth'll do you good," he decreed. "And some bread, too, maybe. I wouldn't mind a bit o' bread and cheese myself, and you should have sommat to eat, too."

Meg nodded and hurried out of the room.

"You lost a lot of blood before I could get that wound stitched up proper," Dobbin remarked as he studied Becca's face. "You just lie still now, or all my work'll have been for naught."

"Where's Sir Blaidd?"

"I don't know."

Dobbin's expression and tone reminded her that he had yet to hear the real reason Blaidd had gone to the brothel. "He wasn't with Hester for the reason we assumed," she assured him. "When he went there after his squire, Hester told him she had important information for him. He returned to the brothel to find out what it was."

For the first time in her life, Becca saw the color drain from Dobbin's cheeks. "What did she tell him?"

Becca could guess why he was upset. She would speak of that in a moment, after she made certain Dobbin knew Blaidd wasn't a lascivious scoundrel like Lord Throckton. "She told him that Danes had come here before, pretending to be Germans. She feared my—Lord Throckton was up to no good and she wanted to warn Blaidd, so he could protect me from the king's wrath. She also told Blaidd that Throckton was her father, to prove what a lustful, greedy man he was."

Dobbin slowly exhaled.

Becca gripped his strong, rough hand, which had tended to her wound with such gentle care. "I know what you thought I was going to say—that you're my real father. Throckton himself told me, before he tried to kill me."

Dobbin flushed, then rose abruptly and walked over to the window.

"Why didn't you tell me yourself?" she asked gently.

Without looking at her, Dobbin said gruffly, "Because I knew what you'd do if I did. You would've left Lord Throckton's household, because you'd never live a lie." He raised his blue eyes to regard her. "But you deserve to be a lady, just as your mother was, and have all that a lady has."

He moved away from the window and spread his hands. "What could I offer you but the rough life of a soldier's daughter? So I contented myself with staying here and watching you grow into a fine lady, like your mother." He lowered his hands and stared straight ahead, not at Becca, but at some vision she couldn't see. "Your mother was the finest, bravest, kindest creature who ever walked this earth, and what she ever saw in me…" His words trailed off as he shook his head.

"A good man, that's what she saw," Becca said with firm conviction. "And you loved her."

"Aye, I loved her," Dobbin murmured as he returned to the stool beside the bed. "Too selfishly, or I never would have gotten her with child. I would have been content to worship her from a distance."

"I'm sure she loved you, too, Dobbin. And if loving you was selfish, I don't condemn her for giving in to it."

"She wasn't *weak,* Becca," he replied. "She was good and kind, but strong as iron, too. She had to be, to put up with the pain your father brought her. He tried to break her spirit, the way he tried to break yours, but he had no more luck with her than he did with you.''

Becca thought of how she'd felt when she first began to believe that Blaidd truly liked her. ''She had your love to give her strength.''

''Not at first. Not for a long time. I admired and respected her from the beginning, of course. And when I realized what was happening, I fought against it. So did she. She was an honorable woman.''

''But she was miserable and she turned to you for comfort, and then love. I'm glad she had you to love her, Dobbin. Very glad.'' Becca reached out and took his hands in hers. ''I'm *proud* that you're my father.''

''And I'm more than proud that you're my daughter.'' Tears glistened in his eyes. ''*My* daughter.''

A silence filled with heartfelt emotions no words could express stretched between them.

Then Dobbin's expression changed, to one of grave concern. ''You can't tell anybody else about this, Becca. This'll have to be our secret still.''

''Why not?'' she asked, dismayed. ''I'm not ashamed to admit that you're—''

''For the people of Throckton. Who else will speak for them, and make sure the king knows nobody else here—not you, not Laelia, not me or my men—was in on that lout's schemes? Laelia may be the eldest, but she's only good for weeping and wailing.''

Becca realized he was likely right. ''Yes, I see,'' she murmured, ''but I don't like it.''

''D'you think I do?'' Dobbin asked, frowning.

"But we've got no choice. You've got to think of the household, and I've got to think of my men."

"Where is Laelia? Did you tell her about—?"

"Last I heard, she was in the chapel, crying. *He* told her what happened."

It wasn't hard to guess to whom Dobbin was referring, and Becca's heart filled with sorrow—for Laelia and also for Blaidd, for having to be the one to tell her about her father's death. "Has Blaidd said anything about what's going to happen now?"

Dobbin shook his head. "Not that I've heard, but he's taken command of the castle. He's ordered the Danes to leave. They rode away at dawn."

"I want to see him, Dobbin, as soon as possible. Will you find him for me?"

They were interrupted by a sharp rap on the door.

"Ah, that'll be Meg with the broth," Dobbin said, slapping his hands on his thighs as he got to his feet.

But it wasn't Meg who walked into the room.

It was a grim, grave Sir Blaidd Morgan, and he was dressed for battle.

Chapter Sixteen

Or so it seemed to Becca, for he wore chain mail beneath his cloak and spurs on his heels, and he carried a helmet under his arm.

His broadsword slapped his thigh as he marched forward more like a soldier on parade than a man coming to see the woman he loved, the woman he'd saved from certain death. "I hope I find you recovering, my lady."

"You do," she murmured, dismayed by his stiff bearing and the cool way he spoke.

"I'm sorry to have to be the bearer of more bad news."

Becca pushed herself up, regardless of the pain her action caused. "What bad news?"

Blaidd's distant, steadfast regard faltered. "I regret to have to tell you this, my lady, but your sister's…" He hesitated, then straightened and went on. "It seems, my lady, that your sister has run away."

"Run away?" Becca cried incredulously.

"So it appears." Blaidd's expression grew even grimmer. "Last night she said she wanted to keep a vigil over your father's body in the chapel. I saw no harm in it, provided one of the servants stayed with her. Apparently the servant fell asleep, and when she awoke, your sister was no longer there. The servant came to me at once, and I ordered a search of the castle. This was found in your bedchamber, which was in some disarray."

Blaidd came forward and thrust a piece of parchment at her. "She *can* write?"

"Yes, although not very well," Becca replied. "I wanted to learn, to keep the household accounts, but she didn't. My fa—Lord Throckton insisted."

"The letters are very shaky."

"Hers always are."

Becca read the messily scrawled words. It was a note of farewell, addressed to her and saying that Laelia was leaving with Valdemar. That Becca could have all her clothes and jewels.

She read it through three times before she could fully comprehend what Laelia had done, and why.

Then she raised her eyes to regard Blaidd before looking at Dobbin's worried face. "She's run off with Valdemar."

"She always wanted to go to court, but I thought she meant the English one," he muttered, not hiding his scorn.

"I'm not convinced she went willingly," Blaidd declared.

Becca spoke to Dobbin again. "Your men would

have come to you if there was anything amiss at the walls or gate, even if you were tending to me, wouldn't they?''

''Aye, my lady. Nobody can get past my sentries.''

''Your sentries didn't catch me going over the wall,'' Blaidd noted.

''Oh, didn't they?'' Dobbin retorted, raising a brow.

Blaidd's face betrayed nothing. ''This still could be a trick, or some sort of revenge on Valdemar's part.''

''If she *wanted* to go and not be seen, there is a way,'' Becca said. ''It's known only to the family, but I'm sure I can trust you with the knowledge, Sir Blaidd.''

She hoped he would appreciate her choice of words and how much she was willing to trust him now. ''There's a secret passageway out of the castle, in case we're ever besieged. The entrance is in the chapel.''

''Maybe the Danes found out about the passageway,'' Blaidd suggested. ''Perhaps Throckton told them. They could have come in and taken her out that way.''

Dobbin snorted. ''Ain't you noticed how she's been looking at the man? After what's happened, she's likely terrified you're planning to have her arrested. No wonder she ran off with him. I wouldn't waste my time chasin' after 'er.''

''You might not, but *I* must,'' Blaidd countered. ''I gave the Danes the opportunity to leave. If there's even the slightest chance they've kidnapped Laelia, I've got to bring her back." Finally, he looked again at Becca, this time with something approaching deference. "You do want to be certain it was her choice, don't you, my lady?"

"Yes, of course, I want to be completely certain Laelia went willingly," she replied, pleased that he was not quite so distant.

"I'll take twenty of your men and head after them," he said to Dobbin.

"There's fifty Danes," Dobbin pointed out.

"So twenty of your well-trained men ought to be plenty if it comes to a fight."

"Twenty-one, because I'm going with you," Dobbin replied.

Blaidd turned to leave, then looked back at Becca. "If she fled because she feared me, she had no cause. I am well aware that neither of you were knowingly involved in your father's plans, and I intend to make certain Henry knows that, too."

When he spotted the Danish cortege not ten miles from Throckton Castle, Blaidd had the grim satisfaction of realizing that Lady Laelia had indeed probably chosen to go with Valdemar. If Valdemar had kidnapped her, he would surely have urged his men to ride at the gallop and been farther away by now. They must have gone at the more leisurely pace Laelia preferred.

Distinguishable by his bearing and his hair, Valdemar was at the head of the entourage. A blond woman clad in a blue cloak rode beside him, another sign that this was no abduction.

In spite of the evidence, Blaidd was still determined to speak to them. As he'd told Becca, he represented the king, and he had to be absolutely certain there was no mischief here.

Shouting an order for Dobbin's men to follow, Blaidd spurred Aderyn Du into a gallop. Trev would be sorry he'd missed a charge like this, but Blaidd had ordered him—forcefully—to remain behind. This was no tournament or practice drill, and he wouldn't risk Trev getting hurt.

Valdemar twisted in his saddle to look behind him when he heard the noise. Around him, his soldiers' horses shifted nervously and whinnied as their riders tried to control them. Some of the men gave up and took off down the road. More joined them, disobeying Valdemar's shouted commands. The woman started to scream.

Blaidd expected Valdemar to flee, but the man stood his ground and stayed beside his companion, who was, indeed, Laelia. By the time Blaidd and his men reached them, they were the only members of his party left. Even Valdemar's baggage cart had disappeared down the road in a cloud of dust.

The Dane positioned his horse in front of Laelia, blocking her from Blaidd and his men.

"I thought I was free to go," he said, still arrogant, still very much the prince.

"You're free to leave England, Valdemar, and the

sooner the better," Blaidd replied. "It's because of the lady I've come after you."

Laelia nudged her horse forward, so that she was beside the Danish prince. "I chose to go with him," she said, and Blaidd could hardly believe the firm, stern voice belonged to the same woman. "You're not my father or brother. You have no authority over me. You can't make me return with you."

"Since you have no father or brother, Henry is your legal guardian until such time as your nearest male relative is found, or you're married, so as Henry's representative, I do have authority over you," Blaidd answered.

"There aren't any male heirs," Laelia replied. "And you're looking at the man I intend to marry."

Blaidd turned his attention to Valdemar, whose horse was prancing nervously. Blaidd saw fear in the man's eyes, but it wasn't as if he feared pain or death. He looked like a man afraid of losing something he held dear. "You're willing to marry her?"

"Yes," he answered firmly, and without hesitation. "I would have this woman for my wife."

"You'll take her without a dowry?" Blaidd asked, although he thought he already had his answer. He didn't doubt that their feelings for one another were sincere. Nevertheless, he felt it necessary to make certain Laelia and Valdemar understood all the ramifications of their actions. "If Laelia goes with you now, you'll get only what she has with her. Her father was a traitor and everything he possessed is forfeit to the crown. The king could take her title, too."

"I want the woman, not the dowry or a title," Valdemar said, as if Blaidd's remarks were barely worth a response. "She will be my wife, a worthy mother of my sons. *Legitimate* sons," he declared with fierce resolution. "I give you my word she will not be a mistress, but a prince's bride."

Blaidd heard the ring of truth in his words, saw the sincerity in his eyes. "I believe you." He even managed to smile. "Maybe you're not a pirate, after all."

Valdemar's shoulders relaxed. "Then you'll let us go?"

"Yes." Blaidd turned to Laelia. "You do understand all that you're giving up?"

Laelia smiled, and never had she looked more beautiful or happy. "I do—and what I'm gaining, too. I love Valdemar, and he loves me."

"You may never be able to return to England, not even to visit."

Laelia's delicate chin began to quiver and her eyes filled with tears. "The only thing I'll miss is Becca. Please tell her I hope she'll be happy, and that one day she'll find happiness with a man she loves, as I have. Tell her goodbye and may God bless her. If He is kind, perhaps we'll see other again someday."

Valdemar reached out and covered her hand with his. Laelia looked at him, and if Blaidd needed any confirmation that he was doing the right thing by letting them leave together, he had it then. "Go to your ship, Valdemar," he said. "I'll take your message to your sister, Lady Laelia."

"What will you tell your king?" Valdemar asked.

Blaidd thought a moment. "That Lady Laelia fell in love with a Viking and fled with him rather than risk her sovereign's wrath." Blaidd gave them another little smile. "He'll like that last part."

"Farewell, Sir Blaidd Morgan," Valdemar said, smiling in return. "I'm glad we didn't meet in battle. It would have been a great pity to kill you."

"I would have regretted killing you, too," Blaidd said.

Then he watched as Valdemar and Laelia turned their horses and headed down the road. Together.

When Blaidd returned to the castle, he tossed his reins to the waiting Trev, leaped from Aderyn Du's back and immediately went to see Becca. Meg opened the door to Lord Throckton's bedchamber and ushered him inside, where he came to an awkward halt. Becca was sitting up in the luxuriously appointed bed, her bountiful, dark brown hair loose about her shoulders. She looked young and lovely and vulnerable, although far too pale.

Sir Blaidd Morgan, knight of the realm, champion of tournaments, friend of the king and supposedly able to whisper a woman to bed, suddenly felt as shy as a lad, and tongue-tied, too.

As he stood there, all his errors seemed to pile up on him. He'd killed her father. He'd wooed her while in her home under false pretenses. He'd as good as lied to her.

The questions that had been haunting him since he'd left this room returned in full force. Would his love make up for all his deceit, and would self-defense excuse him of causing her father's death? Or would she hate him now, thinking him nothing but a deceitful spy and the cause of her family's destruction?

He stood in silence, waiting for her to speak, to say something, to give him some indication of her feelings.

"Meg," Becca said as if he were any other visitor, "leave us, please."

Meg glanced at them uncertainly.

"I want to speak with Sir Blaidd *alone,* Meg."

As the girl went out and closed the door behind her, Blaidd hoped the tension would ease, but he discovered the opposite was true. He wasn't sure what to say to her, or if he should even venture onto personal ground.

The silence lasted until he could stand it no more. Then he took refuge in news of Laelia. "It was your sister's choice to go with Valdemar."

Becca nodded, her expression betraying nothing except mild interest. "I thought so."

"I had to be sure."

"Yes, I appreciate that. And I'm relieved there is no hint of doubt." Her gaze faltered. "I only wish we'd had a chance to say goodbye."

Blaidd instantly regretted not ordering Laelia to return and take proper leave of her sister. "She was upset about leaving you," he told her. "She said you'd be the only thing she'd miss. She also hopes you'll be happy one day."

Becca looked down at her hands, folded in her lap. "I see."

"I truly believe she loves Valdemar, and he cares for her," Blaidd continued, stepping closer, then halting a few feet from the bed. "She has no dowry, and Valdemar was content that it be so. I believe they'll be married. If I didn't, and that she wasn't going of her own free will, I wouldn't have allowed them to leave."

Becca slid him a glance. "*You* wouldn't have allowed it?"

All he could do was be honest. "I do represent the king, my lady."

"Yes, I'm well aware of that."

He immediately wished he'd said something else.

"So what will happen to me now, Sir Blaidd?"

He wanted to say, "Now we'll marry," but he couldn't. Her future depended on Henry, not him.

Even if Henry believed that she was innocent of involvement in her father's conspiracy, he might still be doubtful of her allegiance. To prove her loyalty, she would have to do whatever Henry commanded.

Blaidd hoped to convince Henry of her innocence and persuade the king to let them marry, but if he could not, they'd have no choice but to abide by the king's will. Becca's life could depend upon it.

And if this were so, knowing that he loved her still might only add to her misery. He should keep his distance and say nothing of love, for both their sakes.

"What do you think Henry will do with the daughter of a traitor?'' she asked, echoing his own distraught thoughts. ''Will he imprison me?''

''There's nothing to charge you with,'' Blaidd replied. ''You weren't a coconspirator with your father. I'm absolutely certain of that, so Henry should be, too.''

''You have that much influence with the king?''

''I believe he'll listen to me, my lady. I'll assure him of your innocence.''

''Thank you. Will he take away my title and inheritance?''

''I honestly don't know, my lady. I think there's a good chance that once he's convinced of your innocence, he'll make you a royal ward and allow you to keep your title and at least a portion of this estate, for a dowry.''

How her intense gaze seemed to search his mind! ''Then I suppose that, like most men who have power over women, he'll want me to marry where my inheritance will do *him* the most good. Perhaps Queen Eleanor has a relative who needs a wife.''

Blaidd's heart twisted, and he had a moment's sympathy for the traitor he had killed. ''I wouldn't say such things aloud, my lady.''

''No, I shouldn't. Not unless I want Henry or anybody else to question my loyalty.'' She regarded him steadily. ''Tell me, Sir Blaidd, do you think there'll be a nobleman willing to overlook my father's activities and marry me?''

''No one can force you to marry against your will, not even the king, my lady,'' Blaidd replied. ''It's against the law of the church. However..." He hesitated, upset at what he had to say, but she had to know where her safest course of action lay. "However, I wouldn't recommend that you object, given what's happened with your family. If you refuse a man he chooses for you, or anything he commands, you could risk rousing his suspicions about your loyalty, and perhaps even jeopardizing your life."

She frowned. "So although I wouldn't be imprisoned, I wouldn't be free? If I am so *fortunate* as to become Henry's ward, I'll have to do whatever he says, or my life could be in danger because I'm a traitor's daughter. Is that it?"

Blaidd's mind overruled his heart; his concern for her life overcame his desire. "Yes."

She plucked at the silken coverlet. "What if I were to run off like Laelia? What if there were no heir of Lord Throckton here, what would happen to this estate?"

"Why are you asking this? Are you planning on running away?" He came closer as a vision of the future burst into his head.

"I would be free then, wouldn't I?"

Reality destroyed his excitement, and that unfeasible future died. "No, you wouldn't be free. Henry would surely take your flight as evidence of guilt. Like all kings, he has a fear of conspiracies. He would hunt you down until he found you, and then you would be executed."

Blaidd knelt beside the bed. "He would never believe you were innocent if you run away. You mustn't consider it, not if you value your life.''

''Perhaps I don't believe a life as Henry's chattel will be a life worth living.''

''Don't say that!'' Blaidd cried, afraid that she would do something drastic. ''You'll be alive, at least.''

There was so much he wanted to say, but caution still silenced him. As a loyal knight, he was bound to obey his king, and so must she.

''So what comes next, Sir Blaidd?'' she asked, a quaver in her voice that made him yearn to take her in his arms and never let her go. ''I assume the king will have to be informed of all that's happened here. Will you go yourself, since your duty is done, or will you take command of the castle, send word and wait to be told what to do?''

She made him sound like the king's page. Was that how she thought of him? ''I'll go to the king myself. That will be the best way to ensure his mercy for you.''

''It would be best of all if *I* went with you. I'll plead my innocence to the king myself and personally swear my allegiance to him.''

If she were a delicate, beautiful, weak woman, Blaidd might have agreed, but as he imagined Becca facing Henry as boldly as she'd ever confronted him, he decided otherwise. ''That would not be wise.''

''Why not? Don't you think I can speak for myself?''

"Indeed, I'm sure you can. It's what you might say that worries me."

A muscle in her jaw twitched, and not with laughter. "You think I'll make things worse."

"Becca, I know Henry. You don't. If Laelia could go instead—"

"Well, she can't! She's run off with that Dane!" she cried. She winced and put her hand to her wounded side.

Again his heart twisted, but he didn't dare touch her unless it was absolutely necessary.

"Even if I agreed," he said, "you're too injured to ride to London. I'll speak to the king on your behalf, and I give you my word I'll do all I can to make him see that you're innocent of any wrongdoing and deserve his regard and respect."

She met his worried gaze steadily. "I'm not questioning your good intentions, or your abilities, Sir Blaidd. But as you've reminded me, this is my home, and these are my people. It's my place to speak for them, as well as for myself. Don't deny me that opportunity."

He couldn't deny her anything. "Very well," he said as he got to his feet. "When you're well enough to travel, we'll go to London together."

"Thank you. I should rest now, Sir Blaidd."

"Yes, of course," he said, before he turned and strode from the room.

When Blaidd was gone, Becca closed her eyes and slipped down beneath the covers. She really wanted to roll on her side and give herself over to her misery, but the movement would hurt too much.

She felt so alone. Her unloving, false father was dead, her sister gone, and Blaidd had been so cool, so distant, like a soldier at the changing of the guard. Worse, he'd been willing to relegate her to a minor role, although he was speaking of *her* future. Even at the end, when he'd come so close to her, he wasn't the Blaidd she'd fallen in love with.

She'd gotten the answer to her question about his feelings, and it wasn't the one she wanted.

Whatever had been between them before, whatever dreams she'd dreamed and hopes she'd harbored, no matter how she loved him, things were vastly different now.

Chapter Seventeen

A week later, Blaidd and Trev, Becca and Meg and a troop of ten soldiers arrived in the greatest city in England. Dobbin remained in Throckton to look after the castle and estate until either Rebecca returned or another overlord came to take the late Lord Throckton's place.

Claudia had remained behind, too, Dobbin declaring that under no circumstances should Becca ride until the wound in her side healed more. She and Meg traveled in the back of a wagon, seated on cushions like the inmates of a harem. Becca thought it almost decent to be ensconced in such comfort, with a canvas covering to shield her from rain or sun, and it slowed their pace considerably.

Once in the city, she assumed she and Blaidd would go their separate ways, just as they'd done every time they stopped at an inn as they made the long journey to London. He would find happiness with another woman and climb the ladder of power at court, while she did whatever the king commanded, because her father's treachery had left her no other choice.

In spite of Blaidd's deception when he'd first arrived at her home, she didn't begrudge him any future success or happiness. His feelings for her had not been false, and what came after had been because of Lord Throckton's deception, not Blaidd's. Many times she'd wanted to tell him that, yet she'd been unable to summon the words. One look at his grim visage had silenced her, until she'd convinced herself that it would be better to keep mute. Things were as they were; what good would revealing her anguish do, for him or for her?

The wagon rolled through Smithfield toward the New Gate, and the closer they got to the city, the louder was the noise. A great hum it was at first, before breaking into the familiar sounds of a marketplace, albeit a gigantic one: cows lowing as they were driven toward the Smithfield market, sheep, pigs, peddlers' shouts, people's conversations, raucous laughter, curses, dogs barking, chickens clucking, carts creaking, ropes straining—the hustle and bustle of many, many people doing many things.

"God's teeth, my lady," Meg said beside her, her whispered exclamation echoing something of Becca's own awestruck reaction as she rolled up the canvas covering at the sides, so that they could see everything around them while the canvas roof still shielded them from the sun. "I never seen so many people and livestock in one place in all my life!"

"Neither have I," Becca agreed.

A herd of cattle moved around them like a river. The two women held on to the sides of the cart for dear life, fearing it would tip and they'd be sent tumbling to the ground, to be crushed under their hooves.

"Oh, that was frightening," Meg murmured, and Becca didn't disagree as she gingerly shifted forward to get another look at the mob slowly making its way toward the city gate.

In some places, the wagon could barely move for the crowds, yet as always, there was Blaidd, as calm as if he were riding along an empty country road. Trevelyan Fitzroy was somewhere to the rear, with the rest of the men.

"I wonder how long it will take us to get to the palace?" Becca asked as they halted at the New Gate, where the way narrowed and they had to wait for a large coach to enter first. "Maybe as long as it took to reach this city from Oxford."

Meg looked distressed.

"I'm not in earnest," Becca quickly added.

"As long as it's before dinner, my lady," Meg replied, relieved. "I'm starving."

Becca wasn't. She hadn't had much appetite lately.

The wagon lurched into motion again and she moved back inside, where it was more comfortable.

"Why don't you take a nap, my lady?" Meg suggested. "Dobbin said sleep would be the best thing for you."

"There are too many things to see," Becca replied, although in truth, she was too nervous to sleep. Soon

enough they would be at the palace and her future—
a future without Blaidd—would begin.

They said no more for a long while, both watching
the sights of the city, and the jostling crowds. Peddlers and paupers accosted rich merchants and fine
gentlemen, mingling with every status of person in
between. It was like a whole different world, a foreign
place, and one that had Becca pining for home, and
a swift ride on Claudia with the wind in her hair. To
think Laelia would have given her eyeteeth to be in
this crowded, filthy, noisy place...

Becca tried not to think about Laelia, or begrudge
her the happiness she'd apparently found with Valdemar. After all, hadn't she hoped Laelia wouldn't be
envious of her own happiness with Blaidd, once upon
a time?

The wagon halted again.

"What now?" she murmured as she moved forward to see why they'd stopped.

They were at another gate. A large, ornate gate in
a very large, imposing wall. Blaidd had dismounted
and was talking to the armed guards.

The palace. This had to be the king's palace at
Westminster.

Now that they were here, Becca's heart started to
pound and her hands felt clammy. What if Henry
didn't believe her? What if he imprisoned her in the
Tower?

Blaidd left the sentries and walked back to the
wagon. He looked up at her, his face grave as it always was now. "We'll be staying in my brother

Kynan's apartments in the palace. You won't be seeing the king today. He's gone hunting. It'll have to be tomorrow, or maybe the next day.''

She was glad of the reprieve, but tried not to betray that; and as relieved as she felt, she had a new cause for anxiety. She'd assumed she'd be staying at an inn, not the palace itself. ''Very well.''

''I'll meet you for some refreshment later, my lady,'' Blaidd said, turning away. ''I have to find Kynan and tell him he has guests.''

Dressed in one of Laelia's gowns of deep blue velvet with long cuffs lined in gold, and a gilded leather girdle about her hips, Becca took a deep breath and opened the door into the main room of Sir Kynan Morgan's chambers. Her gaze roved over the trestle table set with a flagon of wine, silver goblets and plates of fruit, bread and sweetmeats, to settle on the man standing at the window. One hand on the frame, he looked out over the walls of the palace and the city beyond, toward the setting sun.

He looked achingly familiar, and yet different, too, probably because of the fine clothes he wore. She'd never seen Blaidd in velvet or other luxurious fabric. Even his boots were embossed with silver. At least he hadn't cut his hair, so he still seemed that intriguing mixture of civilized and savage.

Then he turned and she saw that it wasn't Blaidd, but another man enough like him to be his twin. ''Lady Rebecca, I assume?'' he asked genially.

''Yes. You must be Sir Kynan Morgan.''

"At your service, my lady," the younger Welshman said as he grinned and bowed. He looked very much like his brother and obviously shared the same easy charm and self-confidence.

Kynan gestured at the table. "We've taken the liberty of having some refreshments brought here. Blaidd and I thought you might not want to face the evening meal in the king's hall."

"Since I'm not exactly the king's invited guest," she replied, "I thank you for your consideration, and the repast."

Kynan's grin widened and he put his equally strong hands on the backs of two chairs and dragged them to the table. "Then let's begin, shall we?"

"Without your brother?"

"I'm not sure when he'll be back, so there's no point waiting. He'll understand." He gave her an insouciant wink. "Besides, I'm starving. Aren't you?"

She realized it might be something of a relief to be spared the stress of Blaidd's silent, brooding presence during the meal, so she smiled and limped forward to join him.

As she did, Kynan's glance dropped to her skirts and a little wrinkle of puzzlement appeared between his eyes. "I could have some of this sent to your chamber while you rest if your injury is troubling you."

"Thank you, but I don't limp because of my recent wound," she said as she settled into the chair. "I've been crippled for ten years, ever since I fell out of a tree and broke my leg."

Kynan flushed. "Oh, I'm sorry. I didn't mean…"

"I'm surprised your brother didn't mention it," she said matter-of-factly, wondering why he hadn't.

"He, um, didn't tell me much at all," Kynan confessed as he took the other chair.

She wanted to ask him where Blaidd was, but uncertainty held her tongue. It might be better to keep things to herself, too, if Blaidd wasn't willing to reveal to his own brother all that had happened in Throckton. Instead, she tried to focus on the excellent food and wine.

She discovered she really was hungry, but even so, she could only pick at the items on her plate.

After what seemed a long time, Kynan said in a soft voice that reminded her too much of his brother's, "Don't worry, my lady. Blaidd gave me the general gist of what happened, and I'm sure you'll be all right. Henry's got a temper, but with Blaidd arguing mercy for you, Henry's bound to listen. He trusts Blaidd, you see, as well he should."

Becca nodded and tried to smile. "I'm grateful for any effort he makes on my behalf."

The door suddenly flew open and Blaidd strode into the room.

How had she ever mistaken Kynan for him? Kynan might share his brother's dark good looks and charm, but he lacked that sense of controlled power she'd always sensed in Blaidd, even that first day when he'd appeared at the gate.

Oh, God, how she regretted her lack of faith in

him! If only she could go back in time and repair the damage. Listen to him. Believe him. Trust him.

But it was too late for that. For her.

Not sure what to do, afraid to reveal too much of her hopeless feelings, Becca stared at her hands, limp in her lap.

"Lady Rebecca," Blaidd said brusquely. "I've managed to arrange an audience with Henry for mid-morning tomorrow."

"Thank you," she murmured, telling herself that the sooner her fate was decided, the better.

Still not looking directly at Blaidd, she rose. She couldn't stand being so close to him, feeling as she did. Coupled with her anxiety about her meeting with the king, the strain was more than she could bear.

"I've had enough to eat. It was most excellent. Thank you, Sir Kynan. Good night, Sir Blaidd," she said, and she left the room with a swish of velvet.

After she'd closed the door behind her, Kynan regarded Blaidd as if he were a stranger. "God's wounds, brother, I've never heard you speak so rudely to a woman in my life."

Blaidd threw himself into Becca's vacated chair. "I said nothing impolite."

"Not the words, the manner. I don't care if she's a traitor's daughter or not—"

"I don't need lessons in etiquette from you," Blaidd growled as he grabbed a loaf and tore it in half.

"It seems you do."

Blaidd's only answer was a darker scowl as he reached for the wine.

Kynan remained silent for a few minutes, watching his brother eat and drink. Blaidd pretended his scrutiny didn't bother him, and focused on the food.

"You didn't tell me she was crippled."

"It's not important."

"You might have mentioned it. I thought she walked that way because of her wound, and said something about it. It was embarrassing to have to be set straight, even if she didn't seem to mind."

Blaidd wordlessly selected an apple and bit into it.

"What do you think Henry's going to do with her?"

"I'm not sure," he answered, chewing. "I've been talking with Gervais Fitzroy. He seems to think that if I vouch for her loyalty, Becca—Lady Rebecca—won't be charged with treason. If she becomes a royal ward, Henry will have control of her estate and fortune, and that should help appease him."

"That's good, isn't it?"

Blaidd shrugged. "Until he decides to marry her off to somebody of his choosing, or his wife's. Lady Rebecca won't be able to refuse whoever he selects if she wants to prevent any suspicion of disloyalty."

"Yes, I see that," Kynan agreed. "Still, she'll be free of the threat of death."

But not truly free.

"Her dowry had better be considerable," Kynan remarked. "I can't think of too many who'd be willing to take a traitor's crippled daughter."

The tumultuous emotions Blaidd had been struggling to hold in check for days exploded in fierce anger. The apple splattered into a pulpy mess as he threw it onto the table. Then, scowling, he rose slowly like a god of war roused to battle. "Don't you *ever* call her crippled again!"

Kynan stared at him in disbelief. "God, Blaidd, what's got into…" His eyes widened as understanding dawned. "You like her."

Blaidd fought for self-control. "I respect and admire her."

"It's more than that," Kynan said as he cautiously came around the table, never taking his eyes off his brother. "You *really* like her."

"You've got the Sight now, have you?" Blaidd demanded as he crossed his arms and watched his brother's progress.

"I may not have the Sight, but I can see that you care a lot about her. Aye, too much. What happened up there in the north, Blaidd—what *really* happened?"

"I told you."

Kynan shook his head. "Not all of it, not by a long shot. I've never seen you like this before. Something has turned my charming, jovial brother into a gruff and surly bear. Or should I say, some*one?*"

"I don't want to talk about it."

"No? Then that's another odd thing. Not that you were given to regaling me with your conquests, but at least you'd—"

Blaidd's hands balled into fists. "That's *enough,* Kynan!"

"Not yet. First answer me this question. Do you *love* this woman?"

Blaidd didn't reply, but in his eyes, Kynan saw the truth. "God's wounds, Blaidd," he said with a gasp, "you can't want to *marry* her!"

Kynan had seen Blaidd on the tournament field; he knew his brother's "warrior" face. He'd seen the steely determination that made it impossible for Blaidd to yield, and he saw it now when Blaidd said, "And what does it matter to you if I do?"

Eyes wide, Kynan felt for the nearest chair and sat heavily. "You can't be serious! What will Father say? And Mother? Not to mention the king? Her father was a *traitor,* Blaidd—you know that better than anyone."

"Aye, so I do," Blaidd retorted. "I killed the man, remember? Even though her father's death could be justified because of his actions, *I* was the one who struck the fatal blow. *I* was the one who told her what he was. I lied to her about why I'd come there in the first place. Her sister left the country, in part because of what I did. Now Becca's future is in Henry's hands, and she dare not disobey his commands, for fear of her life. So calm yourself, brother. Even if Henry gave his consent, how could she possibly care for me when I'm the one who brought about her family's ruin?"

Kynan's expression softened with sympathy, and relief. "Well, I'm sorry you feel bad about it, but honestly, Blaidd, it would have been impossible, anyway. She's a traitor's daughter, when all is said and done. And cheer up, there are plenty of beautiful ladies here at court to help you forget her.''

With an utterance of complete disgust, Blaidd marched to the door. ''You've never been in love—*really* in love,'' he snarled as he yanked it open, ''or you'd never say anything so damn stupid!''

Chapter Eighteen

Dressed in her sister's velvet robe and silken shift, Becca turned quickly away from the window as the door to her chamber crashed open.

His dark brows lowered, his expression fierce, Blaidd strode inside, then kicked the door closed. "Becca, do you hate me?" he demanded, his hands on his hips.

She was so taken aback by his arrival, his expression and his question that it took her a moment to find her voice. "No, no, I don't hate you."

His hands fell to his side, and his expression softened—a little. "I could understand if you did."

She stared at him incredulously as the words tumbled out of his mouth.

"I've ruined your life. I killed your father, and your sister's run off with that Dane, and because of me you may lose your title and property and have to do what Henry says—"

He was blaming *himself* for what had happened?

"*You* didn't ruin my life, Blaidd!" she interrupted. "Lord Throckton did. He's responsible because of his treasonous conspiracy, not you." She approached him slowly, warily, and yet with a renewed hope she couldn't subdue. "You did what you had to do to save your life, and mine."

"I lied to you from the start and—"

"Oh, Blaidd," she murmured, taking his strong hands in her own. "Don't you think I can understand that you were obeying the orders of the king? That as his loyal knight, you were obligated to do what he asked? That you were honor bound to unmask a conspiracy against the crown? I assure you, I do. I couldn't hate you for that, and I don't. I don't hate you at all."

His gaze searched her face. Now he wasn't the powerful warrior, but simply a man, vulnerable, hopeful and anxious, looking as if he feared he dared to hope too much.

"As for my father…" She was taking a risk, but she couldn't bear to conceal the truth from him any longer. "My father is very much alive."

Blaidd stared at her as if she'd gone mad.

"Lord Throckton wasn't my father," she explained. "He told me so himself before he attacked me. Dobbin is my father."

"*Dobbin* is your father?" Blaidd repeated incredulously.

"Yes." She straightened her shoulders, once again a lady in dignity, if not in law. "Although my mother was Lord Throckton's wife, I'm the bastard daughter

of a soldier. I didn't want to tell you sooner because
I want to speak for the people of Throckton, to assure
Henry that they are not treasonous.''

Blaidd still looked doubtful. ''If that's true, why
did Throckton acknowledge you?''

She couldn't blame him for being wary, given
Throckton's nature. And she, of all people, could understand how hard it could be to accept something
that seemed, on the first hearing, so unbelievable.
''He couldn't stand the thought that it would become
common knowledge that his wife had given herself to
a foot soldier. But now I know why Dobbin always
treated me as he did.''

She clasped her hands together like a supplicant,
which in a way she was. ''I beg you not to tell the
king, Blaidd. If he thinks I have no claim to Throckton, he'll certainly send somebody else to be overlord.
If I have no claim to the estate, I won't be able to
ensure that the tenants and servants—my friends—are
well and justly treated.'' She regarded him with love
and hope. ''Will you keep my secret?''

Blaidd frowned and began to pace as he mused
aloud. ''If I reveal it, Henry wouldn't consider you
fit to be a royal ward. He'd confiscate all Throckton's
goods and leave you with nothing. And then there's
the shame—''

''I'm not ashamed that Dobbin is my natural father!'' she cried.

Blaidd stopped pacing and his incredible lips lifted
in a breathtaking smile. ''Nor should you be. Some
of my father's best friends are bastards.'' His eyes

seemed to glow as he looked at her. "All in all, if it were up to me, I'd suggest you tell Henry. You'd be penniless, and some people whose opinion doesn't matter much anyway would look down on you, but the bastard daughter of a common soldier wouldn't be considered a threat to his throne. You'll have lost your title and your wealth, but you'll be free to do as you wish."

The liberty, if not the poverty, was tempting, yet she had more than herself to consider. "I can't think only of myself, Blaidd. What about my people? What will happen to them?"

There was an air of suppressed excitement about Blaidd as he answered her question. "I think between Gervais Fitzroy—that's Trev's brother—and me, we could probably persuade Henry to give the estate to somebody who'll be a good overlord. Gervais is a very clever politician, and we can surely come up with a few excellent candidates. So I don't believe you need worry about them. It's time to think about yourself, Becca."

She crossed the room, moving away from him as she tried to keep calm and not read too much into his fervor. "There's always the convent, I suppose. They'd have to take me in, poor bastard though I be."

"I have another suggestion."

She couldn't help her reaction. As he spoke, his deep voice full of barely contained excitement, hope sprung into wild, vibrant life. She faced him, her heart pounding, her breathing fast and shallow, as Blaidd slowly approached her.

"Will you be able to trust me again after all that I've done?" he asked softly as he took her hands in his and looked into her eyes.

"I was wrong not to trust you when you told me about Lord Throckton," she answered in a whisper.

"So you can trust me?"

"I do trust you."

"And you don't hate me?"

"No, I don't hate you."

"I love you, Becca," he whispered, his brown eyes shining. "Is it possible…can you…do you still care for me?"

Her heart soared. Sir Blaidd Morgan, knight of the realm, champion of tournaments, stood before *her*—crippled, homely, bastard Becca—humble and sincere, and offering her the greatest, most precious gift in the world: his love. "I can and I do, Blaidd. I love you with all my heart."

There was an instant's hesitation, a moment where they looked into each other's eyes, seeing the measure and depth of their love. Then joy and hope and laughter and relief exploded simultaneously, and she was in his arms, kissing and being kissed. Happiness fueled her passion and she clung to him tightly, holding him as if she'd never let him go again.

"There is no better woman for me, Becca, and I'll be more than proud to have you for my wife," Blaidd murmured as his lips moved along her cheek toward her ear. "If you will have me."

"*If* I'll have you?" Becca cried, delighted beyond measure. "Of course I will!"

With a tender touch, Blaidd brushed a lock of hair from her face. "We still must have our audience with the king."

"I'll gladly swear any oath of loyalty he chooses," she replied. "And surely your willingness to marry me should help banish any doubts he may have of my allegiance," she added with a smile.

Blaidd didn't smile back. "Even if he agrees you present no threat, he might have his own ideas about who *I* should wed."

Becca slowly ran her hands up Blaidd's chest. "I can think of one way, sir knight, that would make it harder for him to refuse your request. What if you were to marry me tonight, in one form, at least? Wouldn't honor then demand that we make it legal in the eyes of God and the law?"

Blaidd knew what she meant, and the primitive male in him shouted that she was right; that if they made love, the king could not deny them. But the rational part of him wasn't certain. "Many noblemen make love to women they never marry. In the past, I have, too. I'm not saying I'm not tempted to try this plan, because God knows, I am, but—"

"I want to make love with you tonight, Blaidd Morgan," Becca said softly, yet with firm resolution. "Whatever happens, I will have one night with you, whether we wed or not. Please don't deny me."

God help him, he couldn't say no. He simply couldn't, so he gathered her in his arms and said, "I want to marry you more than I've ever wanted anything in my life, Becca, and I'm going to do everything I can to make it happen."

She put her finger against his lips. "I know. I believe you. I trust you absolutely."

More in love with her than ever, more determined to make a future with her, Blaidd thought of one more thing he could do, a sacrifice he would gladly make if it meant Becca could be his wife. "If the king refuses, I'll offer to renounce my title and all the privileges that go with it. He won't have so many objections if I'm not a knight, but simply one of his loyal soldiers."

"You would do that, for me?" she asked incredulously.

He caressed her cheek, as he had that first night in the chapel, and the same thrilling desire trilled through her body. "Without regret. You wouldn't mind a husband who is only a soldier?"

"My true father—and the man I've always loved like a father—is just a common soldier. And I would rather live in a peasant's cottage with you than a palace with anyone else."

He believed her, and the last, lingering doubt and dread dropped away. This was the woman he would spend the rest of his life with, and no man, not even the king, was going to keep them apart.

Now certain, he stopped trying to subdue the heat of his desire. He became acutely aware of her body close to his, and the luxurious garments she wore—the dark green velvet robe, incredibly soft, and the white silk shift, like liquid moonlight against her smooth skin.

He kissed her again, deeply. She relaxed in his arms, leaning into him without restraint as his mouth moved over hers. Her wondrous lips parted, and he insinuated his tongue between them. As he did, he slipped off her robe and let it drop to the floor.

How soft her shift was! Sliding down her back, his fingers grazed the delicate fabric as if it were her naked skin.

Her warm, soft skin, which he wanted to taste. His hands cupped her buttocks as his lips left hers to trail down the slope of her jaw toward her slender neck, then brushed ever so lightly over her collarbone.

Clutching his shoulders, Becca sighed when he nuzzled her shift downward. She moaned softly as he pressed light, yet heated kisses to the tops of her breasts, first one, then the other.

He moved his head lower still. Ignoring the silk, he flicked his tongue across her pebbled nipple before drawing it into his mouth. A gasp, a sigh, a groan escaped her lips as he pleasured her until the silk was damp.

He felt her move, but before he could think about what she was doing or why, she took his head between her palms and brought him upward. Her mouth captured his with a fierce hunger that roused a primitive, intense desire.

He returned her kiss with savage need. His hands stroked and caressed, seeking to arouse and excite her, to make her want him as he wanted her.

She tore at the lacing of his tunic until it was untied and loose, then plunged her hand inside. She explored him, brushing her palm over his skin, sliding it over his nipples until he groaned.

He broke their kiss and tugged his tunic over his head, then threw it on the floor. Panting, aroused, he looked at the woman he adored and craved. His gaze raked her body: her hair disheveled as if they'd already slept together, her shift glowing white in the moonlight, her hardened nipples pushing against the thin fabric, the rapid rise and fall of her breasts, the eager look in her eyes....

He'd never been so inflamed.

Then they were together again, bodies separated by only that thin shift and his breeches. Almost nothing. He could feel her breasts against his chest, and she could surely feel him hard against her.

As if in silent confirmation, she ground her hips against him, more than eager.

Then she stepped away. For a horrible moment, he wondered if she'd reconsidered, until she slid her shift off the other shoulder. With a smile and an undulating movement that made his heartbeat race, she wriggled out of the garment until it was a puddle of fabric at her feet. Bathed in moonlight, she stood before him naked and glorious except for the bandage where she had been wounded.

He had forgotten her injury. "Becca, if I hurt you—"

"You'll be gentle with me, won't you, Blaidd?"

Disappointment flooded through him. "I can make no promise that in my eagerness I won't—"

"As long as you'll try to be careful," she said. She reached out to caress his jaw. "I give myself to you, Sir Blaidd Morgan. My heart *and* my body, such as it is, forever."

"I belong to you, my lady—and, come what may, you will always be my *lady,* forever."

"Then love me, Blaidd. Please. Or I might scream with frustration and rouse the palace guards."

He needed no further urging. "We can't risk that," he agreed as he lifted her in his arms, carried her to the bed and laid her there.

His boots and breeches were quickly discarded and then he was beside her. He slid one arm around her shoulders and pulled her close. His free hand skimmed her warm flesh. Her whole body was as soft as he'd always known it would be.

"I'll be careful," he promised as he bent to kiss her again.

Delighting in his touch, sure of his love and full of faith that they would always be together, Becca knew he would be. If she moved quickly, there was a little pain, but Dobbin had tended to her well, and she feared no serious injury—certainly nothing that would prevent her from giving herself to the man she loved, and the pleasure he invoked.

She began to explore his body with her palms and fingertips. His hot skin. The feel of the taut muscles beneath. The hairs on his chest. The hard nub of his nipples.

He liked it when she touched him there. Slipping lower, she sucked his nipple into her mouth, using her tongue to pleasure the tip, just as he had. He threw back his head and moaned.

She did the same to the other one, delighted at her power to arouse him. It was as if he was at her mercy, a thought that prompted her to play.

Moving carefully, she eased her leg over his stomach and straddled him. His eyes flew open. "Becca, what—"

"Shh, sir knight," she whispered. "We don't want to cause an alarm, do we?"

She ignored a little twinge from her wound as she grabbed his wrists and held them over his head. She leaned down so that her breasts brushed his chest, and began to use her lips and tongue to kiss and lick and nip his face and body beneath her.

She made him squirm, and the movement of his hips goaded her even more.

His eyes opened again, gleaming in the dark. "Let go of me, Becca," he said huskily.

"Perhaps I'm not finished with you yet, sir knight."

"Let go of me, Becca," he repeated, his voice low, but full of excitingly dangerous intent. "I can't let you torture me like this any longer."

"Am I torturing you?"

For an answer, he pushed against her hands, his strength easily overwhelming her. He levered himself up and then, holding her gently, swung her back onto the bed. "I think you should lie as still as possible, my love,'' he said softly as he moved to kneel between her thighs. ''I don't want to open that wound.''

She was about to make some sort of retort, but forgot when he placed his hands beside her head, leaned down and began to pleasure her breasts with his mouth and tongue.

Keep still? It was impossible. She moved instinctively, her body anxious for him.

Leaning his weight on one hand, he cupped her below with the other, moving in a slow rhythm that nearly undid her and made her part her legs even more. His hand shifted slightly lower, and a finger pressed down. As he continued to hold his palm firmly against her, her hips rose to meet it.

Tension grew. She wanted more of that pressure, more and more. She remembered this feeling, remembered what had happened at the end—that wonderful, amazing release.

Then he took his hand away. She opened her eyes, to find him looking down at her as he shifted his body forward. She felt him at the entrance.

''I'll be gentle,'' he promised again in his low, deep voice as he caressed her, making her crave him even more. ''Relax, Becca, my love, my darling. Look at my face.'' He shifted forward a little more. ''Know that I love you, and that I always will.''

He thrust and was inside her. She gasped, feeling a moment's pain, and not in her side.

''Is it too much? Should I stop?'' he asked, his brow furrowing with concern.

''No. Don't stop. Make me yours completely,

Blaidd. Please.'' She reached up to pull him down for another soul-searing, passionate kiss.

Liberated by her words, propelled by her passion, Blaidd began to move.

In a moment, Becca forgot her discomfort. It was overwhelmed by the other, infinitely wonderful sensations.

Her body seemed completely alive, every part aware that he was loving her. They were joined, sharing the pleasure, the desire. Their bodies melded, their hearts linked, united in a glorious tension that made her moan and clench her eyes tight, that built and built beyond anything she'd felt before as he moved faster and faster, deeper, harder....

Until the tension shattered, replaced by waves of incredible, throbbing release. As she cried out, he stiffened, the cords of his neck taut, and a groan broke from his lips.

Panting, sweat-slicked, he laid his head against her breasts. ''Oh, God, Becca,'' he murmured. ''I've never...that was...you're...I love you.''

As her breathing returned to something akin to normal, she brushed back his hair and smiled. ''I've never felt anything like that, either, and I love you, too.''

He raised himself on his elbows and glanced at her bandage. ''I hope I didn't make you start bleeding again. I should check. If I have, Dobbin will never forgive me.''

''If you did, I don't mind. And Dobbin will certainly forgive you. He likes you.'' She gave Blaidd a naughty smile and wiggled a little, still enjoying the sensation of him inside her. Very much. "I could always tell him you've more than made up for it. Surely he wouldn't be angry then."

"If he found out we did this before we're married, he might really want to hurt me."

"Then I won't tell him."

Blaidd moved away from her and gently examined the bandage. "No harm done, it seems."

"I think a very great harm's been done," she said with mock severity. "How can I possibly let you leave this bed now without doing that again?"

"You want to do that exact same thing, my love?" he asked with apparent gravity.

Despite where they were and what they'd just done, she began to blush. "What else could we do?"

"I do know a few other things," he purred, lying back beside her and lazily stroking her hip.

Although her body was already responding, she tried to look baffled. "Other ways?"

"I'll be happy to demonstrate."

"Now?"

"Why not? Do you have something more pressing to do?"

"There is sleep."

"Well, if you'd rather…."

She tugged him down for a kiss that told him quite plainly that she didn't want to sleep.

Chapter Nineteen

Kynan stood outside the door to Lady Rebecca's chamber and hesitantly raised his hand to knock. It wasn't his place to rouse her, but he didn't know what else to do. It was already well past dawn, and Blaidd and Lady Rebecca were supposed to have their audience with the king soon. He couldn't find Blaidd or the lady's maidservant anywhere, and somebody had to make sure she was ready when the time came.

He rapped tentatively. No sound came from behind the door.

This was ridiculous. Surely she couldn't fault him for trying to ensure she wasn't late for a royal audience.

He knocked a little louder and called out, "My lady, are you awake?"

What was that? He leaned closer to the door and strained to hear. "My lady?"

It sounded like…like a struggle. Without stopping to think, he drew his sword and charged into the room.

To see his brother hunched over, one leg in his breeches, looking up at him, red in the face, and the lady covered by only a sheet, staring in surprise.

"Oh, God, I'm sorry!" Kynan gasped as he turned and ran out of the room, slamming the door behind him. His sword dangling loose in his hands, he leaned backward—then nearly fell flat when the door opened behind him.

He managed to get his balance and, turning, found himself face-to-face with Blaidd, now in his breeches and unlaced, unbelted tunic. He held his boots in his left hand, his sword belt slung over his arm.

Lady Rebecca was smiling and somewhat more covered by the bedclothes. With her waving brown hair loose about her slender shoulders and that smile, Kynan could better understand what his brother saw in her.

At the moment, however, it was rather clear Blaidd was in no mood for a genial chat about women. He shooed Kynan outside and closed the door behind them. "You should have waited for somebody to say you could come in," he growled.

"Yes, well, I'm sorry, but it's getting late and I couldn't find the maid, or you, and I didn't want the lady to miss her audience with the king—"

Blaidd gasped. "Damn me, the king!" He looked out the nearest window. "What o'clock is it?"

"Nearly nine."

"Damn, damn, damn!" Blaidd muttered as he dropped his boots and hurried to buckle on his belt. "Why didn't you wake me sooner?"

"I might have if I'd known where you were."

Blaidd paused in his buckling and flushed not with anger, but embarrassment. "I didn't know I was, um, going to be staying the night here," he explained before he bent down to put on his boots.

Kynan regarded him gravely. "There's something else."

Blaidd raised his eyes. "What?"

"Our parents arrived at dawn."

Blaidd straightened and stared as if his brother had just announced the Second Coming was at hand. "They're *here?* Now? Why?"

"To visit me."

"Why the hell didn't you tell me they were coming?" Blaidd demanded as he tugged on his other boot.

"Because I didn't know when exactly they'd be arriving. They made good time, but they could just as easily have arrived a sennight from now."

He was right, of course. No one could say with any degree of certainty how long it would take to get to London from their estate in the marches. There were too many variables: the weather, the roads, a problem with the horses.

"Maybe it's just as well," Blaidd decided. "The sooner they meet the woman I'm going to marry, the better."

Kynan stared. "She agreed?"

Blaidd grinned from ear to ear. "Aye, she did." He clapped his brother on the shoulder, making him stagger. "And after talking with her and...well, other things…I'm hopeful Henry won't object. Where are Mother and Father now?''

Kynan looked as if he had a hundred questions, but had second thoughts about asking them. ''They're with the Fitzroys.''

''I haven't got time to meet them before my audience. Tell them I'll see them after.'' Blaidd turned to go back into Becca's room. ''And don't tell them about Becca and me. I want to do that.''

Kynan spread his hands and backed away. ''No chance of that, brother. I'll leave that little bit of news solely to you.''

Becca smiled lazily as Blaidd came back into the chamber. ''I hope he wasn't too upset,'' she said as Blaidd approached the bed. ''Your brother looked as if he might swoon with embarrassment.''

Blaidd leaned over and kissed her lightly. ''He'll get over it. But now, my love, my wife, get up, or we're going to be late for our audience with the king.''

She started to gingerly shift toward the edge of the bed, for her side was rather sore, when something in his expression made her hesitate. ''Something else has happened, hasn't it?'' she asked warily. ''What? You're not sorry we—''

''I'm certainly not sorry for making love with you or wanting to marry you,'' he said firmly as he caressed her cheek. ''It's just that my parents have arrived. I wasn't expecting them, to say the least.''

''Oh.'' Becca shrank back a bit. She hadn't thought

about Blaidd's parents, or the rest of his family, and how they might react to his announcement that he was marrying a woman they surely would think most unsuitable, in a host of ways.

He gave her a smile and chucked her under the chin. "Don't worry, my darling. Once they meet you, they'll understand everything. Now we'd better make ourselves presentable."

Becca nodded and tried not to show her fear.

There was a flurry of knocks on the door, then Meg came rushing in. "Oh, my lady, I'm so sorry to be late. I never meant—"

She skittered to a halt and her mouth formed an O as she stared at Blaidd, then Becca, undressed and still in bed.

"I'll be waiting for you in the larger room, Becca. Be as quick as you can, my love," Blaidd said calmly as he nodded a greeting to Meg, whose shocked expression slowly changed into a delighted smile.

When he was gone, Meg bounded toward Becca like an excited puppy. "Oh, he's going to marry you, isn't he? I knew he would! He'll make you so happy!"

Becca could hardly disagree, so she smiled, then said with some attempt at being stern, "Where have you been?"

Meg immediately calmed down, and her cheeks colored. "Oh, me, my lady? I've been...sleeping. Yes, I fell asleep and didn't wake in time."

"Where were you sleeping?"

Her blush deepened. "In the palace, of course."

"Alone?"

"It wasn't like that, my lady, honest!" she cried, wringing her hands. "We was just talking, Trevelyan Fitzroy and me, and we were both tired and next thing I knew, I'm waking up with my head on his shoulder. He was just as surprised as I was."

"Trevelyan Fitzroy?"

Meg nodded. "He's a gentleman, my lady, like Sir Blaidd. He never tried anything impertinent. He just wanted to talk, is all. Really. And I wouldn't let him do more than that, anyway."

"I'm hardly in a position to cast stones, Meg," Becca noted as she eased herself out of bed. "Now help me get into my sister's finest gown. I have to look my best to meet the king."

And Blaidd's parents, who might never see her as anything other than the ruin of their son.

Her arm linked through Blaidd's, Becca tried not to reveal any nervousness as they approached the king's hall. She would have been much more tense if this had happened before last night; at least now she was sure of Blaidd's love, and secure in the knowledge that he wanted to spend his future with her.

"I still think it would be best if you let me speak for you," Blaidd said as they drew near the heavy carved doors guarded by two chain-mail-clad soldiers. "Of course you should reply to the king if he asks you a direct question, but otherwise, leave me to argue your case. I know him, after all, and he trusts me."

Becca nodded. At the moment, she doubted more than a croak would come out of her throat if she tried to talk.

After running his gaze over them, one of the guards recognized Blaidd and opened the doors. Becca took a deep breath and willed herself not to look concerned as she limped into the hall.

She barely stifled a dismayed gasp. There were so many people! Men and women filled the large chamber, all dressed in incredibly rich garments of bright reds and greens and blues, with jewels and gold and silver sparkling around their necks and on their fingers. The air was permeated with perfumes. What seemed like a mile ahead were two thrones on a canopied dais, and seated there were the king and his queen. He wasn't very old, but she was even younger, and obviously pregnant.

As they moved forward through the crowd, Becca felt woefully underdressed and plain and pathetic, despite the fact that she was wearing Laelia's most lovely gown. She was very aware that Blaidd looked magnificent in his black velvet tunic, black breeches and polished boots, and he carried himself as if he were a king. He seemed to belong there, while she…she belonged back at Throckton Castle, giving orders to Rowan in the kitchen.

Blaidd reached over and covered her hand with his. She glanced up at him, to see him smiling with love and confidence. She took comfort from that and felt a little better, until he checked his steps.

She followed his gaze. Trevelyan Fitzroy stood beside a man who must be Trevelyan's brother, and beside them was an older couple who were watching them both with an intensity even more disconcerting than Blaidd's could be.

"Those are my parents," he said in a whisper, and she immediately saw the likeness between Blaidd and his father. Blaidd would look exactly like the man in twenty years—older, wiser, but still very much a warrior, albeit with iron-gray hair. Blaidd's mother was a comely woman who must have been even more beautiful than Laelia in her youth.

"Welcome back, Sir Blaidd!"

When the king called out his greeting, Becca focused her attention on him and the woman beside him. Continuing toward the dais, Becca and Blaidd bowed to the king and queen.

"Greeting, my liege," Blaidd said, smiling. "Queen Eleanor. Motherhood becomes you, Your Majesty."

The queen smiled, and who could blame her? Blaidd's deep voice and tone made his observation a great compliment.

Henry likewise looked delighted, but not for long. "I've been apprised of the unfortunate doings at Throckton Castle," he said. He turned his attention to Becca. "This, I take it, is Lord Throckton's younger daughter?"

"Yes, Your Majesty. This is Lady Rebecca, a most loyal subject."

"So you say, Sir Blaidd."

"So I *know,* Your Majesty."

The brow over Henry's drooping eyelid rose in inquiry. "You have proof, have you?"

"Her presence here, and her willingness to swear any oath of loyalty you choose."

"Is that so, my lady?"

"Yes, sire."

Henry looked back at Blaidd. "It could be, Sir Blaidd, that she is as subtle as her father and thinks to trick me by coming here. And a sworn oath is only words."

King or not, this man insulted her honor by implying that she would break her word. Becca forgot what Blaidd had said about keeping quiet, and stepped forward. "Majesty," she said firmly, "I assure you that I am an honest woman, and that I hold my honor as dear as any person in this court."

Henry's brow rose higher. "Do you, indeed, my lady?"

"Indeed, I do, and in keeping with that statement, I will confess that I am *not* Lord Throckton's daughter."

An excited, curious murmuring filled the hall, and the king and queen looked equally dumbfounded. Blaidd fidgeted beside her, but she continued regardless. "I am the daughter of Lord Throckton's late wife and another man."

"You would tell this entire court that you are a bastard?" Queen Eleanor demanded incredulously. "For what purpose?"

"To prove that I am what I claim, an honest woman."

"Then you have no claim to Lord Throckton's property or movable goods."

"None at all."

"You will not be a ward of this court and you'll be left with nothing."

"And thus have no reason to covet power, since my illegitimate birth and lack of wealth means I'll never command any, either."

Henry's eyes lit with comprehension. "Ah, a clever argument."

"And the truth, Your Majesty. I pledge it with my life, as I vow that I am your faithful subject."

"You have nothing to fear from Lady Rebecca, my liege," Blaidd confirmed, reaching out to take her hand. "There's more, sire. I ask your permission to marry this lady."

Another murmur of surprise rose from the assembly.

"Did you not hear her, Sir Blaidd?" Queen Eleanor demanded. "She is *not* a lady."

"By title, no," he agreed. "But in every other way, she is, and therefore worthy to be the wife of one of your knights."

Henry looked a little peeved and ignored Becca as he addressed Blaidd. "You heard how things stand. She has no dowry. No property at all. No title. It will be like marrying a peasant."

"Your Majesty, may I remind you that my father was born a peasant? However, if you think she is too far beneath me, I'll forswear my knighthood. I'll be your loyal subject and dutiful soldier under your command, but I will reject my rank, and the privileges thereto.''

A gasp went up from the assembly, followed by more shocked murmurs, but Blaidd ignored them. ''I'll gladly do so, Your Majesty, if that is what I must do to be allowed to marry her.''

Becca tensed, waiting for the king and queen to protest and voice what everyone else in the hall must be thinking: that he couldn't be serious. That no knight would willingly renounce his title for a penniless bastard who limped.

Henry's brow furrowed and his grip on the arms of his throne tightened. ''You are telling your king to whom you have sworn to be loyal that if I do not allow you to marry this woman, you will leave my court?''

''Although I'll still be loyal to you with my life, you'll give me little choice.''

''You would give your king an *ultimatum?*''

''No, Majesty,'' Blaidd replied. ''I will always be at your disposal, but you must choose whether or not it will be as a courtier or a humble soldier. My absence at court will be no great loss to you, my liege. You have many capable men about you, Englishmen of wise and good counsel.''

Another murmur arose, of pleased English voices and not-so-pleased French ones.

''That may be,'' Henry replied, ''but I will lose a champion of tournaments and one of the rare men in whom I have absolute trust.''

More whispers wafted through the hall, as men wondered if they were among this chosen few, or not.

"Therefore, Sir Blaidd," Henry continued sternly, "I find no need for such an extreme sacrifice." His grim expression turned into a smile. "I accept your choice of bride. May you both be as happy and blessed as Eleanor and I."

Becca wanted to shout with joy and cry with happiness. She might have done both if Blaidd hadn't taken her in his arms and kissed her heartily, right there in the king's court. Trevelyan Fitzroy burst into wild applause, and others followed, while a wave of laughter rolled over them. It seemed the king's decision had pleased more than Becca and Blaidd, who stopped kissing when the king wryly noted, in an audible whisper to his queen, "I've no doubt earned Sir Blaidd's loyalty for life."

"You have indeed, Your Majesty," he confirmed.

Henry rose and came forward. He took Becca's shoulders in his hands and kissed her cheeks. "You must be quite a woman."

Becca smiled into the king's face and saw not a lordly ruler, but a young man with many cares trying to do his best. "He is quite a knight, and will serve you well, Your Majesty."

"I know it, or I wouldn't have agreed to your marriage," Henry said before returning to his throne. When he had sat down, he declared, "We permit this marriage as a reward for Sir Blaidd's activity on our behalf, and as a further reward, we endow him with

Throckton Castle, the lands surrounding it and all the income it provides.''

This time, Becca couldn't restrain herself. She let out a whoop of delight and threw herself into Blaidd's arms, hugging him tightly. Blaidd looked a little nonplussed by her enthusiasm, until Henry started to laugh. ''Kiss her, man!'' he ordered. ''I can tell you want to.''

''As my king commands, I obey,'' Blaidd said with a joyous smile. He pulled Becca into his arms and, regardless of the people watching, kissed her with passionate fervor until she was breathless.

The king cleared his throat. ''Sir Blaidd, I fear the other ladies of the court are on the verge of swooning because of that demonstration. If you wish to continue expressing your love and happiness, I suggest you take your lady elsewhere. We'll discuss the recent events and the conditions at Throckton in more detail some other time.''

''Yes, Your Majesty,'' Blaidd said humbly, bowing. ''Thank you, Your Majesty.''

Holding hands, Blaidd and Becca departed from the hall, amid many curious glances, a few envious ones from young ladies, directed at Becca, and much excited whispering.

Once the heavy doors had closed behind them, they hurried past the stone-faced guards and ducked into a window alcove, where they kissed again. And again. And then once more.

''I can't believe he gave you Throckton,'' Becca said when they stopped to draw breath.

"I never expected that, either," Blaidd said, grinning merrily.

"Nor did I," said a deep voice very like Blaidd's, with a heavier Welsh accent. "I thought you'd lost your mind in there, boy."

Blaidd and Becca broke apart as Blaidd's parents, with Kynan, Trev and Gervais Fitzroy behind them, approached.

Still smiling, Blaidd faced them squarely. "Father, Mother, this is Rebecca. Becca, this is my father, Sir Hu Morgan, and my mother, Lady Liliana. That's Gervais Fitzroy with Trev."

Feeling more nervous than she'd been while talking to the king, Becca bowed with all the grace she could muster. "Sir Hu, my lady, Sir Gervais."

"I assure you, Father, I'm very much in my right mind," Blaidd said when the introductions had concluded.

"Or as much as a man desperately in love can be, I suppose," his father replied, breaking into a familiar grin. "Look you, taking years off my life, you were, when you said you'd forswear your knighthood, and after all the trouble Urien had training you. And your mother was nearly swooning with the shock."

Lady Liliana gave her husband a wry look and went to Becca. Taking the younger woman's hands in hers, she smiled pleasantly. "I've long ago ceased to be shocked by anything these men do, my dear," she said kindly. "I've despaired for years that Blaidd would ever find a woman to wed. Now it seems he has, and quite on his own, too. If my son loves you enough to give up his knighthood, then you're an exceptional woman, and one I will be proud to call my daughter.''

Overcome with happiness and not a little relief, Becca hugged Lady Liliana as enthusiastically as she had Blaidd in the king's hall. Blaidd's loud throat-clearing made her draw back quickly, and she feared she'd acted improperly.

"My mother doesn't need such, um, demonstrations," he quietly explained.

Liliana frowned at him. "I don't mind them, either," she retorted. "They are *such* men, these Morgans, aren't they, Becca?" She gave her a saucy wink. "Which is one reason we love them, I suppose."

Any fear Becca had of her future in-laws dissipated, while Blaidd slipped his arm around her and held her close. "If I've fallen in love with a bold, brave woman who speaks her mind and seems to have no respect for my rank and battle prowess, whose fault is that?"

Lady Liliana laughed and slid her hand into her husband's. "Will you be joining us for some wine, my son, or do you have things to discuss, such as a day for the wedding?"

"Aye, Mother, we do. We'll meet you later."

As Sir Hu and his wife strolled away, into the breach stepped Kynan, Gervais and Trev.

"I tried to tell Gervais what was in the wind, but he wouldn't believe me," Kynan said. "Maybe now he'll listen to somebody else for a change."

The middle son of Sir Urien Fitzroy scowled, but his eyes danced with laughter. "I don't think I can be faulted for being skeptical about all this. I mean, Blaidd goes off on a journey and comes home with a wife—who'd have thought it?" Then he stopped attempting to look disgruntled. "Not that I mind being wrong. I'm glad you're getting to keep your knighthood, though. *And* you've got an estate, too. That's excellent."

Blaidd looked at Trev. "What about you, Trev? Do you approve of my choice of bride, and are you willing to move north with me and stay my squire?"

The boy looked as if he'd just been given a present. "I'd like that, Blaidd. Dobbin's got a few tricks with a lance he promised to show me. Wouldn't it be something if I could show my father a thing or two with a lance?"

The men exchanged knowing looks and chuckled.

"Sir Urien gets particularly fierce when it comes to training with lances," Blaidd explained to Becca.

"That's one way to put it," Gervais muttered.

"We can talk about Sir Urien some other time, I think," Blaidd said. "Now, if you fellows don't mind, I'd like to spend some time with my future wife. As Mother pointed out, we've got a lot to talk about."

Kynan grinned. "Talking, yes, of course. We'll leave you to it."

He nudged Trev to head down the corridor, the way Sir Hu and Lady Liliana had gone.

"Plans for the wedding can wait a bit, can't they?

I want to hear more about what happened at Throckton,'' Gervais protested.

"Later, Gervais," Kynan insisted as he grabbed him by the arm and started to pull him away. "Can't you see they want to be *alone?*"

Gervais's baffled expression changed to one of embarrassed realization. "Oh, yes, I—I see," he stammered. "Later, then, Blaidd. Delighted to meet you, Lady Rebecca!"

The moment the young men were out of sight, Blaidd drew Becca into his arms again. "Alone at last."

She glanced over her shoulder at the sentries standing by the door to the hall. "Not quite."

"Enough that it's not going to stop me from kissing you," Blaidd murmured, bending toward her.

"Nor me from kissing you, either, sir knight. I'm going to kiss you every day for the rest of my life, too," she replied as she raised herself on her toes and met him halfway.

And let it be recorded that she did.

*   *   *   *   *

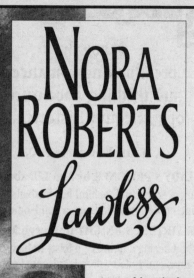
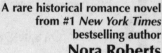

Your opinion is important to us! Please take a few moments to share your thoughts with us about your experiences with Harlequin and Silhouette books. Your comments will be very useful in ensuring that we deliver books you love to read. *Please take a few minutes to complete the questionnaire, then send it to us at the address below.*

Send your completed questionnaires to:
Harlequin/Silhouette Reader Survey, P.O. Box 9046, Buffalo, NY 14269-9046

1. As you may know, there are many different lines under the Harlequin and Silhouette brands. Each of the lines is listed below. Please check the box that most represents your reading habit for each line.

Line	Currently read this line	Do not read this line	Not sure if I read this line
Harlequin American Romance	❑	❑	❑
Harlequin Duets	❑	❑	❑
Harlequin Romance	❑	❑	❑
Harlequin Historicals	❑	❑	❑
Harlequin Superromance	❑	❑	❑
Harlequin Intrigue	❑	❑	❑
Harlequin Presents	❑	❑	❑
Harlequin Temptation	❑	❑	❑
Harlequin Blaze	❑	❑	❑
Silhouette Special Edition	❑	❑	❑
Silhouette Romance	❑	❑	❑
Silhouette Intimate Moments	❑	❑	❑
Silhouette Desire	❑	❑	❑

2. Which of the following best describes why you bought *this book?* One answer only, please.

the picture on the cover	❑	the title	❑
the author	❑	the line is one I read often	❑
part of a miniseries	❑	saw an ad in another book	❑
saw an ad in a magazine/newsletter	❑	a friend told me about it	❑
I borrowed/was given this book	❑	other: _____	❑

3. Where did you buy *this book?* One answer only, please.

at Barnes & Noble	❑	at a grocery store	❑
at Waldenbooks	❑	at a drugstore	❑
at Borders	❑	on eHarlequin.com Web site	❑
at another bookstore	❑	from another Web site	❑
at Wal-Mart	❑	Harlequin/Silhouette Reader	❑
at Target	❑	Service/through the mail	
at Kmart	❑	used books from anywhere	❑
at another department store or mass merchandiser	❑	I borrowed/was given this book	❑

4. On average, how many Harlequin and Silhouette books do you buy at one time?

I buy _____ books at one time	❑
I rarely buy a book	❑

MRQ403HH-1A

5. How many times per month do you shop for any *Harlequin and/or Silhouette* books?
One answer only, please.

1 or more times a week	❑	a few times per year	❑
1 to 3 times per month	❑	less often than once a year	❑
1 to 2 times every 3 months	❑	never	❑

6. When you think of your ideal heroine, which *one* statement describes her the best?
One answer only, please.

She's a woman who is strong-willed	❑	She's a desirable woman	❑
She's a woman who is needed by others	❑	She's a powerful woman	❑
She's a woman who is taken care of	❑	She's a passionate woman	❑
She's an adventurous woman	❑	She's a sensitive woman	❑

7. The following statements describe types or genres of books that you may be
interested in reading. Pick *up to 2 types* of books that you are most interested in.

I like to read about truly romantic relationships	❑
I like to read stories that are sexy romances	❑
I like to read romantic comedies	❑
I like to read a romantic mystery/suspense	❑
I like to read about romantic adventures	❑
I like to read romance stories that involve family	❑
I like to read about a romance in times or places that I have never seen	❑
Other: _____	❑

*The following questions help us to group your answers with those readers who are
similar to you. Your answers will remain confidential.*

8. Please record your year of birth below.

19 _____

9. What is your marital status?

single	❑	married	❑	common-law	❑	widowed	❑
divorced/separated	❑						

10. Do you have children 18 years of age or younger currently living at home?

yes ❑   no ❑

11. Which of the following best describes your employment status?

employed full-time or part-time	❑	homemaker	❑	student	❑
retired	❑	unemployed	❑		

12. Do you have access to the Internet from either home or work?

yes ❑   no ❑

13. Have you ever visited eHarlequin.com?

yes ❑   no ❑

14. What state do you live in?

_____

15. Are you a member of Harlequin/Silhouette Reader Service?

yes ❑   Account # _____   no ❑   MRQ403HH-1B

ITCHIN' FOR SOME ROLLICKING ROMANCES SET ON THE AMERICAN FRONTIER? THEN TAKE A GANDER AT THESE TANTALIZING TALES FROM HARLEQUIN HISTORICALS

On sale September 2003

WINTER WOMAN by Jenna Kernan
(Colorado, 1835)

After braving the winter alone in the Rockies, a defiant woman is entrusted to the care of a gruff trapper!

THE MATCHMAKER by Lisa Plumley
(Arizona territory, 1882)

Will a confirmed bachelor be bitten by the love bug when he woos a young woman in order to flush out the mysterious Morrow Creek matchmaker?

On sale October 2003

WYOMING WILDCAT by Elizabeth Lane
(Wyoming, 1866)

A blizzard ignites hot-blooded passions between a white medicine woman and an amnesiac man, but an ominous secret looms on the horizon....

THE OTHER GROOM by Lisa Bingham
(Boston and New York, 1870)

When a penniless woman masquerades as the daughter of a powerful marquis, her intended groom risks it all to protect her from harm!

Visit us at www.eHarlequin.com

HARLEQUIN HISTORICALS®